Acclaim for *The Trial of True Love*:

'Nicholson's critically acclaimed last novel, *The Society of Others* and Oscar-nominated screenplays, *Shadowlands* and *Gladiator*, prove his talent . . . Hopefully *The Trial of True Love* will make his name as famous as his work' *Glamour*

'A quirky and enjoyable read' *Spectator*

'He is an expert in understanding and depicting human emotions. His ideas and language are wonderfully involving and perceptive. This novel is a real find: clever, funny, subtle and hopelessly romantic. I loved every word . . . The key to this novel's success is that it asks all the best questions. Does love at first sight really exist?' *Daily Express*

'A mixture of existential thriller and romantic discourse . . . rich in artistic allusions' *Mail on Sunday*

'A love story that explores the many different beliefs between men and women' *The Sun*

'There are some nice twists . . . its real strength lies in the near-beauty and astuteness of Bron's musings as he tries to get closer to what love really means' *Big Issue*

Acclaim for *The Society of Others*

'This extraordinary book, a sort of wild combination of Kafka and *The Catcher in the Rye*, whirls its catonically dysfunctional hero into a maelstrom of violence and danger to learn from oppressed strangers what really matters in a human life, and to face the most terrifying of interrogators, the self. The reader will not escape unchanged'   Jill Paton Walsh

'William Nicholson is a successful writer of film scripts, plays and an award-winning children's trilogy. He has explained that while he was writing this first novel for adults a muddle of wild ideas came tumbling out of him … the result is urgent, spontaneous and exhilarating'   *Sunday Telegraph*

'The story may be metaphoric but the tension of being hunted is real enough … the constant unexpected twists, like a conjuror pulling yet another handkerchief out of an apparently empty box, keep you reading to the end'   *The Times*

'A book brimming with ideas … it is at times almost dizzying. Before you realise what has happened, you are in a fantasy world whose landscape is shaped by great works of art and whose inhabitants are dangerous extremists. The interior and exterior narratives mix seamlessly as the central character tries to escape an all-too-recognisable figure who is haunting him'   *Independent*

'There are some laugh out loud moments … the tone is as droll and deadpan, the prose as crisp and well-turned as one would expect from a writer who earns his living in movieland'   *Irish Independent*

'There is certainly no shortage of ideas in William Nicholson's thought-provoking and multi-layered new novel

... a modern day fable, written in the style of a fast-paced thriller but carrying more messages than a sackful of mail'
Yorkshire Evening Post

'Exciting, funny, wise and beautifully written ... that a middle-aged author should so successfully enter the mind of a twenty-two-year old man is impressive, and is here portrayed with a beautiful economy and precision. Nicholson writes with such panache that *The Society of Others* transcends genres: it entertains us while it reflects with great profundity on the human condition ... We accept the narrator's vision – life as 'the dwindling away of dreams' – yet are drawn by the very cynicism and disillusion into accepting the novel's positive conclusions. [Nicholson] has to my mind established himself with this first work of adult fiction as one of the best novelists around'   Piers Paul Read, *Spectator*

'Part philosophical treatise, part spy story, part reflection on loyalty and statehood ... There are echoes of Albert Camus in Nicholson's wonderfully perceptive story ... displays the full range of the exceptional talents of the creator of *Shadowlands* ... It is thrilling in every sense, but also hypnotic, fast-moving and intellectually challenging and it twists and turns, leaving you confused, uncertain, even uncomfortable and yet utterly hooked. A philosophical masterclass, it is quite staggeringly good'   Geoffrey Wansell, *Daily Mail*

'An intriguing story, a suburban drama that quickly unfolds into a surreal tale with big ideas and meaning ... thought-provoking'   *Daily Mirror*

'*The Society of Others* is a novel that demands attention. William Nicholson is someone we are going to hear a good deal more about'   *Catholic Herald*

By the same author

THE WIND ON FIRE TRILOGY:
THE WIND SINGER
SLAVES OF THE MASTERY
FIRESONG

THE SOCIETY OF OTHERS

THE TRIAL OF
TRUE LOVE

William Nicholson

BLACK SWAN

THE TRIAL OF TRUE LOVE
A BLACK SWAN BOOK: 0552772895
9780552772891

Originally published in Great Britain by Doubleday,
a division of Transworld Publishers

PRINTING HISTORY
Doubleday edition published 2005
Black Swan edition published 2006

1 3 5 7 9 10 8 6 4 2

Copyright © William Nicholson 2005

Extract from *By Myself* by Lauren Bacall, published by Jonathan Cape,
1979, © 1978 Caprigo Inc.
Extract from *To Have and Have Not* by Ernest Hemingway, published by Jonathan
Cape, used by permission of The Random House Group Limited.
Screenplay by William Faulkner and Jules Furthman for the Warner Bros. film based
on *To Have and Have Not* by Ernest Hemingway (New York: Scribner/Simon &
Schuster, 1937). Copyright 1937 by Ernest Hemingway. Copyright renewed © 1965 by
Mary Hemingway.

The publishers have made every reasonable effort to contact the copyright owners of
the extracts reproduced in this book. In the case where they have been unsuccessful
they invite the copyright holder to contact them direct.

Set in 11.5/15pt Granjon by
Falcon Oast Graphic Art Ltd.

Black Swan Books are published by Transworld Publishers,
61–63 Uxbridge Road, London W5 5SA,
a division of The Random House Group Ltd,
in Australia by Random House Australia (Pty) Ltd,
20 Alfred Street, Milsons Point, Sydney, NSW 2061, Australia,
in New Zealand by Random House New Zealand Ltd,
18 Poland Road, Glenfield, Auckland 10, New Zealand
and in South Africa by Random House (Pty) Ltd,
Isle of Houghton, Corner of Boundary Road & Carse O'Gowrie,
Houghton 2198, South Africa.

Printed and bound in Great Britain by
Cox & Wyman Ltd, Reading, Berkshire.

Papers used by Transworld Publishers are natural, recyclable products made from
wood grown in sustainable forests. The manufacturing processes conform to the
environmental regulations of the country of origin.

THE TRIAL OF TRUE LOVE

1

Here where two rivers meet by an island, in the early morning, shortly after dawn, there is a mist along the valleys. The sun rises over the railway bridge, white as a moon, and everything is still. I stand before Taw pool, watching the water eddy round the island, my breath cloudy and my thoughts far away. I do not anticipate. And yet there is a moment before the moment, that is both a preparation and a culmination. What is about to happen to me is long longed-for, familiar, out of reach, needed, despaired of, completely imagined, but never known: so first, and memorably, comes the intimation that it is about to happen. The light falling from an opening door on to a winter's street. The silence before a phone begins to ring. Anticipation, in the razor-cut of time before it bursts into fulfilment.

The Barnstaple train, headlamp furry in the mist, booms suddenly over the bridge. Rooks rattle out of invisible trees, cawing up into the sky. The premonitory sounds disperse into the slow tumble of the rivers, into my own quiet breaths. The smell of soaked grass and the sharp white air that makes me shiver and the silence after the train.

And then I see her.

*

This is a story about falling in love. The time is 1977, a generation ago. I am twenty-nine years old, and waiting for my real life to begin. I am engaged in this waiting process in the very small second bedroom of a very small flat in Cross Street in north London, owned by my friend Anna.

She comes back earlier than usual and pours herself a glass of wine, which is not like her, not at five in the afternoon, and says we must talk. So I have a glass of wine too, and we talk.

'The thing is this.' She moves her hands carefully before her as if describing an invisible object about the size of a box-file. 'This is the thing. I have to think of myself. I have to think of the future. I'll be thirty in January. Which is meaningless, of course. But I would like, one day, to have children.'

Anna is home early because she's been visiting a friend who has recently had a baby.

'How was Polly's baby?'

'Like a baby. This isn't about that.'

'Yes, it is.'

'Alright, it is, then. The thing is this. For a baby, one needs a man. And one hasn't got one.'

She makes a comic-sad face as she says this, which makes me laugh. Also she's making me nervous.

'I don't know what to tell you, Anna. This is how it is these days. Everyone free to be with who they like, and everyone alone.'

'Well, I've decided to do something about it.'

Anna is small, slightly built, with a friendly, puzzled sort of face and short hair of that colour that has no name, between brown and blond. She's quick-thinking and funny and honest, and has no luck with men. There was a man called Rory who was part of her life for years and we all assumed they would get married, until he went to Johannesburg and married someone else. This in the apartheid era. Anna knew she was better off without him, but she still cried every night for weeks.

She calls me her walker. We have what is in some senses the perfect relationship, because the sex is behind us. There was a clumsy fumbling sort of affair at college, which went through what are for me the usual phases of eagerness, gratified vanity, claustrophobia, guilt, evasion and disappearance.

'Bron doesn't do break-ups,' Anna says. 'He does vanishings.'

She calls me a coward, but I've never pretended to be a war hero in the battle of the sexes. What am I to say, faced with the wounded eyes, the question why? Not the truth: that this can't be it, that this can't be enough, that there must be more. All love affairs are understood to be for ever, and the one who walks away a deserter from the human race.

In the case of Anna, time the great healer worked its magic, and there were other boyfriends who behaved yet more disgracefully, so by the time we met again I was received as an old comrade-in-arms. Since then I've seen her through the long lean years of the unspeakable Rory, and the short turbulent months of an affair with an artist called Jay Hermann. Anna deals in corporate art, which means she sources art works for hotel lobbies and company headquarters. This makes her a modern Robin Hood, who takes from the rich to give to the poor. Few of her artists are grateful. She tells them they are working in the tradition of the Florentine masters, all of whom painted to commission, but the model they identify with more readily is the Mexican artist Diego Rivera. Rivera, an ardent communist, accepted a well-paid commission from John D. Rockefeller to create a mural in the new Rockefeller Center in the 1930s. In order to prove that he hadn't sold out to the arch-capitalist of all time, he included in his mural a portrait of Lenin, hiding among many other figures. When Rockefeller found out and objected, Rivera hoisted the banner of politico-artistic integrity, and refused to paint Lenin out. Rockefeller paid him in full, and destroyed the entire vast mural.

Jay Hermann, a small aggressive sculptor, created large aggressive structures out of steel, which Anna sold to property developers. During their affair, he was remorselessly unfaithful to her, and on principle refused to conceal the fact. I had my own take on this.

'He's a prick.'

'It's his way of saying I haven't bought him. He minds terribly about his independence.'

'Tell him to fuck off.'

'I expect I will. But I do like him. And I don't want to have no one. And he's no different to other men. And at least he's honest.'

So like Anna. It may sound like masochism, but it isn't. Anna is a realist, and has long been in the habit of making the best of what's available to her.

So Anna has decided to do something about being alone.

'I'm not giving out the right signals. I'm like a taxi with the For Hire light turned off.'

'Are you? Why?'

'Because of you.'

This I have not seen coming.

'Me?'

12

'Think about it, Bron. You're a sweet, friendly man, you get my jokes, I don't have to pretend I'm someone else when I'm with you. You're really quite attractive, in your shabby way. And I'm living with you.'

'Yes, but we're not—'

'Sex isn't everything. Though it is a first step. If you want to have children.'

I feel bewildered.

'So what are you saying?'

'You're in my way. You've got to go.'

'But we're just friends.'

'No we're not. We're like an old married couple. It's disgusting.'

I'm tallish and darkish, with a mass of dark-brown hair and dark-brown eyes, thin and nervy, quick to smile, except I never see my own smiles. The self I see is grave, peers back at me in reflections without lightness or grace. I dress like a student: jeans, T-shirts, loose sweaters. I am a writer, none of whose writings have yet been published. However, I now have a commission, a real contract with a real publisher naming real sums of money, to write a real book. This book will not be one of my three completed novels, all of which lie in a cardboard box alongside letters ending 'but I would be interested to see your next work'. It will be a work of non-fiction. I call it, for the present, The Book of True Love. It deals with the phenomenon of love at first sight. For this, a publisher is paying me £2,500, half on signature, meaning £1,250: enough to keep me alive for maybe six months. I am therefore very poor.

'You could always get a job,' says Anna the brutal.

'Of course I could get a job,' I reply. 'But in return for the money I'd have to do the work, yes? Nine to five, yes? Leaving me knackered, yes? So when do I write?'

I have chosen to be time-rich and cash-poor. This has a romantic air about it in a student or a very young man. But soon now I will be thirty years old, and my lifestyle will begin to look sad. So I am in a hurry.

As for The Book of True Love: the subject has not been chosen at random. Love at first sight fascinates me. In my own love life I appear to suffer from the standard-issue male malady called commitment phobia. It has never presented itself to me as a phobia. Far from hating and fearing commitment, I long for it. But it doesn't happen. Each love affair begins with a flurry of enthusiasm, but soon dwindles into the so-so, the acceptable, the could-be-worse. The prospect of promoting such half-measures into marriage and children appals me. There must be more.

This pickiness baffles Anna.

'What exactly is it you're looking for, Bron?'

'I don't know. I truly don't know.'

I don't know. So I conclude that I am fated to repeat the familiar cycle until some outside force stronger than my power to resist blasts me out of my bunker. I conclude that I need to fall in love.

People use a conventional metaphor for falling in love at first sight. They say, 'I was struck by lightning.' I am in the position of a man who wishes to be struck by lightning and so walks about hatless in storms.

Freddy Christiansen, of whom more later, is vastly amused that I was compiling a book on love at first sight at the time that I myself fell in love. He teases me in Latin, calling me *praeceptor amoris*, the teacher of love, after Ovid, and *exclusus amator*, the lover shut out. But of course he too knows that it is no coincidence. In Devon, that October of 1977, my mind was crammed with true-life love stories, to which I was more than ready to add my own.

I pour myself another glass of wine. So does Anna.

'Look here, Anna. This is all wrong. Why do I have to go? Why can't men and women be friends?'

'I don't know, Bron. I think maybe it's because of sex.'

'That's a terrible admission of defeat.'

'Yes, it is rather.'

'So don't give in.'

'No. I've thought about it very carefully, and I'm sure I'm right. You have to go.'

'Thanks a lot.'

I feel ill-used.

'Now you're cross.'

'I just don't think me being your friend has anything to do with this other thing. It would be a sad world if we were only allowed to be friends with one other person all our lives.'

'You're cross because you don't know where you'll go to live. I've thought about that. You can go to Bernard's place, in Devon.'

'You're tidying me up.'

'You could do your book just as well in Devon as here. Probably better.'

'That's all sorted then, isn't it?'

More wine.

'Oh, Bron. You know I don't want you to go. Don't be mean to me about it.'

Her hand on mine.

'Oh, hell.'

'You do understand really.'

'Yes. I suppose I do.'

Oh yes, I understand. If I loved her more, I would be the man she's looking for: the husband, the father of her children. So why don't I? Because I'm not in love with Anna. There it is again. The mystery ingredient.

'You'd be a lousy provider, anyway.'

'You don't know that. I'm just a late developer, financially speaking.'

'Actually I don't mind about that. I meet enough rich men in my work.'

'Have one of them.'

'They're all dull and old. Even the young ones. Oh Bron, wish me luck. It's so fucking hard.'

'Good luck, Anna.'

I raise my glass and she raises hers and we drink and refill.

'So you will go?'

'Alright, alright, I'll go. You want me to go right now?'

'No. Not right now.'

'Do you realise we've drunk a bottle of wine in a quarter of an hour?'

'It's because I'm tense.'

'So I must be tense too.'

'Are you still tense?'

'No. Now I'm drunk.'

'Me too.'

We look at each other and grin like fools.

'Anna, if I'm going to fuck off out of your life for ever—'

'I didn't say that.'

'I'll re-phrase. If I'm to go—'

'No. I do want you to fuck off out of my life. Just not for ever.'

'Until you're hitched up.'

'Exactly.'

'After which I take it the occasional friendly intimate moment will be out of the question.'

'Entirely off the menu.'

'So this is our last chance.'

'Don't even ask.'

She opens a second bottle of wine, unoffended.

'Just a thought.'

'I do have some pride. I don't want to be the easy fall-back option. The one who'll do when there's nothing better around.'

'No,' I protest, gallantly and also truthfully. 'You're the best. A man can dream.'

'Quite a small dream, Bron. A dream of short duration.'

'Only because we're friends. Or not-friends. Or whatever it is we are.'

'Only because you're not in love with me.'

No answer. Pour the wine. But Anna drunk can be very direct.

'And by the way, why not? Why aren't you in love with me?'

'Oh God. I don't know.'

'You look so moronic when you say that.'

'I feel moronic. I'm not doing this deliberately. I'd be in love with you if I could. And anyway, you're not in love with me.'

'That's because I don't want to do it on my own. It's too fucking miserable, being in love on your own. I've been there.'

'So have I.'

'Liar.'

'I have. When I was younger.'

'Oh, sure. For ten minutes.'

'So anyway. I'll call Bernard.'

'I already called him. He said you could have the gate-lodge. He sounded pleased.'

'Well, fuck you.'

But she doesn't. So we eat takeaway pizza and watch *Goodbye, Mr Chips* on television and cry at the end. The next morning I move out.

2

I wrote in the kitchen of the gate-lodge, the only warm room. The iron range was roaring, I had banked it high and opened all its vents. There was condensation on the inside of the window-panes. I had a cloth, a blue-and-white tea towel, with which from time to time I wiped the window clean. I liked to look out at the trees, and the gap in the trees that was the beginning of the path through the wood. By my right hand there stood a mug of coffee, brim-full and smoking; by my left hand, the careful stacks of index-cards, my file of aphorisms, quotations, anecdotes. The top card read: 'The ivy clings to the first tree it meets,' which was Napoleon's description of the business of falling in love. Before me, pinned to the window frame, were Dante's words on first seeing Beatrice: *Ecce deus fortior me, qui veniens dominabitur mihi.* 'Behold a god stronger than I, who comes to rule over me.' And just below, my own selection of lines from Marotte's letters: 'I leave doors open to feel closer to you ... Please obtain slower clocks ... I need only a warm room, a still mind, and you.'

I was at work on my book.

It is always with an excited curiosity that we hear of a couple who fell in love at first sight. At once two questions spring to mind: what was it they recognised in each other so quickly? And, did it last?

Salvador Dali, when a boy, had a dream of a little Russian girl swathed in furs riding in a sled pursued by wolves. Many years later, in 1929, he met Elena Diaranoff, known as Gala, the wife of the surrealist poet Paul Eluard, and recognised in her the child of his dream. 'We fell in love instantly,' he has written. His courtship, conducted largely on the beach at Cadaques, was both passionate and childish. He wore a red geranium behind one ear, and laughed when there were no jokes. Gala seems to have understood. 'My little boy,' she told him, 'we shall never leave each other.' Dali invented tender names for her: bee, squirrel, fur bell, noisette poilue, lionelle. Whimsical though their love must have seemed at the time, they remained devoted to each other for over fifty years.

After three months of research, I had begun to write the book itself: and so at once I came face to face with the two great flaws in my scheme. The first was that my mass of love anecdotes, all fascinating and all true, had all been previously published. If there was no original material in my book, it would be no more than an anthology. The second flaw was that I had no thesis. When all the stories were told, what would I conclude? That love at first sight was the product of delusion? My case histories said no. Many lasting unions had begun with a *coup de foudre*. But if it was real, what exactly was going on? Why didn't everyone experience it? Why didn't I?

These questions weren't new to me. They'd been lying in wait throughout the time of research. They'd been the reason

I'd delayed so long in starting work. Now, impatient at my own uncertainty, I had decided on a new approach. I would write, and as I wrote I would discover what I thought about it all.

I decided to take, as my first extended case history, the least well known of my lovers: the French post-Impressionist painter Paul Marotte. Marotte was a favourite of mine, because it was the moment of falling in love at first sight that became the focus and core of his art.

I began with the known facts.

In 1889, when he first met a young English governess called Kate Summer, Paul Marotte was a physician working in Amsterdam, who painted only as a hobby. By the turn of the decade he was an acknowledged member of the Pont-Aven group of artists that included Paul Gauguin and Emile Bernard and called themselves the Synthetists. The catalyst for this change was his love for Kate Summer.

The artist and the governess lived together for eleven years, until his death in 1899. In the 1940s some fragments of Marotte's journal came to light, including a curiously detached account of that first fateful meeting. The style puts one in mind of the medical practitioner; but this factual manner was in accordance with a conscious artistic policy, sometimes called 'formalised emotion', which he developed most fully in his painting.

'At nine o'clock last Tuesday morning I was following my usual route to the clinic along the Keizersgracht, and had just reached the bridge which crosses the Leidsegracht, when my attention was caught by a small child with a blue ribbon in her hair. She was hopping rapidly towards me over the bridge, first on one foot, then on the other, with an expression of great concentration on her face. It seemed that her little brown boots must land in certain spots, and not in others. I heard a voice call to her. She stopped and turned round. I then saw a young woman in a pearl-grey coat. She wore a flat cream-coloured hat with a reddish-brown band, and her brown hair was coiled at the nape of her neck. I believe I stared at her, but she was concerned only for the child, and did not notice me. In a dozen steps she came up with the child, and took hold of the obediently offered hand. In a few steps more, both were gone by me over the bridge, and I continued on my way.

'On arriving at the hospital I found myself in a state of inexplicable excitation. After a while, this condition was replaced by its opposite, a lassitude so penetrating that my limbs could hardly sustain me. Thinking myself ill, I drew the curtains in the examining room and lay down. At once, as if it had been waiting only for my eyes to close, there sprang into my mind the picture of the young woman in grey. Accompanying this picture was a sensation of tranquil delight. I lay still, and I saw the young woman's face in the eye of my mind, exact in every detail, as if she stood before me. I was filled with wonder and thankfulness. I knew, without the possibility of doubt, that I loved her. This knowledge was profoundly satisfying to me.

'In a little while I found the feebleness had left me, and I returned to my interrupted work.' Here a sentence has been added, at some later date. 'From that day on, this woman, about whom I knew nothing, became everything to me.'

As I copied out Marotte's journal entry, with its quietly magnificent last words, it struck me that many questions remained unanswered. What was it about the governess that enraptured him so instantly? What was his state of mind before the meeting on the bridge? Was he dissatisfied with his life? Was he lonely? Was he sexually frustrated? Neither the slim biography of Marotte, nor the collection of letters and journals, gave me answers to these questions.

So it was here, on the first working day of my exile in Tawhead, that I decided to place Paul Marotte at the heart of my book; a decision which would, of course, require more research. And no sooner had I reached this decision than an event took place that changed my perceptions on the subject, and indeed, changed my entire future life. I had my own meeting on a bridge. I too became enraptured.

She was standing a little way away from me, looking down at the water, wearing a wide-shouldered belted trench coat that was too big for her. The sleeves covered her hands. Her golden hair fell forward across her face. No more than a trick of the mist, and her secretive way of walking, but I was stupid with surprise. She had come from nowhere.

She turned then, to look at me. She said nothing. But she smiled: an unwarranted smile. That surely was the moment for a little banality. For this reason if for no other I hold her responsible too, because of that silence, because of that smile. No more than a tremble of the eyes, a shared joke, a reference to a joint past that did not exist. It amused her to be discovered in the mist in Bernard's raincoat, like the heroine of a wartime movie.

And I, I fell in love at first sight. At the age of almost thirty, never having known since adolescence an unqualified desire, I dropped like an amateur skydiver from a plane, turning over and over into the helpless equilibrium of free fall.

Now, by the river, by the island, she was gone again. There was no mystery to it, the meadow path led back to the road.

But she made so little of the business of going that again I was surprised. The mist received her silently: our first meeting and our first parting, an efficient fantasy. It could not have been done in a shorter space of time.

I returned along the familiar path, climbing out of the meadow up the roomy staircase of the oak wood. No mist here, and dry ground. The picture of the stranger began to shiver and fragment in my memory. With each few steps I attempted to build the image again, starting from my own surprise and ending with her smile. Each time I retained less of her. Then, at about the point where the woodland path joins the tractor way, I lost the memory completely.

> I've got an arrow here;
> Loving the hand that sent it,
> I the dart revere.
>
> Fell, they will say, in 'skirmish'!
> Vanquished, my soul will know,
> By but a simple arrow
> Sped by an archer's bow.

Emily Dickinson wrote many poems that seem to describe the experience of love at first sight, but she remained unwed to the day she died. However, from the age of thirty she wore only white, as if dressed for her own wedding. Was she living a solitary illusion? Is falling in love, in its most intense form, a game only one can play?

3

Early that evening, I left the gate-lodge and made my way through the trees to the big house. The sky above was fading, the air mild. It was dark in the wood, and I walked fast. At the end of the path through the wood, where the long hillside begins to fall away down to the river and the railway and the road, there comes a sudden spectacular view. The encroaching trees seem to swing open to reveal, stretching as far to the west as the eye can see, the valley of the Taw, and the folded hills beyond, and the immense sky. Here the woodland path meets an old stone wall, the boundary of the private grounds of Tawhead. There are two gates in the wall, a wide iron-barred gate for vehicles, and beside it a little wooden gate for those on foot. I had fallen into the habit of pausing by this gate each evening, and admiring the view, before taking the footpath across the paddock to the big house. On that evening too I stopped, and leaned my arms on the top bar of the wicket gate.

It was just that time of day when the sun has dropped behind the hills, and the shape of things, the house and the high woods and the overlapping hills, the formed world itself, begins to release its definition into the soft afterlight. The western sky was already tinted rose, watercolour pale; a bank of cloud rested on the horizon, its under-surface lit gold, the upper part pearl grey. As I watched, this relationship of quiet colours, the grey and the rose and the gold, began to change. The band of bright gold retreated, and the shadowy cloud grew thin, permeated by the pinkness, as if warmed by the sympathy of the sky. I watched for five minutes or so.

As the last glimmer of golden light died, I felt for the iron latch, and pushed on it. It was stiff, and yielded with a sudden click. The gate, on which I was still leaning, swung open a little way. In that moment, as I turned with the turning gate, I was pierced with an emotion so powerful, so full of longing and the conviction of loss, that my whole body flinched. Because I had been watching the sky, I thought at first that this emotion was called into being by the bright glow of the cloud's rim: as if that golden light was somehow precious to me, necessary, even as it faded away. But then there flashed into my mind, clear and complete, the memory of the stranger in the mist, of her grave face, her smile. I sensed her close by me, though too close to see. I wanted to speak to her, but did not know her name. I felt my hand shake on the latch, with the surprise and the wonder and the ache of her nearness. Not a presentiment: I did not guess how soon she and I would meet again. The sensation was immediate as hunger.

There was a bird calling insistently from the chestnut tree in the paddock, its cry three notes long: *chip-chip-chee*. The pink in the sky was now deepening to red, and other higher clouds were revealing themselves over the hills. I felt then that I stood before the doors of the world; that if I stepped forward, or even moved at all, I would be safe no more.

As I write this, I stop to question myself. Did I really feel so much so soon? Or do I read my knowledge of what was to come back into those first days? Impossible to answer. Impossible to tell a story from the past without memory of the future. No doubt I reshape my life in the telling: for this, there are explanations, which must wait their time. For now it is enough to note that before I saw her in the library, standing with her back to me by the tall windows, I had already found her again; so perhaps I was not as surprised as I should have been.

I remember that I performed each stage of my entry into the house with undue care, as if to assure myself that nothing had changed. I stood my boots by the scullery door, and put on the slippers that waited for me there. I greeted Dora, at work in the kitchen, and asked what was for supper. I lifted the lids of the pans steaming on the Aga, and smelt the flannelly smell of cabbage. Dora had received a postcard from her son, a merchant seaman, posted in Tonga, 'the Friendly Isles'. 'Friendly, Dora. We all know what friendly means. Coffee-coloured grandchildren. Tiny grass skirts.' Dora's circular face creased into a delighted smile. 'You wild man,' she said. 'You wild man of the woods.'

Everything was familiar, yet I was no longer in the same relation to it all. The morning's encounter, or the emotions it had released in me, which I had not yet learned to respect, had somehow rendered my current life provisional. I climbed the back stairs and emerged into the corridor that runs the length of the house, lit by a window at the north end, and this bare passage with its giant radiators and its many doors, down which I was about to walk as I had walked each evening for a month, was radiant with the promise of change: round any corner, through any door, the chance of a new life. The expectation had no sensible basis; yet it transformed my perceptions.

So I padded in my warm slippers down the corridor to the open library door. Music was playing, romantic opera to match the sunset. I felt my heart beating more rapidly as I stepped into the library and saw, through the four tall west windows, the same rosy vault I had left behind me at the wicket gate. There were no lights on in the dusky room. The eye was drawn instinctively to the windows, which, by splitting the sunset into panels, made of the sky a display that was at once framed and uncontrollable. Within one such frame she stood, the familiar stranger, with her back to me, silhouetted by the light of the sky. The image remains with me still: four bright strips, and her proud high-shouldered form, unmoving: no capitulation, no helplessness.

Bernard was at work building a fire. Seeing me, he stood up, his kind face flushed, rubbing his hands over corduroy thighs.

'Hello, Bron,' he said. 'How's love?'

That at least should have made her curious, but she did not turn round. The dogs came up and pushed at my shins. I scratched their necks, then squatted down to make a fuss of them.

'Good boy, Bracken. Good boy, Bramble. Good boy.'

They became excited by my attentions, and began to bounce and prance, licking my face.

Bernard introduced us, giving only a first name.

'Bron, this is Flora.'

I said, 'We've already met. This morning, in the mist.'

'So that was you.'

Her voice was low, detached, as I had known it would be. She turned then and looked at me, and in her eyes I saw, or thought I saw, a look of collusion, a secret message that said, *No need for Bernard to know what's happened between us*. This

28

look exactly matched my own feelings, but it also astonished me, and flooded me with concealed excitement. So from the very beginning my love was intensified by secrecy.

She moved away from the window to the fire, and lit a cigarette. I was now able to see her in the light of a lamp. She looked to me to be about my own age. I learned later that she was four years older than me. She was wearing a tailored tweed suit, square on the shoulders, slim at the waist. She held her cigarette in her right hand, at face height, her right elbow cupped in the other hand.

'Did I speak?' she said. 'I don't think I did.'

'No. You didn't speak.'

'You stared.'

'I was surprised.'

'Yes.' She tilted her head, and with a quick flick, threw back the fold of golden hair that fell forward over her cheek. This little gesture made me shiver, as if I had seen her do it before. She said, 'I thought maybe it hadn't happened.'

'Flora is one of my myriad cousins,' said Bernard. 'A refugee, like you. How about a sun-downer?'

I poured drinks while Bernard gave this unexpected cousin a short error-laden version of my life.

'Bron and I were at school together. He's writing a book about love. His girlfriend's kicked him out.'

'She's not my girlfriend.'

'Alright. The girl you were living with.'

I felt unreasonably irritated by this, but couldn't think of a short and casual way to explain my relations with Anna, so I said nothing. I gave Flora her drink.

'So what are you a refugee from?'

'People,' she said.

'People in general?'

'Pretty much.'

Bernard began to wave his arms about in the air in time to the music issuing from the ancient speakers.

'A Traviata sky tonight,' he said; and began to sing the aria along with the tenor.

> *'Di quell'amor, quell'amor ch'è palpito*
> *Dell'universo, dell'universo intero—'*

Then, abandoning his duet for a moment: 'Bron's the expert on love. We're counting on him to disprove it.'

Flora was restless, and moved back to the windows. I joined her there, and we watched the last colours of the sunset soften into night. We talked, or rather, I talked; not the conversation of old friends, since we had only just met, nor the conversation of strangers, but a sort of nonsense with which I tried to fill up the space between us. I wanted her to look at me again with that secret look.

I talked about the crystal spheres.

'There's one that holds up the clouds, and beyond that one that holds up the moon, and beyond that one that holds up the sun, and beyond that one for all the stars. You can see them, if you look for them. Up there, where the stars are appearing, that's the next sphere. That's the dome of the stars.'

She said, 'What happens after the dome of the stars?'

'Then there's the dome of night.'

'What happens after the dome of night?'

'Beyond the dome of night you reach the dome of silver-crystal, which is a perfect mirror.'

'What happens after that?'

'There aren't any more spheres after that. That's the end of all space and all time. That's where you enter infinity. The silver-crystal sphere gives such a perfect reflection that you can enter it, and travel back through the night and the stars, down past the sun and moon and the clouds, and find yourself home again.'

She said, 'Are you making this up as you go along?'

'No.'

'But it's not true.'

'It's true if you want it to be.'

'I don't think I want it to be. I don't like your domes. They make me feel trapped.'

I asked her how well she knew Bernard, and she shrugged her shoulders as if to say, I make no claims to know him.

We turned, both at the same time, to look at him: he stood with his staring hair and baggy trousers, his eyes closed and his arms outstretched, venting his ungainly emotions in the amplifier's amber glow.

She said, 'Aren't you much younger than Bernard?'

'No. Exactly the same age.'

I told her how Bernard and I had slept in adjoining beds in the cold school dormitory, and he had whispered to me across the lockers: 'Listen, Dearborn. Hello? Listen.' So many unwanted secrets that I, ashamed of his need, did not reciprocate. 'Listen, Dearborn. I can drink a pint of beer in one swallow.'

We ate in the dining room, by the light of candles in silver candlesticks. This was in Flora's honour. Bernard's mother joined us, also because there was a guest in the house, though she ate very little. She was not well. In her shyness at Flora's presence, Mrs Eyre called me by my proper name, which is John.

'John!' said Flora, surprised. 'You're not a John.'

'Aren't I?'

And there it was again: that sudden collusive look that bound us together in secret against the world.

'You don't seem to me to be a John at all. Bernard doesn't call you John.'

'He calls me Bron. It was my school name.'

I told her about our rhymes and anagrams and dyslexic distortions of each other's names, the manufacture of secret selves in instinctive resistance to institutional life: how Dearborn became Darebron, which was abbreviated to Bron.

Bernard said, 'Bron was the wiz at acronyms.' He then recited the sentence I had made of his own family name, which was Fortescue-Eyre: 'Frustrating or resisting the ego-self commonly undermines every experience you really enjoy.'

Flora laughed and said, 'What awful little boys you must have been.'

I said, 'Egotism was fashionable when we were sixteen.'

'Do an acronym of Flora, Bron,' said Bernard.

'Flora.' I played with words for a few moments. Then: 'Far away, lonely, out of reach, apart.'

'That's not very nice,' said Bernard. 'And it makes Faloora.'

Flora herself said nothing, but her blue eyes turned on me. *You don't fool me*, her eyes said. This must have been towards the end of dinner, because she was smoking a cigarette, holding it up high, near her mouth, even when she was not drawing on it. One of her favourite poses.

Have I said how beautiful she was to me from the very first? When I travel back in time to that first day, I see her pale face shadowed by candlelight, reflected in the dark polish of the dining-room table: the clear high forehead, and the oriental eyebrows that slant upwards, and the eyes wide-spaced, smoke-blue, immense. She let me hold her eyes for a brief moment; then the lion hair fell back between us.

4

Restless with thoughts of the day gone by, I lay awake through that long night. A little before dawn, mildly intoxicated by lack of sleep, I rose and dressed and walked through the chill woods. The black oaks closed around me like a sea. I remember only parts. I stood on springy turf, beneath high chimneys, aimless, tree-wrecked. I wanted to be near her.

Softly treading gravel, a thief of love, I found the window of the room in which I guessed she was sleeping. I reached up as tall as I could go, rose on the cold air, gently spiralling, until through the gap in the curtains I could look down on her in bed. There was no sexual content to this imagining; I watched over her with tender respect, as if she was a child dear to me. I close my eyes now and see once more the stone mullions of that window in the pre-dawn light, and the faint white outline of the sash frames, and a blur of condensation on the inside of the glass: so high did I reach. She was within the stretch of my arm.

There were lights on in the kitchen, illuminating the stable yard. The door opened and shut. I heard the clump-clump of boot-steps and saw Bernard on his way to the farm. He wore a sheepskin body-warmer and a fur hat, like a Russian. I ran to catch up with him, and he smiled to see me. 'Up early, Bron.'

The cows lowed to greet him, pressing against the barn gates, burgundy coats steaming. 'Sally, Molly, Meg,' he said, rubbing the tight white curls on their brows. He climbed the ladder to the loft, and a single bulb came on, lighting up the beams and rafters of the vaulted roof. The cows waited, staring at me, shamelessly curious, blinking their lustrous lashes. They roared softly, like expensive engines, issuing jets of steam from their nostrils. Then as the hay fell, sliced from the bale like giant toast, they lumbered away.

I heard the rivers flowing into Taw pool at the foot of the hill, and the blue-bottomed sheep coughing on the hillsides. I heard a bird calling: *chip-chip-chee*. I heard her move in her sleep, the soft scuff of sheets.

The light went out in the hayloft, and Bernard descended. 'Best time of the day,' he said. In his heavy boots, over the tops of which showed thick grey woollen socks, he strode back and forth with a swinging gait, lumbering, grand; of course, just like his beasts. The spiky hair that stuck out from under the Russian fur hat was Hereford red, the deep dark madder he had bred into the Tawhead herd. This was Bernard on his own ground, unafraid. 'Fidelity among the beasts, Bron.'

Tell me about Flora. How is it possible that she's your cousin?

But I did not yet ask my questions. Flora filled my mind, but greater than any impulse of curiosity was the impulse to reveal myself to her. That was how it was at first. Knowing so little about her, I could only imagine showing myself to her, like a child proud of a newly mastered skill: Look at me. I'm loving you.

Bernard scattered straw over the night's dung, followed

about by a stocky, inquisitive calf. There was light now in the sky, a rim of white over the hills, soaking upwards into the night black. I saw Flora asleep, the bedclothes crumpled around her; I felt the cut of the air in her room. I pictured, seated by her bedside, how some scatter, some fine spray of the dawn would follow me into her room between the incompletely drawn curtains, lie lightly on her sealed eyes, her lips parted in sleep breath, frowning at dreams. Summoned from a great distance by these motes of morning, I watched her embark on the gummy wriggle into consciousness.

Because she was strange to me, yet loving her, I obliged each passing sensation to speak to me of her. The wind rose up in the farmyard, flapping the blue plastic fertilizer bags nailed to the barn's gappy sides. I saw her head turn into the wind, her hand reach up to brush blown gold hair from amused blue eyes. Again: Bernard had hold of a calf, he was straddling it, rubbing its child-soft coat, saying to me, 'What do you say to my little Don, then? My Giovanni, my breaker of hearts?' And I, I saw Flora, seated, and in her lap, lightly circled by her arms, a blue-eyed child, neither boy nor girl.

Bear with me. Worship before knowledge, icons before photographs, dreams before memories. This is how it goes.

Bernard and I walked back to the house together and ate a breakfast of tea and porridge in the cavernous kitchen, by the changing light of the dawn. Bernard never turned on lights unless absolutely necessary. He pretended this was to save electricity, but the truth was that bright light saddened him. He knew his way round Tawhead like a blind man, from long familiarity. He ate standing, leaning against the Aga rail, bowl in one hand. His dogs lay at his feet, their backs pressed to the warm oven doors.

Here, in the quietness of the early kitchen, I asked him to tell me about his beautiful cousin. He answered warily, as if under some obligation not to tell too much.

'She's come down for a rest. I think things have been getting on top of her. She asked me not to ask questions.'

'Where does she live? What does she do?'

'I think they have several places. He's very rich.'

This was the first I had heard of a 'he'. I was ridiculously disconcerted. But a moment's thought would have told me that a woman as beautiful as Flora was unlikely to be living alone.

'Who's he? Her husband?'

'I think he's her husband.'

'Does she have children?'

'No. No children.'

He stopped, and looked at me with guilty eyes.

'Go on,' I said.

'Why do you want to know?'

'Why do you think I want to know? She's beautiful. I'm dazzled. I'm curious. Don't do this to me. I swear I'll throw my porridge at you.'

'She is beautiful, isn't she?'

'Very.'

'You know, Bron, I've had a crush on Flora for years and years. But don't tell her. She feels safe down here. She is safe.'

'Safe from what?'

'Oh, you know.'

'From her husband?'

'Her husband. Men in general.'

'She wouldn't be hiding away down here if there wasn't some sort of problem with the husband.'

'I expect you're right.'

37

I persisted, and under pressure Bernard told the little he knew.

'He's some sort of businessman. His name's Axel Jaeger. I think he's a lot older than her. He doesn't like her to show interest in other men.'

'Does she show interest in other men?'

'No. She says not.'

I pondered this information. It made no sense. There were no children. Nothing obliged her to stay with this husband.

'Why doesn't she leave him?'

'I don't know. The money, I suppose.'

'Is that what she's like? Is money what matters to her?'

'No. I don't think so. She used to be a kind of hippy. Then she was with Mick Jagger for a while.'

'Mick Jagger!'

'And David Bailey. She's still got one of his pictures of her. Ask her if you don't believe me.'

'I believe you.'

It was not so hard to believe. Ten years ago she would have been even lovelier. She would have been able to pick any man she wanted. And now here she was, stepping out of the mist and into my life, and in her eyes that secret gaze. No wonder she filled my dreams.

I have dreamed women all my life. In the memorable winter of 1963, when the snow lay until Easter and the country lanes were impassable except by foot, I fell into an adoration of a girl named Mary Sexton. I was just fifteen years old, she fourteen, the daughter of a farmer in a nearby village. She had black curly hair, and looked like Natalie Wood. We went for a walk together, and she kissed me. After the kiss she took my hand, and as we returned over the squeaky snow she told me

I was her twenty-third boyfriend, which made me proud. I went back to boarding school. There were some letters. By the end of term, when I was home again and the snow was long gone, I had been replaced.

I don't remember that this much dismayed me: there had been enough reality in that one winter day. I treasured every part of the memory of the kiss, how she had stood on tiptoe, how I had felt the press of her young breasts against my coat, how the touch of her lips had been so little and yet the feeling so big. To me, she was an angel, bright with light from another world.

Is fifteen a little old to receive a first kiss, and to be so satisfied? I have no way of telling. Boys exchange information of the geographical kind, as if the discovery of girls were a matter of mapping; nothing of the wonder and gratitude that was born in me with one kiss.

The way in which I loved Flora was formed by all those other loves: all the women I have adored, feared, needed, exploited, disappointed, since I walked with Mary Sexton in the snow. Much of what I write may seem strange to my female readers, because they live in a world where the power is still mostly in the hands of men. But if my story is to have any value, you who read this must believe that my perception of women is not some private distortion: it is a view from the heart of the castle-city of men. That castle-city is built on a hill, and from its high walls the watchmen see for miles.

If the men have power, why are they so afraid? If independent, why the dread of dependence? If free, why so little love?

As a boy, I was fascinated by fortifications. The South Downs, where I grew up, were pocked with abandoned wartime installations built to oppose an invasion from France

39

that did not come: concrete blockhouses, pillboxes, gun emplacements, all now overgrown with brambles and gorse. These military burrows were my secret places. I sat within them, among the newspapers and the empty bottles and the stench of urine left behind by tramps, and peered out through the slit windows at the golfers on the fairway. The satisfaction of being so well protected mingled with the fear of being trapped. Were the enemy to dodge my machine-gun fire, and to clamber on the concrete roof, and to appear in the narrow downward-sloping tunnel that formed the doorway, I would be unable to escape. Therefore I never hid for long. After a few minutes the panic would strike like an arrow, and I would burst out on to the immense bald-browed hills, from any one of which, as I ran like a crazed rabbit, I could see for miles.

Bernard brought his cousin to visit me in the gate-lodge: the writer at work. I was seated at my mug-ringed table when they appeared through the trees, and my pen was in my hand, but I was not making progress with my work. All morning I had been drawing shapes on paper, arcs and eggs and spirals, and writing among them, over and over again, the name 'Flora'. When I saw her out of the window I crumpled up the crowded sheet and put it into the stove. So she came in upon me wielding the riddle-iron, making secret heat from the letters of her name.

She was wearing Bernard's raincoat, as before, and a long red scarf. My kitchen was warm. She unbuttoned the coat and let it flap open, and unwound the scarf. Bernard displayed my way of life as if I were famous.

'The writer's bed. The writer's armchair. The writer's pen. These cards, they're all the men and women in the entire history of the world who've fallen in love at first sight. One card each.'

Flora looked and said, 'How far have you got?'

'I've only just started the book itself. It's all been research so far.'

She moved about the room, curious and restless. Whatever drew her attention she reached out and touched with one finger, lightly, as if to hold it steady to her gaze. On one of the internal walls, which were timber partitions, I had pinned various lists and notes and stray quotations. There was my postcard of Gauguin's woodcarving, on which he had cut the injunction: *Soyez amoureuses, vous serez heureuses* – Be in love, you will be happy. Beside it was my list of alternative titles for the work in progress: A Simple Arrow, Lovestruck, At First Sight, True Love, Mirrors of the Self, The Enslaved Heart, A God Stronger Than I.

'It really does happen, then?' she said, intrigued. 'Love at first sight.'

'Oh yes, it happens.'

'Has it happened to you?'

Before I could answer, Bernard smacked his great hands together and burst into laughter.

'That's the big joke,' he said. 'Bron's the original heartless bastard.'

I protested at this. 'I've been in love.'

'When?' said Bernard. 'Fifteen years ago?'

'Even so, that was love at first sight. Well, hope at first sight, anyway.'

She sat down in my armchair, pulling her legs up and hugging her knees. She fixed her eyes on me, as if she knew already what I was going to say.

'What's hope at first sight?'

'Oh, you know. Being ready to fall in love with anyone. The emotional equivalent of taking your toothbrush to a party.'

Her face broke into a smile, but her eyes were looking past me. Turning round, I found Bernard behind me pointing at me in an exaggerated way and clowning admiration.

'A bon mot,' he said. 'I told you he was a writer.'

Bernard was not acting typically that day, any more than I was. Flora's presence among us had an irritant effect that came out in him as an incongruous playfulness. The shadow over Bernard's life has always been his relations with women: I have seen his agonies of shyness, and his subsequent furious self-contempt. To my knowledge, Flora was the first woman he had invited to Tawhead since Zoë left him, seven years ago, after just three days of married life. He has a joke about his disastrous marriage: 'What's the difference between me and Jesus Christ? On the third day Jesus Christ came back from the dead.'

They did not stay long, not wanting to disturb me. As Flora left, her eyes fell on one book among the many stacked on the table, and she said in surprise, 'That's Freddy's book.' She picked it up and turned it over in her hands, as if it were familiar to her.

'Who's Freddy?'

'He wrote it. I know him. I often go and stay with him.'

The book was *The Collected Letters of Paul Marotte*, edited by the art historian E. F. Christiansen.

'Have you read it?'

She shook her head.

I took the book from her, saying, 'It's wonderful stuff. Very moving. He fell in love with a governess called Kate Summer.' I turned the pages until I came to the Left-Hand Letters. 'He

42

died as a result of a street accident. The accident paralysed him down his right side, and he lost the power of speech, so he wrote her these messages with his left hand. He knew he was dying.'

I showed her one of the pages.

Eyes dry with not seeing you.

And: *I need only a warm room, a still mind, and you.*

I watched Flora and Bernard out of sight through the trees. As they disappeared there came the roar of a low-flying jet streaking down the valley. There was an air-force training school at Chivenor, not far away, and the local people were used to the flights. To me it was still a source of wonder, the way the little grey planes entered the valley at treetop height and were gone again in the blink of an eye, trailed by their dilatory sound; as if for one, two, three seconds the placid Devon landscape had intersected with another universe.

When the roar of the jet had faded away, I said aloud:

'I love you, Flora.'

There was nobody to hear, yet the words were spoken. They had taken on an existence outside me, as vibrations in the air. In this manner I decided to suspend my resistance to the obsession that had come upon me, and to surrender to it, without security and without understanding. I decided to overlook the absurdity of feeling so much with so little basis. I accepted with due gratitude this gift of the gods, this smiting, this bolt of lightning. And I vowed to do all in my power to make the beautiful stranger love me in return.

5

Over those days at Tawhead, every encounter with Flora shocked me. I carried her with me so completely in my imagination that each first sight gave rise to a sort of scuffle, a churning of water, as in the basin of Taw pool where two rivers meet. Not Flora and I, this convergence of rivers, but the dream and the experience: my love affair had outpaced the reality of our dealings with each other. For all the sudden seduction of her secret looks, nothing had passed between us that made us more than new acquaintances.

I decided to move slowly. Some instinct warned me that she would startle easily, like a wild creature. If I were to reveal the intensity of my feelings, she would take fright and run. She had come to Tawhead as to a kind of sanctuary, and I must take care not to violate it. At the same time I played the game that she herself had begun, that something was happening between us that must be concealed.

One afternoon, when Bernard was taking his mother to the doctor, Flora and I played Scrabble in the library. There was no bag for the letter-tiles, so we laid them face down on the table and picked up our replacements from these rows; and I was cheating. Flora was chain-smoking, tapping each cigarette on the back of her hand as she took it out of the packet, flicking her hair to one side, scraping a flame from her old Zippo lighter; then leaning forward as she drew on the cigarette, stroking her right shoulder with her left hand, guarding and comforting herself.

We talked as we played, about Bernard, and his mother, who was very ill, and laid out a pattern of unadventurous words: PLUME, HEAL, MOON.

She said: 'Did you ever meet Bernard's father?'

'Oh, yes. Several times. He died while we were still at school.'

'Oh, long ago.'

'Nearly twenty years.'

In my little wooden rack I saw the letters L,V, B, and the sequence recalled to me one of my index cards. When my turn next came I used it to exchange the other four tiles in my rack for four that lay with their backs to me, peeping when I could. This exchange gave me two more of the seven letters I sought.

'Bernard says he's known you since you were little,' I said.

'Yes. But we were always somewhere else.'

'So which of your parents is related to Bernard?'

'Oh, Mummy.' She spoke as if it could only have been her mother. 'She's Bernard's father's sister.'

'That's close. You're a true cousin.'

I surrendered my turn once again, and in the exchange of tiles added one more to my tally.

'Aren't you going to make a word?'

'Not yet.'

'I'm playing with myself here.'

'Bernard's never told me about you before.'

'Why would he? He hardly ever sees me. This is maybe the third time I've ever been here in my life.'

'So where do you live?'

'Oh, here and there.'

'With your husband?'

'When he's there.'

I exchanged my final tile, this time picking up the letter I needed to complete the group. I arranged all seven in correct order.

She could tell from the look on my face that I had got what I wanted.

'Well? What is it?'

I turned my rack of letters round to face her.

I, L, V, B, I, D, T.

She read them, frowning, trying to make them form a word or group of words. Perhaps she even guessed at an acronym, but could not pull any sense out of it.

'I don't understand. What does it mean?'

'Crown Prince Rudolph of Rumania had those seven letters engraved on an iron ring that he gave to his mistress. *In liebe vereint bis in den tod*. In love united unto death.'

'Oh. One of your love stories.'

'She wore the ring on a chain round her neck.'

'So were they? United unto death?'

'Absolutely. They committed suicide together, in a hunting lodge in the Vienna woods.'

'That's one way out, I suppose.'

'Did you really go out with Mick Jagger?'

'Yes.' She didn't seem surprised by my question. 'I did a lot of stupid things.'

'What was stupid about going out with Mick Jagger?'

'Oh, Mick was alright. But you know how it was. Too many drugs.'

'Sounds wild.'

'Yes, I suppose so. But none of that's real.'

I liked that. Fame and wealth, sex and drugs and rock'n'roll, all unreal. Here and now, she and I were real.

'So you didn't fall in love with Mick Jagger?'

'Oh, no. We were far too cool to fall in love.'

'Didn't you want to fall in love?'

'Not then. Now, yes. I'd give anything to fall in love now.'

'What's stopping you?'

'I don't know. Too much past, I think.'

Suddenly she jumped up, as if unable to sit still any longer.

'Can't we go out somewhere?'

'We could climb to the top of the Head,' I said. 'Let ourselves be blown away by the wind.'

'Blown away by the wind! That's perfect!' Her eyes shone for me, thanking me for guessing so exactly what she wanted to do. 'Let's be blown away!'

On the long summit of the hill above the house no trees grew, and sheep grazed on the springy turf, and half of Devon lay in our sight. We walked the ridge path into the wind, so that her blue eyes watered and her golden hair streamed behind her like a wave. The shadows of clouds swept over us, piling up rain in the west. She held my arm, and we pushed against the wind all the way to the lip of the hill, and there we turned our backs to the wind and I took her in my arms and kissed her. Her lips accepted mine and yielded to me, all her brittleness and distance melting away, and I felt how fragile she was, and how full of need. Then she drew away from me, not unkindly, and we walked back the way we had come, with the wind now hurrying us home.

We did not speak. The kiss had no words. It had happened on the hilltop, where we were blown away.

When the trees began again we turned downhill, and so met the tractor way that led to the lodge. She sat in my armchair, as she had done before, her feet pulled up under herself, her baggy raincoat loose about her. I boiled a kettle and made us mugs of tea. Rain began to fall outside, heavy drops blown by the wind against the window-panes. This was the start of the record rains that fell over Devon without ceasing for ten days; until Flora left Tawhead. I was happy with the rain. It locked us in together. I was happy because we had kissed, and everything was now changed.

'Tell me about your book,' she said. 'Tell me about real people who fell in love at first sight.'

I was sitting at my work table, so I looked through my research cards for an illustration. I chose Richard Burton, the nineteenth-century explorer, and Isabel Arundell. In the greying rainy light I read to her Isabel Arundell's account of her first meeting with Burton on the ramparts at Boulogne.

One day, the vision of my waking brain came towards us. He was five feet eleven inches in height, very broad, thin, and muscular; he had very dark hair; black, clearly defined eyebrows; a determined-looking mouth and chin nearly covered by an enormous black moustache. I have since heard a clever friend say that he had 'the brow of a god and the jaw of a devil'. But the most remarkable part of his appearance was two large black flashing eyes with long lashes that pierced me through and through. He had a fierce proud melancholy expression; and when he smiled, he smiled as though it hurt him, and looked with impatient contempt at things generally. He was dressed in a black, short, shaggy coat, and shouldered a short thick stick, as if he were on guard. He looked at me as though he read me through and through in a moment. I was completely magnetised, and when he had got a little distance away, I turned to my sister and whispered to her, 'That man will marry me.' The next day we met again, also on the ramparts. He produced a piece of chalk, and wrote, 'May I speak to you?', leaving the chalk on the wall. I took up the chalk and wrote back, 'No, mother will be angry'; and mother found it, and was angry.

I smiled at this, as I always did when I read it.

'Don't you think that's a wonderful message? "No, mother will be angry."'

'Why?'

'Because it's a no that's really a yes.'

'What happened to them?'

'She married him, just like she said.'

'Did it last?'

'Oh, yes. For thirty-one years. Till Burton died.'

She pondered this information.

'She can't have stayed magnetised all that time.'

'Burton was quite a wild character. Being in love with him seems to have been a career in itself.'

I read from another file-card Isabel Burton's best-known lines: 'I wish I were a man. If I were, I would be Richard Burton. But being only a woman, I would be Richard Burton's wife.'

'How strange,' said Flora. 'Wanting to be a man.'

'I suppose it's because men were so much freer than women in those days.'

'They still are.' She looked up at me and smiled. 'That's my name. Did you know? Freeman.' Then the smile faded. 'Not-free, not-man.'

'You seem free enough to me.'

'That's all you know.'

'Give me time.'

'No,' she said. 'No.' And she looked away. I could feel her withdrawing, retreating back into that inner sadness I had met before, a place where she would not let me follow her. *Too much past*, she had said.

But she had let me kiss her. That was real.

She said, 'Don't you get lonely here?'

'Yes.'

'Don't you get tired of just writing about love?'

'Yes.'

'But that's what you are, isn't it? A writer.'

'Yes.'

I did not defend myself, though her criticism was plain enough: writing is not living. I wanted her to go on asking me questions.

She said, 'Some things are better not put into words.'

'Why is that?'

'I don't know why. It's just better not to talk about some things.'

'Words are how people know each other.'

'You have to say that. You're on the side of words. You're the writer.'

'What side are you on?'

Her answer amazed me, though she has told me since that she meant nothing by it, spoke the first words that came into her head, wanting only to deflect my question. But I do remember her rueful smile.

'I'm the subject,' she said. 'I'm the one you write about.'

It amused her to tease me, to romanticise herself in my eyes; but she gave away more than she knew. In guarding one secret she exposed the rest. Too much vigilance is revealing.

The rain had become heavy by the time we left the lodge, so we returned to the big house under the shelter of a black wood-framed umbrella that I found in the lodge entrance. The track through the woods was dark, the daylight fading fast. The sound of the rain falling on the trees cocooned us in a steady soothing murmur. We walked close, to share the umbrella's protection, and I felt the warm press of her shoulder against mine. We did not speak.

This was my time of innocence, I suppose; my few days in the garden. Like Adam, like Eve, I was restless and full of questions. With knowledge came the fall from grace. When I walk again through the rain and the trees with Flora in my dreams, I have no questions.

The rain falls; the two rivers flood the meadows. Bernard in the back kitchen stamps mud from his boots, his every entry heralded by wet dogs. Mrs Eyre opens doors, peeps into empty rooms, in search of her husband who has been dead twenty years. Flora stands, cigarette in hand, forever guardian, before the tall grey windows. I have no sense of time, of the numbers or names of these days. They have seeped together into one arrested moment, in the course of which certain things happen, and certain things do not happen, and we wait.

The moment is, say, late afternoon. The day is draining away, but is not gone. The lights are not on, and the long rooms are shadowed, secretive. I am entering the library, and for a few moments I cannot tell whether she is there or not, she stands so still.

I say softly, 'Flora?'

There are conversations and parts of conversations.

'I hated school,' she says. Or, 'I don't believe in love.'

Bernard tells me, 'My mother fell in love with my father. You should put them in your book.'

Flora persuades Mrs Eyre to talk about her husband. I think the subject will distress the old lady, but Flora understands better than I.

'George was very tall,' Mrs Eyre says. 'That was the first impression, you see. My hat, how tall he was. He said to me, You must be the beautiful Miss Hampton. Of course, it was nonsense. I was what we used to call a plain Jane. We were a couple of ugly mugs. George said, a mug and a cup.'

'Did you know you would marry him?' Flora asks. 'From the start?'

'Well, my dear, I thought I might.'

'He was your first love.'

'My first love, yes; and I his. George was never a talker. When we reached an understanding, he clapped his hands together and said, That's that and no more bother about women.'

George Fortescue-Eyre lies buried in the churchyard at the foot of the hill. Standing beneath umbrellas in the rain we read the headstone: *We shall be reunited in a better place*. We return slowly up the road, and along the oak avenue. Mrs Eyre clings to Bernard's arm.

'Bernard, your wife should come to church.'

'Zoë has gone, Mama.'

'No, dear. I saw her this morning.'

Bernard's great frame leans towards the tiny figure of his mother, who is shrinking day by day in her illness. Flora and I walk behind, each with our own umbrella, not close.

Also within the same moment, the dogs lie spread before the library fire, and Flora sits cross-legged between them, stroking their golden coats. I sink far back in a deep chair, listening, saying little. We are alone, and Flora is telling me about her childhood. I look not at her but at the fire, fearful that the intrusion of my gaze will silence her. I want her to trust me. I want her to come closer to me. I want her to kiss me again.

'I have a memory of my mother from when I was, oh, four years old. She's sitting at a table by a window, writing. My father's in the room too, but indistinct, further away. She's writing in her diary.'

I learn small items of information from these fire-lit memories. Little by little, as in all my other researches, the picture is forming. I am beginning to tell her story.

'She showed me her diary, years later. I read a page, and skipped through a few more pages, but it was too sad. She was still writing about Daddy, every day. He'd left years ago.'

'How old were you when he left?'

'Seven. They say that when a girl is seven years old, her father is the perfect man. So my perfect man left.'

She shrugs, without bitterness.

'But you must have seen him since.'

'Yes. He visited me at school. I was seventeen. My friends thought he was gorgeous.' But her tone is not one of pride, or of pleasure remembered. 'So naturally I'm screwed up about men, and best avoided.'

This is a clear-enough warning. I ignore it.

'Except for your husband.'

'Axel?' She laughs. 'Axel knows what he wants. Which is rare.'

'Do you love him?'

'Do I love him? No. I don't think so.'

'Why do you stay with him?'

'Do I stay with him?'

'Have you left him?'

'Too many questions. You make me nervous.'

She doesn't sound nervous. She sounds weary.

'I'm curious.'

'No you're not. You're just the same as all the others.'

'What do you mean?'

'I don't suppose you've got any grass?'

'What?'

'Dope. Hash. Mary Jane.'

'No.'

'I shouldn't anyway.'

The intimate moment has passed. I curse myself. She's leaning over the dogs, stroking them, her hair falling gold on gold in the golden firelight. I want so much to touch her.

'I'm just interested in all that stuff,' I say. 'I'm writing about it, remember?'

'Well, leave me out of it.'

'You're the subject. That's what you said.'

'You shouldn't believe everything I say.' And then, before I can respond, 'Are you really as clueless as you make out?'

This hurts, and I am silenced. What can I say? The truth is I do feel clueless about Flora, but it's the last thing I'm going to admit. Clueless is not sexy.

Now it's Flora's turn to feel guilty.

'Let's not talk about me,' she says, and she reaches out one hand and touches my knee. Not a caress exactly, but a peace offering. 'Talk about you.'

'What do you want me to tell you?'

'Anything. Are you happy?'

'Sometimes.'

'What makes you happy?'

I decide to avoid all talk of love. I look out of the windows at the rain, and I tell her about the raft.

'I used to lie in bed at night, before going to sleep, and imagine I was on a big raft. It was square, and made of wood, and had a house in the middle. The house was just a hut, really, only small, so that there was room to walk all round it. There was no engine, no tiller, no sail. The raft just drifted, very slowly, down a wide river bordered by trees. I liked it best when it was raining. Then I would sit in the little hut and listen to the drumming on the plank roof and look out at the rain on the river and the trees sailing slowly by. That always made me feel happy.'

'Were there other people on your raft?'

'No. Just me.'

'Didn't you get lonely?'

'Yes. But it didn't matter.'

'I like your raft.'

So now we're friends again.

The house grows damp, stains form in high corners. At night the ancient radiators knock and tick like prisoners. Mrs Eyre takes to her bed. Bernard sits with her for hours at a time. I come every day.

'You shouldn't be here,' says Flora. 'You should be writing your book.'

'I'll go back to my book when the rain stops.'

'I can tell. Your heart's not in it.'

'No. My heart's not in it.'

And our eyes meet: those secret faraway smoke-blue eyes. It's become a game between us, a dance of courtship. She wants me to want her, but she does not yet want to give herself to me. Or so it seems to me. Why else these quick collusive looks? Why else her hand on my arm, left there just long enough to contain promise? Why else the wordless message to me, contained in her eyes, in her tone of voice, in her silences, that if she is unavailable to me it is for reasons beyond her control?

One kiss, that's all so far. I'm living on one kiss.

She says one day, when I speak of Bernard and the burden he carries, 'At least he's living his own life.'

'What do you mean?' I say. 'Aren't you living your own life?'

'No. Not really. Mostly I live other people's lives.'

'Why?'

'Because it gets me what I want.'

'What do you want?'

'Safety. Love. Not to grow old. The usual bag of tricks.'

The less I understood, the more I was fascinated. In my own defence, I could hear, as insistent as a heartbeat, the cry for help that sounded beneath the deliberate mystification. This allowed me to invent her as the beautiful fragile creature held prisoner by an evil power. The absurd myth of the knight-errant lay potent within me, undimmed by post-modern irony. I wanted to rescue her, because then I would be worthy of her love, and she would love me. It's no accident that so many ancient stories translate love into a hunt, a pursuit that involves danger and weapons that wound and kill.

A simple arrow sped by an archer's bow.

6

In the course of those few days and nights in October more rain fell on north Devon than had been recorded over the entire previous year. The water level in Taw pool rose so high that the island disappeared, leaving only the three trees standing like paddlers in a lake. The meadows lay under water as far as the hanging woods; and the entire bulbous oak-clothed promontory between the rivers, the Head itself, became enisled.

This relentless onslaught found the gaps in the house's defences, and water came trickling through into corridors and rooms. Bernard placed an assortment of buckets and pots under the leaks, some of which filled up so rapidly that they had to be emptied morning and night. The drips made their descent at different intervals, sounding on impact at varying pitches, according to the size of the collecting vessel, so that the old house rang with changes like a bell tower.

The claustrophobia of those days was so suited to my obsession that I came to believe I had willed the weather. Rain shut us in, closed doors pushed us together. I grew rash with nearness. I was restrained by the unspoken rules of our intimacy from saying aloud to Flora, 'I love you.' The paradoxical consequence was that I longed to say these three words, with a compulsion that became almost intoxicating. To put this in context: I had never before said 'I love you' to anyone, not since the long-gone bedtime litany of childhood. It had become a matter of almost phobic resistance. Why? I think I was afraid that the unadorned statement carried a commitment I could not honour. It was this very issue that had ended my affair with Anna, back when we were both nineteen years old.

The argument had been about flowers.

Anna and I had been going out together for a year, which is a long time at that age. Anna's best friend Polly had been sent a bouquet of flowers: a serious bouquet, wrapped in cellophane, with an arch little note from the sender, an older man who had fallen for Polly. I was there when the bouquet arrived, and witnessed Polly's lack of enthusiasm, and so felt able to speak freely.

'Flowers, for God's sake! Next he'll ask you to come up and see his etchings.'

Polly just said, 'He can afford it.'

Anna said, 'I don't understand. What have etchings got to do with it?'

'It's prehistoric, sending flowers. This guy needs to update his seduction technique.'

'It's just a gesture,' said Anna.

'It's like waving money at a girl,' I said. 'Do you know what that bunch of flowers cost? Probably five pounds. He's saying, I'm spending five pounds on you, so now you owe me.'

'Yes,' said Anna hesitantly, 'but aren't all gifts like that?'

'Flowers are in a league of their own.' I was warming to my theme, quite unaware of the forces driving me. 'Flowers deliver a message that's unambiguously romantic, for which read sexual. He's trying to buy sex with Polly for five pounds.'

'I'd rather have the five pounds,' said Polly.

'But you like getting flowers, don't you?' said Anna.

'Oh, yes. I love flowers.'

Later, when we were alone, Anna returned to the subject.

'You shouldn't have sneered at Polly's flowers, Bron. You spoiled it for her.'

'What! She didn't give a damn about those flowers! I was watching her.'

'That was just for show. Everyone likes to be sent flowers.'

'I don't.'

'Well, all women do.'

'I can't believe this! It's one thing to pick flowers from your own garden, but phoning a florist, someone else does all the work, all you have to do is pay. It's the laziest, least personal, least imaginative gift there is!'

'I like flowers.'

'Wrapped in cellophane? With a message written in capitals by an illiterate shop assistant?'

'Yes.'

'You'd like me to send you flowers?'

'Yes.'

'They cost a fortune, Anna! And all they do is die.'

'Not right away.'

She was responding in a more muted way than usual. I sensed the reason for this, and it only made me more insistent.

'Well, you won't be getting any flowers from me.'

'I had noticed.'

'I can't afford it.'

'I suppose you could always pick some.'

'Where? Someone's front garden?'

'I don't know. A field.'

'You want me to go hacking across the countryside looking for buttercups?'

'Not if you don't want to.'

'I don't see the point.'

'It's what you said. It's a romantic gesture.'

'There are better romantic gestures than flowers.'

'Alright,' said Anna. 'I'll have one of those.'

I had backed myself into a corner.

'Look, Anna. Why are we even having this argument? We see each other every day. We don't need these things.'

'I suppose not,' said Anna. 'It's just that *these things* make people feel good.'

'What do you want? Poems? Serenades?'

'Yes please.'

'People don't do that any more.'

'So what do they do?'

'They talk. Like ordinary normal people.'

'Do they say "I love you"?'

'Of course they do.'

'But you don't.'

'You know it anyway.'

'So why not say it?'

'Because saying it when you've asked me to say it makes it not a free expression of feeling.'

'So if I don't ask, will you say it?'

'You've asked now. It's too late.'

'Too late for how long? For ever?'

'Oh, come on, Anna. Give me a break.'

'Give you a break?'

'Just leave it alone, okay?'

'Did you hear what you just said? You said, "Give me a break."'

'So?'

'So maybe I should give you a break.'

Ridiculous to recall now, but our relationship never recovered from this little exchange. Anna told me many years later that it was on that day that she began to prepare her exit. You may suppose that this experience made me readier to send flowers or to say 'I love you' to later girlfriends. The opposite is the case. I became unable to say it at all.

Picture then my astonishment at finding myself at Tawhead daily forming the forbidden words with my lips, longing to utter them, with a guilty compulsive longing. The sensation of helplessness, the loss of control over my own future, which had always in the past so frightened me, now became the heart of my delight.

On several occasions I almost spoke; but some instinctive sense that the moment had not yet come held me back. I remember one time when Flora and I were alone in the kitchen, and the radio was playing a lunchtime concert. We sat on either side of the wide wooden table, and she cut up an apple with a big triangular-bladed cooking knife. The chamber music ended and there was a weather forecast, and then the one o'clock news. She frowned with concentration as she chopped the apple into ever-smaller pieces. I wanted to put my arms around her, to rock her, soothe away the tension that she discharged down the knife; but the wide table lay between us. *I love you. I ask nothing. Being with you is enough.*

My words did not make a sound in the kitchen, but for me they filled the world.

*

During this time of rain, little Mrs Eyre fell into a coma. It had been expected. 'There's been so much pain,' Bernard said.

We sat with Bernard, Flora and I, in the old lady's bedroom. There were blankets nailed over the window against the draughts, and three paraffin heaters to warm the high-ceilinged space. This was the room in which Bernard's parents had slept all their married life. The bed was high, antiquated, vast. The old lady's child-sized body lay propped on a pile of pillows, completely still, occupying barely a corner of the hummocky expanse. Bernard sat on a chair drawn close to the bedside, and held his mother's hand in his, and stroked it. The dogs lay by his feet, pressing their flanks against the chair-legs, panting softly. The paraffin heaters threw flickering blue flowers on to the ceiling. From time to time he spoke to her, forgetting our presence.

'Mama,' he told her. 'Mama, it doesn't matter if you can't hear me. It doesn't matter if you can't answer. I'm only talking to help you sleep.'

With his big careful hand he parted the hair on her brow and kissed her as she slept.

'I just want to tell you how much I love you. Everyone has to have someone who loves them.'

The old lady slept on, her face showing some weariness, some peace.

'We've had some good walks together, haven't we, Mama?'

Later: Flora and I alone in front of the library fire. Because the old lady was dying, it seemed to me that I should speak the truth, as a sign of respect; which is to say, to tell what was most true of me in that moment. But my truth was like a clumsy stranger, waiting outside the door. I needed a process of introduction.

She was standing with her left hand clasping her right shoulder. I looked up to speak, I forget what I had in mind to say; but it was then that I caught the likeness that had been in the back of my mind ever since I had met her.

'You don't have to act with me, Steve,' I said. 'You don't have to say anything and you don't have to do anything. Not a thing. Oh, maybe just whistle. You know how to whistle, don't you, Steve? You just put your lips together and blow.'

She looked round at me, her eyes bright with amusement, and gave me back other lines from the same script.

'You know, Steve, you're not very hard to figure. Sometimes I know exactly what you're going to say. The other times . . . the other times, you're just a—'

She couldn't remember. Her face scrumpled up in a puzzled grin. 'What is it? Rotter?'

'Stinker.'

She laughed softly.

'Stinker.'

My heart began to beat so fast it frightened me. How many people knew the dialogue of that particular old movie as I did? How many, knowing it, could cross-cast the lines to say so much?

Flora repeated, relishing the term, 'Just a stinker.'

I said, 'I knew it. I knew I was right about you.'

'Don't count on it.'

I saw it so clearly now, in her high square shoulders and the curve of her golden hair, the consciousness of the look. Howard Hawks had directed the young Lauren Bacall with these words: *No capitulation. No helplessness.*

The silver hiss of the falling rain. The golden hiss of the fire. No more evasion, no more distance. I kissed her, and she kissed me back like someone who wants to be loved.

63

I said, 'It's even better when you help.'

Another quotation. She shook her head, turning away.

I said, 'I love you.'

As soon as the words were out of my mouth, I felt a surge of elation, a buoyancy of the heart. This came as a complete surprise, a reward not conditional on the response. So I said again, 'I love you.'

She said, very low, 'You wouldn't if you knew.'

Too much past.

She took out her cigarettes and lit one and inhaled deeply. 'It's not a very good moment, is it?'

'You knew anyway.'

'It's different once it's been said.'

'Yes, it is.' So I said it again. 'I love you, Flora.'

'You don't know anything about me.' She pushed the hair from her eyes with an impatient hand. 'I wish you hadn't said that. It's better not to say things.'

'I wanted you to know.'

'I always know.'

She gave me such a strange look then, wistful and longing and sad, so that it seemed to me she would have loved me, but for – but for what?

'You know Bacall and Bogart fell in love while they were making that movie? They called each other Slim and Steve. In real life, I mean.'

'You know too many love stories.'

We shared so little past. I had to use such material as came to hand. It's the past that provides the tools of intimacy: memory and misquotation, history and revisionism.

But already the space was opening up between us. It was maddening. Each moment of intimacy was followed by a retreat. This was not a woman exercising guile to win my heart – my heart was won already. This was true ambivalence. I did not feel rejected as a lover: I felt that love itself was rejected. But I did not know why.

I don't regret that second kiss. I don't regret the speaking aloud of the feared and magnificent words, part-spell and part-prayer. But there is a sort of aggression in unconditional love, and Flora fled before it.

Now, in retelling this story, I accept responsibility. Here from my index-cards is a line from a letter by Rilke, which I offer as a confession of sorts:

> I sometimes ask myself whether longing cannot so stream out of a man, like a storm, that against it, in opposition to this outgoing current, nothing can reach him.

When I next walked through the woods to the big house, Flora was gone. There was no parting message. She left my life as abruptly and absolutely as she had entered it.

There were other concerns at Tawhead that took precedence during those days. As the rain at last ceased, and a late-autumn sunshine brightened the sodden valleys, little Mrs Eyre died, having never awoken from her long coma. I remained with Bernard until the funeral, and saw her buried beside her husband in the little graveyard beneath the Head. My friend was more bewildered by his mother's death than grief-stricken, at times forgetting that she had died at all.

'Bron, just now I came in through the conservatory, and I was bending down to pull off my boots, and I looked up to where the vines hang down over the door, and they were swinging as if somebody had just passed. I called out, Mama? It was so strong, the feeling that I'd just missed her. That she'd been there, watering the vines.'

I too saw ghosts at Tawhead, though I did not tell Bernard. Often, when I entered the upper library, I thought I saw Flora standing before the tall windows, looking out at the railway and the river and the hills. Once I said out loud, 'So you came back.' But she did not come back.

I spent much of my time with Bernard among his cows. He had a little farm office above the feed store, reached by an out-side staircase, and here there was a kettle and the makings for tea. He preferred to sit in the farm office than in the library, or any of the other silent rooms in the big house.

He told me he was losing his memory of his mother as she had been most recently, her hair grey and her frame dwindled by illness. In its place came older pictures.

'Sometimes I see her coming down the corridor humming to herself. Her hair's how it always used to be, dark and springy. She's plump, and has her spectacles on a string round her neck. The dogs are following her, Bella and Sam. Bron, Sam died while we were still in school. I try to remember her the way she was in these last years, but I can't. All I see is that frowning face she put on when she'd forgotten something, and the way she pushed her hands through her hair, and the dogs getting in the way of her feet.'

Bernard said to me many times after his mother's death, 'I don't make sense on my own.' Over these days I spent alone with him, I came to understand what he meant. He saw himself as part of a process that was larger than himself, his existence made purposeful only because he occupied a place in a line. Tawhead, the house, the farm, the fields and woods between the two rivers, this was his place; he felt no desire to leave it, even for a time, as I urged. Here he belonged. But he had no wife, no children; the line was cut, and he was adrift.

It is only through loving that I have learned to honour

bonds; I who was so long in transit. Bernard is right, none of us makes sense on our own; but there is a price to pay for belonging to others, and I watched my friend pay it.

As for me, all the time I thought of Flora. In my mind she became the nineteen-year-old Lauren Bacall, leaning on the piano in the Hotel Marquis, while Hoagy Carmichael plays 'How Little We Know'. I was her audience, watching in the darkened cinema, seduced by the tension between her self-mockery and self-assurance, her defiance and surrender.

I read again, from the photocopied pages in my files, willing the same happy ending, Lauren Bacall's account of how she and Bogart stole time alone together as the shooting progressed: an oddly innocent road map of love, traversed in a 1940 grey Plymouth coupé:

> We drove over Highland Avenue, turned right on to Hollywood Boulevard to Franklin, then another right on to Selma Avenue, a small street that was curved and very residential – almost no traffic would pass through. We'd pull over to the side and he'd come over to my car. There we would sit, holding hands, looking into each other's eyes, saying all the things we couldn't say at the studio. We'd sit on our street for fifteen or twenty minutes, dreading the moment of parting, then he'd get into his car and off we'd go, making the turn at Laurel Canyon Boulevard to Sunset Boulevard, continuing on until we reached Horn Avenue, where Bogie lived. As he made the turn he'd wave his hand out of the window, I'd do the same, and go on to Beverly Hills.

I stayed at Tawhead until the first frost came, and the grass stiffened, and the ground turned hard. There were clear skies, sharp and starry at night, and fine dawns.

One evening Bernard spoke about his cousin, as if remembering quite suddenly that she had come to Tawhead, and stayed as a guest, and left again.

'I don't really know why Flora came, or why she went. Though it can't have been much fun for her here.'

'She didn't say anything to you?'

'Anything about what?'

'When she said goodbye.'

'Did she say goodbye? I don't remember.'

Not much forwarding information there.

'I suppose she's back with her husband,' I said. 'Do you think she's alright?'

'No, not really,' said Bernard. 'People who come down here and stay are never alright.'

He saw surprise on my face. I was surprised to find Bernard more insightful than I supposed. But he drew a different interpretation.

'Apart from you, of course. But you're a writer.'

'A writer who isn't writing.'

'Yes, I'm sorry. It must have been distracting for you. My mother and everything.'

I had already decided I must leave. Not for my work: that was in suspension, or even possibly in disintegration. Life had overtaken it. I had to leave to find Flora again. But how? Bernard was no use.

'You must have a phone number, at least.'

'No, I don't. She phoned me.'

'What about your aunt?'

'Flora's very private. She doesn't give out phone numbers. Just leave her alone, Bron. It's what she wants.'

'Doesn't she want friends?'

'You don't mean to be her friend.'

This was true. I was relieved to be able to abandon my front of casual interest.

'Is it so obvious?'

'Just about every man she ever meets falls in love with her. She can't handle it, Bron. Forget her. You're better off with Anna.'

'Anna is not my girlfriend. How many times do I have to say it? We're friends, okay?'

'Well, I don't understand you. I would have thought a girl like Anna would be enough for anybody. What's wrong with her?'

'Nothing's wrong with her. I'm just not in love with her.'

'Would she go for someone like me, do you suppose?'

'I don't know, Bernard.' I found this talk of Anna exasperating. 'Since when were you so keen on Anna? You've only met her once.'

'Twice. But I thought she was with you.'

'Well, she isn't. She's got a modern artist.'

'Oh.' Bernard took this news philosophically, long accustomed to having his romantic hopes dashed. 'So that's that, then.'

Strictly speaking, Anna was no longer going out with her artist, as far as my most recent knowledge went. But by now there was probably someone else. There was no point in getting Bernard's hopes up. And anyway, they weren't right for each other.

7

I returned to London. Anna let me stay in my old room in Cross Street on the understanding that the arrangement was temporary. She was at her best, warm, high-spirited, funny, because she had just met a new man.

'So you see, I was right.'

'The taxi is for hire.'

'Exactly. Or it was.'

'What did he do? Flag you down in the street?'

'More or less. We met at a private view.'

This new man was called Harry. He was an architect, working for the Ove Arup Partnership, and he collected art, rather than made it. All this sounded promising.

'And does he appreciate you?'

'I think so. It's all very new.'

I said nothing about my own romantic adventure in Devon, partly because I was aware that it would sound like a fantasy of my own making. But I thought about Flora all the time. I had only one clue to her life beyond Tawhead: she had said she was a friend of the art historian E. F. Christiansen. I wrote Christiansen a letter, through his London publisher, and delivered it by hand. My letter described the book I was writing, and begged an hour of his time to discuss Paul Marotte. No mention of Flora. I gave my address as Cross Street.

While I waited for a response, I tried to get on with my writing, but could not. So, as a holding measure, and in hope of a favourable reply from Christiansen, I read all I could about Marotte and the Pont-Aven school.

The artists who adopted the little town of Pont-Aven in Brittany, and the nearby fishing village of Le Pouldu, were surprisingly diverse in age and background. They came from France, England, Holland, Switzerland, Denmark, Ireland and Poland. Gauguin had been a stockbroker; de Hahn a businessman; and Emile Bernard was barely out of school. Marotte, of course, had been a doctor. Together they achieved what perhaps none of them could have done on his own, which was a distinctive new way of seeing the world. Armand Seguin's name for this, 'synthetism', fails to convey the impact of the canvasses that came out of Pont-Aven. The colours are startlingly bold, applied in big flat blocks, in the fashion of the enamel decoration called *cloisonné*; also much influenced by Japanese art. The framing is strange, with human figures sometimes pushed to the edges, or cropped mid-body. Faces are often indistinct. The artists' self-declared project was to paint 'by heart': to re-create a scene from memory, allowing the visual details to be overlaid by the retained emotions.

I was charmed to discover that one of their favourite gathering places was a woodland overlooking the town called the Bois d'Amour. They all painted scenes here, the best known being Emile Bernard's *Pont-Aven vu du Bois d'Amour*. Paul Marotte, true to his obsession, painted several portraits of his mistress in these woods – woods of love indeed. One of his letters, reprinted in Christiansen's book, gives a word picture of these few idyllic summer days in Brittany:

I like to be in the woods not because nature is in itself more beautiful than manufacture – why should this be so? a roof tile is as complex and full of wonder as a rock in a woodland stream – and for flowing water I have sunlight – how the sun shines here! It makes me drunk each day! I sit in Turkish shade, drinking wine so new it is more blue than red. Kate lies on the rug and mocks the glittering of my spectacles. I have been painting myself, you will be astonished to learn, this for my Kate of course. She demands an image of me. Why? I say to her, You have the original. Have I left you for even one day since we joined our lives together? (I have not. She cannot deny it.) Still she asks for my likeness, there being no photographic portrait for her to frame and kiss when she is tired of kissing me. So I am at work on an image of myself, painted true to our united creed not from a looking glass but from my own memory of myself. No, I must correct that assertion. I have a mirror of a kind, which is my own Kate, who I require to sit before me as I paint, and look on my undistinguished face. In this way I see something of myself in her now studious, now amused gaze. I feel my features moulded by love and gratitude, and this I paint. The lunatic on the canvas grins back at me like a hair-oil salesman. It can't be helped. The air is warm, the wine is mellow, and I have no notion of the time of day.

On re-reading this letter I find I never concluded the opening sentence. I like to be in the woods because – because here there are no mirrors, no shop windows, no danger of a sudden encounter with that most hated and most feared of all ghosts, my own reflection. As a scientist, so now as an artist, I look intently at all that is not me, because I do not want the returning gaze. Emile calls me the Invisible Man. I wish it were so.

This self-portrait intrigued me. Marotte was well known to have refused to sit for his fellow artists, or even to be photographed. There is no picture of him: the Invisible Man indeed. And yet this letter describes the painting of a self-portrait. The editor's note says simply, 'The painting referred to here is presumed to have been among the works destroyed by fire in 1944.' I made a note to ask Christiansen about this fire, if he proved cooperative.

As I made myself familiar with Marotte's life, I became ever more amazed at the change that had come over him on that Tuesday morning in early December 1888. It was as if a hammer had struck the brittle matter of his life, and broken it in two. He did not evolve from meticulous scientist to passionate artist: he exploded. I longed to see a picture of this extraordinary man – any picture. I wanted to look into his eyes, and feel what he felt. I wanted to believe that what had happened to him could happen to me.

That was when I found the key to my thesis; which had been before me all the time, unnoticed. I was writing a book about *transformation*. Marotte's encounter on the bridge changed his life, his work, even his personality. Deep in our hearts, we don't believe in the possibility of transformation. We fear that as we are now, so we will be to the day we die. Paul Marotte's story, and my book, would offer a challenge to this numbing fatalism. You too can be born again. For was it not, even now, happening to me?

With these thoughts in mind, I began my book again:

73

What if the act of falling in love at first sight is something more than a romantic surrender? What if it is a radical declaration of true selfhood, an act of liberation, a coming-out? If this is so, then the dramatic moment of first meeting that seems to strike like a bolt from the blue is in fact the culmination of a process long in the making, the bursting of the chrysalis that reveals the winged and brightly coloured being within.

There is only one work by Marotte in a public collection in England, and that is a portrait of Kate Summer in the Courtauld Institute. Anna and I went to look at it one Sunday afternoon. On the way there Anna, who sees the art world in business terms, introduced me to the concept of Marotte as a tradable commodity.

'Strictly speaking, he's a minor figure in the Pont-Aven school. The work now looks derivative. He has a very narrow range. But that's not how the art market works. The art market is driven by celebrity. Look at the high prices paid for Van Gogh. What do you know about Van Gogh?'

'He cut his ear off.'

'There's celebrity for you. And by the way, he did it while Gauguin was staying with him. Gauguin moved from Pont-Aven in Brittany to Arles in Provence to live and paint with Van Gogh, and it all went horribly wrong. Van Gogh went for him with his razor, and ended up cutting his own ear, and now fetches higher prices than Titian.'

'Higher than Gauguin.'

'Gauguin's not done too badly. He has his own Unique Selling Point, as the ad men say. What do you think of when you hear the name Gauguin?'

'Tahiti.'

'Bright colours. Sexy native Polynesians. The longing of over-civilised man for a pre-industrial Eden.'

'Be fair. He did go to Tahiti.'

'He went, and he found petty French officials, and petty French priests. He gave the Polynesian girls syphilis. He hated it all so much he took arsenic, only he took too much and vomited it up. He would have stayed in Paris if anyone had bought his pictures.'

'You just like being cynical about art.'

'I'm not cynical. Van Gogh and Gauguin are good painters. I'm just making the point that people aren't interested in art theory, they're interested in people. They always have been. They looked at Titian's paintings, back in his day, and they thought he must have used some kind of magic, because his painted figures were so like real people. And as for Marotte – what does everyone know about him? That he was a Synthetist who rejected Impressionism? I don't think so. What they know is that he fell in love on a bridge.'

'And his mistress killed herself.'

'Suicide always adds value.'

She looked at me, and we both laughed.

'I'm not really an art-bitch,' she said. 'I'm sorry she did it.'

'At least she knew love.'

'You've been doing your book too long.'

Anna then gave me the prices commanded by recent sales of Marotte's work.

'One of the bridge meetings, a hundred thousand dollars and up. Anything with Kate Summer in it, close behind. A still life, twenty thousand if you're lucky. Unless Kate Summer bit one of the apples, and you've got a letter authenticating the bite.'

*

We found the one portrait we had come to see hanging to the right of a door, on its own, outshone by the riotous jungle of Gauguins on the other walls. I recognised Marotte's mistress at once: the pale oval face, the heavy eyebrows, the brown hair drawn back from her brow. She had the look of a Quaker matron, not the bohemian libertine you might expect.

Anna said, 'She was a governess when he met her, right?'

'Yes.'

'Gauguin's wife was a children's nanny.'

'So?'

'What is it about these men who fall in love with nannies?'

I declined to answer. Anna studied the portrait, frowning.

'What do you think he saw in her?'

'What does anybody see in anybody?'

'Well – what?'

'How should I know?'

'Because you're the one who believes in it. I don't. This love-at-first-sight business. I think it's all bollocks.'

'Bollocks?'

There were only two other people in the room. Both turned to look at us. We lowered our voices.

'If you ask me,' said Anna, 'it's obvious. He fell for a governess *in her uniform*.'

'That's enough.'

'He knew he'd been a naughty boy.'

'I said, that's enough.'

But my eyes met Anna's, and we both burst into suppressed laughter.

The chill air of Woburn Square sobered our spirits.

'You have no heart.'

'No heart? I like that! Am I the one who thinks Valentine's

Day is a trick to make people spend money? Am I the one who chokes on the word love?'

I couldn't tell her how everything had changed for me. I didn't exactly know why, but I couldn't. It felt as if it would be taking something away from her.

'Still,' said Anna, clearly feeling she'd been too hard on me, 'you're on to something with Marotte. His life choices do get people talking.'

'I think it's all about transformation.'

Her lips came together, and I caught her in time.

'Don't say bollocks again.'

'Why not?'

'It's juvenile.'

'Oh. Alright.'

She took my arm as we walked down the street towards the Tube station.

'So what's a mature way to say it?'

'Rubbish. Balderdash. Baloney. Piffle. Tosh.'

'Piffle? Tosh? No, somehow it's just not the same.'

As we returned to the flat, the phone rang. I could tell from Anna's voice that it was Harry, the promising boyfriend.

'Oh, hi,' I heard her say. And, 'Not a problem.' And, 'Whatever's good for you.'

Then she put down the phone and said in a light and off-hand way, 'That was Harry. We were going out, but he can't make it. Some work crisis.'

'It happens.'

'So are you booked this evening, Bron?'

I was not. We went out and had pasta at the Portofino in Camden Passage, and a bottle of Chianti, all paid for by Anna, because I was as usual penniless. Only later, as we were walking back up the Essex Road, did Anna refer to what should have been her evening's date.

'I'm afraid Harry may turn out to be a mistake.'

'You think so?'

She was sounding philosophical. I stayed neutral.

'He said he'd call me during the week.'

'Then I expect he will.'

'He tells me he has a crisis at work. He says, I'll call you during the week. And I say, No problem. Why do I say that?'

'What else could you say?'

'I could say, I'm busy all next week. I could say, If you want to see me again you're going to have to summon up a bit more enthusiasm than that. I could say, You don't break a date an hour before you're due to show up, you inconsiderate jerk.'

'True. You could have said that.'

'Oh, Bron. Why is it always like this?'

I realised her eyes were filling with silent tears as we walked. I took her hand. Unfortunately, I knew the answer all too well.

'Do you want me to tell you?'

'No. I know. I've been there before. He thinks he's getting in too deep. He's cooling me off. Oh, God. I'm so tired of it all.'

She let the tears come, and we walked down the road hand in hand, and there was nothing I could say.

Back in Cross Street, Anna looked up Gauguin in her art books and read out to me the following quotation from his *Intimate Journals* of 1903:

As you perceive, I do not know love. To say 'I love you' would break all my teeth . . . I wish to love, and I cannot. I wish not to love, and I cannot.

He sounded just like the old me. He sounded like Harry.

'Fuck Gauguin,' said Anna. 'I've gone off him in a big way.'

Two days later, I was in the flat alone when the doorbell rang and it was Harry. Anna wasn't back from work yet, so I let him in and made conversation. He looked normal enough, except that his clothes were too clean, too pressed. We chatted about this and that, and then I thought of Anna crying in the Essex Road, and I got serious.

'So how long have you been going out with Anna?'

'Oh, just a few weeks,' he said.

'And is it the real thing?'

'What do you mean, the real thing?'

As soon as he said that, I knew Anna was doomed.

'Do you think the two of you will make it all the way?'

'What do you mean, all the way?'

He didn't fool me. I could smell the fear. It takes one to know one.

'I'm not criticising. I'm only asking.'

He shrugged and avoided my eyes.

'I'm not about to propose marriage, if that's what you mean. It's just a few dates. I hardly know her. Why does everything have to get so heavy?'

It was like listening to myself.

'Okay by me,' I said. 'Only Anna's one of my best friends. I happen to know she's looking for a lasting relationship.'

'So am I,' he said.

'But not yet.'

He nodded, and his eyes met mine for a moment, and we shared the shame.

Anna came back from work, and was surprised and pleased to find Harry there. I could see that she was reading

79

this as a more promising sign than it was. I couldn't bear to watch, so I withdrew to my room. They went out together, and much later they came back, and Harry stayed the night. I could track every inch of Harry's journey, from sitting with me, shrugging and looking away, saying, 'It's just a few dates,' to sharing Anna's bed: a little alcohol, a little neediness, a little lust, a little why-not?, and the anaesthetising of further thought.

Christiansen replied.

'Dear Mr Dearborn. Your book sounds interesting. When you next come to Amsterdam, I would be happy to meet you and discuss our mutual interest in Paul Marotte.'

8

In the early seventies, by means of a public subscription, and with the generous sponsorship of the Nederlands Credietbank, the house in Amsterdam in which Paul Marotte had lived was purchased and restored and opened to the public as the Marotte Huis. Keizersgracht 519 was, and is, a narrow five-storey brown brick house, topped by the ornamented neck-gable typical of the early eighteenth century; no more than one room wide; and looking on to the beautiful tree-lined canal just below the Spiegelstraat bridge. Here was assembled a collection of sketches, letters and memorabilia, and a small number of paintings, for an admission price of three guilders.

It was Christiansen's suggestion that we should meet at the Marotte Huis, which, he said, was within easy reach of his own home and gallery.

'You appreciate, Mr Dearborn,' he said as he showed me round the lovingly restored rooms, 'that such paintings as we have here are of the second rank, even third rank. They are more of biographical interest, I should say. We do have two fine Marottes here in the Rijksmuseum. For the rest you must go to the private collections.'

'I know very little about art, Mr Christiansen,' I said. 'I'm more interested in the biography.'

'So I understand.'

From our very first meeting, Freddy Christiansen showed an unexpected curiosity in me. When I spoke, he stood still and focused on me the attention of his steady deep-set eyes, in a way that was both flattering and unnerving. I found him impressive: a tall, well-dressed, infinitely careful man, who spoke always in a soft courteous voice, with the accent of one who has learned his English among Americans. I guessed his age to be around sixty.

'It is love, you understand,' he said, referring to my project, 'that made Paul Marotte into an artist.'

He showed me the original of one of Marotte's letters to Kate Summer, known to me already from the collection he had himself edited. It was displayed under a glass frame on the bureau that dominated the second-floor study.

'Not, alas, the actual bureau at which he worked on his case histories. You know he wrote a monograph on facial characteristics and mental instability in women? He deserved more recognition than he ever received. For his neurological work, I mean.'

The ink was somewhat faded, the paper grey, but it was easy to imagine those neatly penned words forming fresh on the page, straight from his heart. Beneath the original letter, for the benefit of those like me who could not easily follow the French in which it was written, there were translations into Dutch, German and English:

Today I have been working on the bridge again. The form of
it is secure in my mind, yet for two hours this morning I stood
at the canvas, the paint so stiff my brushes could hardly work

it. Slowly, slowly it yields. This is how it seems. There comes the time when the sense of it, and the form it will take, and the paint itself are joined, and the effort ceases. You know those pumps that draw on deep wells? I must work the lever for some time, until at last the fresh water gushes out. Then it continues to flow, though I do nothing.

I paint not from nature but from love. My subjects are nothing more than shapes for the sense of love. I need only a warm room, a still mind, and you. Are we not man and wife, Kate, by the ceremony of the heart?

On the wall beside the bureau hung one of the 'bridge' paintings, almost certainly not the actual one referred to in the letter; though, as Christiansen said, all the paintings in that particular cycle resemble each other closely. I studied the canvas with some emotion, touched by the reading of the letter. The bridge itself was short, humped, so that the woman and the child stood at a higher level than the canal beyond. The strong vertical lines of the lamp-posts framed the scene, one at each of the bridge's corners; in the background, casually sketched, the tall houses on the far side of the canal, and a leafless tree. The colours of the painting were strong, non-naturalistic, the sky a dense yellow, the street blue, applied in impatient strokes; all the care given to the organisation of line and colour so that the eye was drawn to the figure of the woman. The dark railings of the bridge led to her; the tree behind made space for her; the bright-blue ribbon in the child's hair was her harbinger. By the ordering of the light, together with a sudden wildness in the brush strokes, the artist had succeeded, even in so part-formed a work, in packing this one figure with energy, so that she seemed to hurry towards the eye of the beholder.

'There is a better version of the scene in the Rijksmuseum,' said Christiansen. 'Also, one of the better portraits of Kate Summer. The best, in my opinion, is in my own collection.'

He told me then of his private collection, which was in Switzerland, where he had a house. As if in apology for such good fortune, he added, 'My collection dates from the end of the war, as perhaps you know. Marotte was not as fashionable then as he has become since.'

He drew my attention to a display of sketches, called the Ziekenhuis Studies: crayon drawings, done around 1887, of female mental patients.

'Even as late as 1887 Marotte was not thinking of himself primarily as an artist. He was looking for points of re-semblance in facial expression.'

I asked about the lost self-portrait, and the war-time fire.

'A collector of Marotte's works, his first patron, in fact, was a mill-owner in Pont-Aven called Medellin. He built up quite a private collection. His heirs didn't share his interest in Marotte. The paintings were stored in a stable loft. The stable burnt down.'

'How many paintings were lost?'

'Nineteen or twenty.'

'The self-portrait among them?'

'Ah, that we don't know. It's a reasonable guess. It's never been found.'

He opened the door to a small office, where a young woman sat at a desk, frowning over a mass of papers.

'Good morning, Camille.'

'Good morning, Freddy.'

She answered in French-accented English, not looking up. A plain young woman in a shapeless brown jersey.

'Camille,' said Christiansen as we headed on down the

stairs, 'is doing a post-graduate thesis on Marotte. She is suffering the misfortune of full access to the archive.'

'Why is that a misfortune?'

'The archive has never been properly catalogued. Nothing is in order. There is no money to pay for the work. As you see, the Marotte Huis is not the city's premier attraction.'

We were the only visitors to the steep-staired house. When the tour was completed, Christiansen invited me to walk back to his gallery, which was on Spiegelstraat near by. The building stood on a corner, and leaned a little into the street. An external flight of steps climbed up to a first-floor door, the stone threshold of which was cupped with age. This was the gallery; above it, Christiansen's apartment. It was modest in size, and sparsely furnished, though in expensive taste. As far as I could tell, he lived there alone.

He offered me a drink, and then a toast to my project: to love at first sight.

'I have been asking myself, Mr Dearborn, whether or not you have a personal interest in the subject of your book.'

I said, 'Surely everybody is interested in love.'

'Of course. But I think perhaps you too have had a meeting on a bridge. Am I right?'

'Why do you say that?'

'A guess. It seems to me you are a romantic.'

I laughed. 'I never would have called myself a romantic. But you're right. Very recently, as it happens. But not a meeting on a bridge.'

'A meeting of another sort?'

'A meeting of another sort.'

'Good. Your book will be the better for it.'

This was my opportunity, even if it gave away more than I wished. Christiansen was my only link to the vanished Flora.

'I think you know her. She saw my copy of the Letters. She said she knew you.'

'I have many English friends.'

'Her name is Flora Freeman.'

I caught a flash of surprise in his eyes, just as quickly overlaid with the smooth and even manner that was his habitual mode.

'Flora? Yes, I know Flora.'

'I met her at her cousin's house in Devon.'

'I see.' He refilled my glass, and then faced me with a quizzical stare. 'So your meeting of another sort was with Flora.'

'Yes.'

'She is a very beautiful woman. Men have a way of falling in love with her.'

'She's also married.'

'That seems to be no impediment.'

'You mean she has affairs?'

'No, no. You misunderstand me. I mean to say that even though she is married, men other than her husband contrive to fall in love with her. Though there's nothing new about that. The greatest poets of romantic love, the troubadours of the court of Provence, all celebrated the passion of under-employed young men for married women.'

'You yourself are clearly not a romantic.'

'A matter of regret, I assure you.'

He raised his glass to me, and drank.

'I get the impression,' I said, trying to sound casual, 'that all is not well with her marriage.'

'I have the same impression,' he replied. 'Though other people's relationships are infinitely mysterious.'

'I would very much like to see her again.'

'Of course you would. May I ask – is it your belief that she would like to see you again?'

'I'll be honest with you. I'm not sure. I think she would like to see me again if circumstances were different.'

'What circumstances?'

'I can only guess. Her marriage, perhaps.'

'Her marriage. Yes.' He seemed to deliberate within himself, and then to reach a decision. 'Her husband is a man who is used to getting his own way. An interesting man. A plain speaker.'

'And rich.'

'Yes, rich. But he has made his own fortune. That gives a man great self-confidence. As for the source of his wealth – did Flora tell you?'

'No.'

'One could call it a charming coincidence, given Flora's name. Axel Jaeger is a flower king. His companies ship fresh flowers in refrigerated containers to all parts of the world.'

'Flowers!' Dim memories surfaced, of Dutch tulip fields in bloom, of the famous tulip fever of the seventeenth century. 'So he is based here, in Holland?'

'Of course. He is one of my best customers. He met Flora Freeman here, in my gallery, at one of my parties.'

'So would Flora be here now?'

'That I don't know. But I can telephone her house. I have her number. Would you like me to?'

'No.'

My answer was too immediate. Christiansen smiled.

'You think she will run away.'

'I'd rather meet her more casually. In the street, or something.'

'On a bridge?'

87

'I expect I appear a little ridiculous to you. The truth is, ridiculous or not, I do seem to have – that is, I owe it to myself—' I stopped, and drew a breath, and started again. 'If it's all an invention of my own, I must find that out. And if it's not, well, I must find that out too.'

My incoherence seemed to touch him. He spread his hands, as if to say, Away with mockery.

'What would you like me to do for you?'

'Her address. That's all. And if you meet her, don't tell her I'm in town.'

He drew a small leather-bound pad out of a drawer, and wrote down an address. As he gave me the little sheet of paper, he said, 'I ask in return only that one day you tell me what happens.'

I walked down the Singel and noted Number 265, a substantial double-fronted house with a dark-grey door. I did not stop, or stare in too obvious a way. Then I walked back down the opposite side of the canal, and allowed myself a more detailed look. With its symmetrical facade and its curtained windows and its neat iron railings, the flower king's Amsterdam residence looked like a doll's house. I loitered on the Singel for half an hour or more, but nobody came and nobody went. The house seemed to be closed down.

What else had I expected? A chance encounter? Truth to tell, I had more than expected it; I had willed it. Christiansen's revelation that Flora's house was here in Amsterdam had reinforced a secret belief in me, which was that I was destined to find her again; that we were destined to be together. This conviction was driven solely by the power of my obsession. How could I want something so much unless I was, in some mysterious way, being caused to want it by its own magnetic power? The logic may seem false, but it was instinctive. Just as the pull of gravity, the sensation of falling, assures us that the earth exists and that we will certainly meet it, so the intensity of my own love caused me to believe in its fulfilment.

Those scenes in movies where the hero and heroine, still virtual strangers, find themselves thrown together by chance in the same railway carriage, or seated at adjoining tables in a restaurant, and turning, discover each other, all innocent confusion and surprise – 'You!' – 'What are you doing here?' – such scenes, far from being weak plot contrivances, are surely dramatisations of the will in action. The hero and heroine, we know it at once, have willed that they should be in the same place at the same time. It is no coincidence; unless coincidence is the name we give to the fruits of those acts of will which, in a sort of shame, we choose not to own.

What to do next? I went back to the Victoria Hotel on the Damrak where I was staying, and wrote up the notes I had taken in the Marotte Huis. Then I counted my guilders and calculated how much longer I could afford to stay in Amsterdam. Not long at all. One more night, if I was frugal with my meals. This had the effect of focusing my mind. Since I was in Amsterdam to see Flora again, I must return to Singel 265, and either trust to fate to bring us together, or knock on the door.

On my return, I settled on a canal-side bench, a white wooden bench placed by a tree, looking across the canal at the house of the flower king. I hoped that passers-by would not find my vigil suspicious. As soon as you become static in a street you discover that you are drawing attention to yourself. Streets are designed for the movement of people and cars, and, in this case, boats. The only people who sit on benches for more than five minutes are homeless tramps. On the other hand, since the only people who see you sitting on the bench are themselves in passage, perhaps each one thinks you have sat down for a brief rest, before continuing on your purposeful way.

So the thoughts idled through my mind, and the dark-grey door remained resolutely shut. Suppose the door opened, and Flora stepped out on to the street: what would I do? Would I jump up, and place myself so that our paths crossed, and so let her discover me by chance? But the door did not open, and Flora did not appear. None of the front doors opened, in all that stretch of canal houses, in all the time I was watching. It then struck me that such millionaires' houses were unlikely to have only the one entrance; more, that somewhere round the back there would be a way in and out for the millionaires' cars.

I left my seat and crossed the canal by a bridge called the Heibrug. There, near Singel 265, an alley called the Ramsteeg cuts through to the back of the tall houses. I went down it, and turned left into Spuistraat, which runs parallel to the Singel, behind its grand seventeenth-century residences. Spuistraat too had its own houses, but here and there a vacant lot opened to the rear of the houses on the Singel. The double-width house that was Singel 265 had its own back yard, and in it stood two cars: a silver Mercedes convertible, and a black Range Rover.

Here I had even less excuse for loitering than on a bench by the canal. But there was no one in sight. The little I could see of the rooms through the back windows showed no activity. So I risked entering the yard itself, and peered into the Mercedes convertible. Had anyone been watching, I would have been taken for a car thief. I was a thief of sorts. I was stealing information.

There on the shelf above the car's instrument panel, beneath an open packet of cigarettes, lay two theatre tickets. The performance was for the Nederlands Dans Theater, at the Stadsschouwburg, that night at seven thirty pm.

By the time I was patrolling the Leidseplein, it was raining. Only a drizzle, but cold. My coat had a thin hood, of the kind that rolls up inside the collar, and I had it over my head, so that I looked like a mugger. However, there were others outside the theatre, waiting under the long pillared portico for friends to arrive, and I hoped that I passed as a young dance enthusiast. Seats could be had for as little as five guilders, so this was not implausible.

I was looking out for the silver Mercedes, and so very nearly missed them. They came on foot, under a blue umbrella. I recognised Flora from behind, though she looked very different, because she had her hair up. By her side was a big man of fifty or so with short fair hair. They made a striking couple.

I walked rapidly towards them, calling out Flora's name. She stopped in the theatre doorway and turned and saw me. I felt at once the unbridgeable chasm between our lives: she so sophisticated, so glamorous, so grown-up; I so young and cheap and wet. But I had begun, and could not retreat now. I waved in what I meant to be a casually friendly way.

'What are you doing here?' I said, smiling.

The big man now turned and looked me up and down. He was not smiling. Flora clearly had no idea who I was.

'I'm here to see Christiansen for my book,' I said.

Flora peered at me. I pulled my hood down.

'Bron?'

'Yes!'

She turned to her husband. 'A friend from England. John Dearborn.' And to me, 'Axel. My husband.'

The big man offered me a big hand, but still no smile.

'It's amazing to see you!' I went on, grimly clinging to my pretence. 'What brings you to Amsterdam?'

'We live here,' said Flora.

'I'm afraid we must go,' said Jaeger. 'The performance begins soon.'

'Yes, of course,' I said. 'Are you free any time tomorrow? I'd love to have a coffee with you, and catch up on the news.'

'I don't think so,' said Flora, glancing towards Jaeger. Jaeger shrugged, as if it were a matter of indifference to him.

'Or maybe we could meet at Christiansen's gallery.'

This was meant by me to be an offer of safe neutral territory. It turned out to be a mistake.

'You are a friend of Freddy Christiansen?' said Jaeger.

'Yes.'

'No,' said Flora at the same time.

Jaeger put one hand into his breast pocket and drew out the tickets and gave them to Flora, with a nod that was almost a bow.

'Why don't you invite your English friend to take my place? I find that dance bores me this evening.'

He handed her the blue umbrella, and turned and strode away into the rain.

Flora bent her head so that she was looking down at the ground. I couldn't see her face.

'I'm really sorry,' I began. 'I had no idea—'

'That's right,' she said. 'You had no idea.'

Then she looked up, and her face was twisted with fear and anger. She never raised her voice, but her words were sharpened and meant to wound, and they did.

'I don't know what you think you're doing, following me about, but if you imagine it gives me any pleasure, you're wrong. I don't want you fucking up my life any more than it's fucked up already. Am I speaking plainly enough?'

'Yes,' I said.

'And keep away from Freddy.'

With that, she went on into the theatre without a backward glance.

9

I was in shock. What offence had I committed? Why such withering contempt? She had spoken to me as if I was half her age. So her husband was jealous: he had walked away. She could at least have been civil to me. Puzzled and hurt, I made my way past the tawdry gift-shops of the Leidsestraat, allowing myself to be herded with the other pedestrians. When I reached the Singel I turned in the opposite direction to the house I had watched for so long, and soon found myself passing the tower in the Muntplein. Wanting still to be walking, I crossed the Amstel and dived into smaller streets. My hood remained down, and the drizzle soaked into my hair, but I felt nothing. The further I walked, the angrier I became. What right had she to speak to me like that? To say to me, 'Am I speaking plainly enough?' And why had I stood there like a guilty schoolboy before the head teacher and said, 'Yes'?

Away to my right I caught sight of the grey steeple of the Zuiderkerk, with its red-and-gold clock telling me the time: the dance programme would now have begun. One empty seat beside her. She could at least have invited me to join her.

Now rambling, circling round smaller curving streets, in flight from my humiliation, I passed dark canals and coffee-shops loud with rock music, and so entered the cluster of narrow streets round the Oude Kerk which is Amsterdam's red-light district. Here, quite suddenly, there were brightly lit windows, and in the windows, bored young women in their underclothes, selling sex. I began to walk more slowly.

I had been saying to Flora in my head, *Fuck you, fuck you, fuck you*, in time with my footsteps. Now, faced with truly available sex, I realised that the last person I was likely to fuck was Flora; and that there were other options. At this, all my shame and anger took a new direction, and the energy released in me by the few moments outside the Stadsschouwburg turned to sexual desire. Why not? Since my higher emotions were labelled infantile fantasies, I might as well indulge my more basic needs. Only, did I have enough money?

The rain was now falling heavily. I found myself standing outside a bar called Le Boudoir. Its door was open, and some framed photographs inside showed naked women dancing, which I took to mean the bar offered more than drinks. I realised I had become very cold. I went in.

There was an inner door, and here stood a doorman with his hand out for money.

'For the first drink,' he said.

I pulled out my slender bundle of Dutch notes, and he pointed to a blue ten-guilder note, so I gave it to him. Somehow it didn't seem possible to turn round and go back out into the rain.

The bar was dark and warm, like an underground burrow. There was a long curving counter, padded on its upper surface, behind which worked two young women. One had long straggling black hair, the other short brown hair and spectacles. Both were entirely naked.

I sat on a bar-stool and felt the cushiony top of the bar with my hands. The woman with the long dark hair came over to me. She had big breasts and a wide mouth and was giving me a friendly smile.

'Want a drink?' She swayed lazily to the beat of the bar music. 'It's free. You've paid for it already.'

'So it's not free,' I said.

'Okay. It's not free.'

I asked for vodka. It came ice-cold, in a tiny glass. I drank it all at once.

'I'm Monica,' she said. 'Want a show?'

Seeing that I did not understand, she pointed to her right. 'Like that.'

At the other end of the bar a man sat with his back to the bar and his head laid on the padded surface, like one who suffers from a nose-bleed. Folded over his nose was a blue ten-guilder note. The woman with the short brown hair and spectacles stood on the bar above him, her bare feet on either side of his head. As I watched, she lowered herself carefully on to his face, and sat there for a few moments, rocking from side to side. When she rose, the blue note rose with her, as payment for favours received: nose money. My sexual desire evaporated.

'No thanks,' I said.

'Okay,' said Monica.

There were no other customers. I suppose Monica was bored, and I seemed harmless. She stretched herself out on the bar before me, lying on one side, her head propped up on one elbow, and we carried on a conversation of sorts. The situation was so surreal that I responded without self-consciousness. I liked her long uncombed hair and her generous lips and the absurd smears of make-up round her eyes and her comforting body and her jungle of black pubic hair.

'You're wet,' she said.

'It's raining.'

'Raining? You don't say.'

'I was walking.'

'It's raining, and you were walking.'

'So I came in here.'

'Out of the rain.'

'Out of the rain.'

'No rain in here.'

'No rain.'

'You sure you don't want a show, angel?'

'No thanks.'

'Okay.'

The man at the far end of the bar was now feeding a red twenty-five-guilder note to the woman in spectacles.

I said to Monica, 'Does he mind me seeing him?'

Monica answered, 'Do you mind him seeing you?'

I shut my eyes.

We who go into nude bars are all guilty. Because I am a man I too pay nose money. I turned then a sudden corner in my mind, and saw beyond it a long unforgiving street, in which men stood on one side in white sunlight, and women on the other in blue shade: an actual memory, of a small town in Mexico, which had been waiting in me for the day when it could surface, transformed into a metaphor of sexual segregation. And I was there among the men in the burning light, indistinguishable from the rest, longing for love.

Must I be a belligerent in this unending war? Is it always and forever impossible for men and women to love each other?

Monica saw the confusion on my face, and was intrigued. While her colleague sat on the nose of the man who was after all much like me, she drew out of me, perhaps also to give me my money's worth, my reason for walking the streets of Amsterdam in the rain. I answered her questions, and drank chilled vodka, and became intoxicated enough to let her put my hand on her naked body, and then to stroke her breasts. I suspected that I would have to give her money for this before I left, but I was beginning not to care. She was a good listener, and I had a story to tell about true love.

'So have you fucked her?' asked Monica.

I shook my head.

'You fall in love but you don't fuck.'

'Yes.'

'And now she doesn't want you.'

'Yes.'

'So what are you going to do?'

'I don't know.'

'What do you want to do?'

'I want to see her again.'

'So you can fuck her?'

'No. Not just that. More than that. Less than that.'

'Now you lost me, angel.'

'I'd like to, oh, be with her. Talk to her. Touch her. Push back her hair, where it falls over her neck. Stroke her neck.'

'Oh my, oh my.'

'You think I'm some kind of fool?'

'Hey, angel, what do I know? Seems to me you want to be the only man who doesn't fuck her, so you can be special.'

That made me smile.

'You may have something there.'

My eyelids closed again. Due to my restricted funds I had made the journey to Amsterdam by overnight coach, which saved the cost of one night in a hotel, but I had not been able to sleep. A combination of exhaustion and vodka now took possession of my body, and I realised I was going to sleep whether I wanted to or not.

When the bar closed, and Monica was dressed and ready to leave, she woke me gently and told me that I must pay more money. It was almost five in the morning. I gave her all that I had, which was pitifully little.

'You don't have no more, angel?'

I shook my head.

'I wouldn't take it for me, but the house got to be paid, okay? The house always got to be paid.'

So my money went.

I returned to my room at the Victoria Hotel and slept until ten. I woke sluggish with failure. I washed and shaved and dressed with slow care, building a shell of respectability over my destitute condition. I left the hotel without breakfast, knowing I could not pay my bill. There seemed to be only one recourse open to me. I called on Freddy Christiansen.

He was sympathetic.

'So you're short of funds? What the English call, I believe, embarrassed?'

'Very embarrassed,' I said.

'It's a sad world, Mr Dearborn, that can't provide even a modest living for its scholars. I would be happy to help you.'

He reached for his wallet.

'If you could just loan me enough to pay my hotel bill. I have a return ticket back to London.'

'Of course. So you've completed your business in Amsterdam?'

'No. Just run out of money.'

'I see.'

He pondered for a moment.

'This book you propose to write. A publisher is interested?'

'Yes. I have a signed contract.'

'And Paul Marotte will play a significant part in the book?'

'I plan to put Marotte at the centre.'

'Well, now, Mr Dearborn. I own a number of Marotte's works. I have what is almost certainly the largest collection in private hands. My collection is my capital. My security. I have, you might say, an interest in Marotte's reputation.'

'Yes, I understand.'

'Your book will add to the general public's awareness of Marotte. That will enhance the value of my collection.'

'I hope so.'

'Therefore it would be appropriate for me to assist you in your researches. I don't see that the sum involved need be very great. If, that is, you would find a few more days in Amsterdam useful.'

I had more than one use for a few more days in Amsterdam.

'You may wish to look into the Marotte archive; though I fear you'll find little of value. Camille will be delighted to have company. You read French?'

'Enough.' I trusted to total immersion to bring my schoolboy French up to the necessary standard.

'And your other business?'

He kept his expression studiously neutral, but his eyes were bright.

'Unsuccessful.'

'Terminally so?'

'I don't know. Possibly.'

'A few more days might clarify matters there also. Would you like me to – to make discreet inquiries?'

'I would like very much to speak to her again.'

He smiled then, and drew from the wallet a sheaf of notes.

'For your expenses,' he said. 'As for accommodation, I have a small guest bedroom here, which I place at your disposal.'

Camille, I discovered, was Canadian, funded by McGill University in Montreal. Her thesis was on facial characteristics as indicators of mental states. It was Dr Marotte the neuro-graphologist who interested her. This meant that there was no conflict between us. Marotte the artist and lover was outside her terms of reference.

As Christiansen had predicted, she welcomed my company.

'A book on true love? That's going to be a short book.'

'You don't believe in true love?'

'I think mostly I don't believe in belief.'

'So you won't be buying my book.'

'Nothing personal. You asked.'

Camille was a pure reductionist. She was convinced that all human impulses were driven by biology, which included evolutionary biology, or by chemistry. Emotions came under biology. Free will came under chemistry.

'Every decision you take is driven by chemical needs in your brain. If you take drugs, that changes the chemical equation. That's as far as free will goes.'

Her take on Marotte's transformation was similarly brutal.

'Peak level of stress brought on by overwork. Adrenalin build-up in the blood. Shallow sleep, leading to reduced flow of oxygen to the brain. Caffeine shock – he'd just had his morning coffee. Result – metabolic crash.'

'That would be the falling in love?'

'Read his journal. *Inexplicable excitation. Penetrating lassitude.* He thought he was ill. Sure he was ill.'

I found all this curiously refreshing. I felt no need to take Camille's theories seriously, because I had my own reductionism to explain her outlook. She was a very plain young woman. As such, she was not a player in the great game of love. That stocky frame, that mannish face, was never likely to strike a passing stranger on a bridge with the thunderbolt of love. But for all that, Camille was not bitter. She looked with a lofty pity on the lesser beings who were the subjects of my book, who misinterpreted their glandular fluctuations as romance, and then became baffled when their effusions were not reciprocated.

'It's all about timing,' she told me. 'Women are only really sexually receptive when they're ovulating.'

I said nothing to Camille about Flora. Marotte was something else.

'Have you come across anything new about Marotte's private life?'

'Not a thing. Though I've not turned up every document in that freeway wreck they call an archive.'

I shared the rear room with Camille, sitting at a table with my back to her, an electric fan heater humming away on the floor between us. The whole house was cold, kept at a low temperature to economise on heating bills. The few visitors who paid their three guilders to tour the open rooms soon departed, chilled into silence.

Not wanting to think about my humiliation in the Leidseplein, I plunged into the Marotte archive, hoping to discover some original material that would give weight to my work in progress. The papers, ledgers and notebooks, in French and Dutch, were stored in file cartons in rough date order, but were not divided into any subject categories. Case notes lay beside monthly accounts, letters relating to the running of the clinic alongside tradesmen's bills. All personal letters had been weeded out long ago, along with the journals, and were now housed at the Bibliothèque Nationale in Paris.

Camille asked me to look out for doodles.

'Any graphic stuff you find, show me. He was always sketching his *folles*.'

'His what?'

'His crazy ladies. His patients.'

'Were they all female?'

'So it seems.'

'Why?'

'Think about it. You're bourgeois, you're female, and it's the 1880s. What can you do except go nuts?'

I found a book of accounts that covered the years 1882 to 1889, and flicked through its stiff pages. The entries had been made by different hands over the years, presumably book-keepers employed by the clinic, and tracked expenditure on staff wages, laundry, lamp oil, coal. I scanned the pages with no object in mind. The only curiosity was that over the winter of 1887/8 the coal bill more than doubled. It must have been an exceptionally cold winter.

'Or,' said Camille, 'they decided to sit around with their clothes off.'

My notebook in hand, I traced the route taken that December morning by Marotte along the Keizersgracht. When I reached the bridge over the intersecting Leidsegracht I took out my print of Marotte's painting of this bridge – one of his many paintings of the bridge – and moved back and forth until I was standing, as best as I could work it out, where he had stood. Of course, the painting was not a photograph. The perspectives were all out of line. But after some study I found

I could match the line of black iron railings on my left, the single tree on the far side, and the distinctive gables of the old houses along the Keizersgracht. Because the houses were still there, just as they had been in Marotte's day, I was able to block from my vision the parked cars and the modern street signs, and imagine myself back to that morning that changed Marotte's life. I pictured the child coming towards me, hopping from one foot to the other. I heard the woman's voice call. I saw the child stop and turn. And there behind her, in a pearl-grey coat and a cream-coloured hat, was Flora.

Only my little act of self-indulgence.

'From that day on,' I murmured to myself, 'this woman, about whom I knew nothing, became everything to me.'

10

Steel-framed enamel-hard canvasses hung on the white brick walls. I recall *'58 T-Bird Meets '60 Corvette, No Survivors*, in which the detail of the crashed automobiles was rendered with loving care, and the mutilated bodies of the drivers sketched in with a few contemptuous strokes. This was the work of Christiansen's most recent discovery, a local artist called Ger Bakker. There was nothing else to look at in the gallery as I waited, so I walked up and down the scenes of glamorous devastation.

At the far end of the gallery a receptionist sat at a desk reading a book. She was well dressed, her face shiningly made up, as if to match the paintings. Freddy Christiansen was late returning. It must have been a longer conversation than he had anticipated. However, when he came at last, his report to me was brief.

'I'm to tell you she thinks it better that you do not see her again. I'm sorry.'

I concealed my disappointment.

'Oh, well. It was worth a try.' I turned and pointed to one of the canvasses. 'Do they sell?'

'Certainly. Ger Bakker is quite the thing. He's considered

very talented. And, of course, very young.'

I passed along the paintings as if considering a purchase.

'So she won't even meet me for a coffee?'

'I'm afraid not.'

'I just want to talk to her. An ordinary conversation.' Then, feeling the sadness and the frustration rising in me, 'Go on about this Bakker.'

'There is a story about him that might amuse you.' Christiansen understood my need for distraction. 'Ger Bakker is a supporter of animal rights. I call him, out of pure mischief, our militant vegetarian. There is a famous old restaurant here in Amsterdam called Dikker en Thijs, and Dikker en Thijs have opened a second establishment on the Apollolaan, near the Hilton, which caters for businessmen on expense accounts. Very expensive, very much for show. It is called De Kersentuin, the Cherry Garden. Now one evening, eighteen months or so ago, Bakker made an attack on De Kersentuin, a raid – a smash-and-grab? – at about nine o'clock, when the restaurant was full. He stole every steak in the restaurant, right from the plates of the diners, from beneath their raised knives and forks, you might say. The next morning he and other supporters of the same cause processed to the Oosterbegraafplaats, one of our old cemeteries, and buried the steaks according to the rites of the Lutheran Church. There was quite a sensation.'

'He sounds mad.'

'No, not mad. He has rage, but also style.'

I said, 'I have to talk to her.'

'I'm sorry. What can I do?'

'I don't understand why she won't see me. I'm not going to misbehave.'

'I am only the messenger.'

'Do you have a message?'

'Only what I have already told you.'

'What did she say, exactly? What were her exact words?'

'That it was better for you not to see her again.'

'Better for me?'

'Yes.'

'What else?'

Christiansen considered, and then evidently decided to tell.

'She said, Make him understand.'

'Understand what?'

'I think, that you should forget her.'

'I can't.'

I sat down on a canvas-backed chair among the paintings of blood and steel, not knowing what to do next. 'Is it true, what you said about the steaks?'

'Perfectly true. Perhaps you would like a cup of coffee?'

The receptionist brought us coffee, and Christiansen sat with me, patient and attentive.

'So you are unable to put Flora out of your mind.'

'I just can't do it.'

'Even though she has made her wishes so clear.'

'I don't believe her.'

'Ah. You don't believe her. You know her own feelings better than she knows them herself.'

'Something's stopping her seeing me. She's afraid of something. Or someone.'

'Yes, I see. The jealous husband.'

'Maybe.'

'So what do you propose to do now?'

'It's not like I'm asking her to run off with me. I just want to have an ordinary conversation with her. I just want to talk to her.'

I knew I was repeating myself, but Christiansen was tolerant. It seemed at the time that he was sympathetic to my case. Certainly he found me interesting. To me he was no more than a bystander, a witness; in my obsession I did not even look at him with any attention, and so have only a faint impression of him sitting before me in his gallery: a grey suit, unwavering eyes. Like all lovers, I found nothing strange in being the object of other people's gaze.

He said, 'I think if you truly wanted no more than an ordinary conversation with her, she would make no objection. But she does not believe that is what you want.'

'It is. I swear it. I want to get back to being friends. I hate leaving it like this. It's so unnecessary. We got on really well in Devon.'

Frustrated, I fixed my attention on one of the paintings on display before me. It showed a beautiful blonde with her mouth round the muzzle of an automatic rifle. The detail was so precise that I could see where her bright-red lipstick had smeared the silver alloy of the gun barrel.

'What happened to Bakker after he stole the steaks?'

'There was a court case. Quite a *cause célèbre*. A fine, which he refused to pay. He served a short prison sentence, in Haarlem. His paintings doubled in value.'

'What do you advise me to do?'

'Complete your researches. Leave Amsterdam.'

'If I could only talk to her before I go. Just once.'

He looked at me thoughtfully for a moment or two.

'I can't arrange a meeting,' he said at last. 'But I can make a suggestion.'

It was a good suggestion, and I followed it, though even at the time I was aware of the irony of the situation: that in order to plead the cause of true love, I had first to lie.

He said, 'Tell Flora you don't love her any more. Tell her your pride has been hurt by her rejection of your overture. You are not in the habit of pressing yourself where you're not wanted.'

'How does that help me?'

'Then you can talk to her.'

'Then she'll talk to me?'

'I think so. It's true love that frightens her off.'

I said simply, 'That's what I have to give her.'

'I understand. But have you ever gone into a paddock, Mr Dearborn, to catch a horse? The method is to keep the halter out of sight behind your back, because the horse does not want to be caught, and to hold the sugar lump in full view, because the horse likes sugar lumps.'

'I don't want it to be like that.'

'No, of course not. That would not be true love.'

Christiansen teased me over this, as if true love was some amiable superstition. He did not yet appreciate that my certainty was my source of power. I was not so much afraid of losing Flora as I was afraid of losing my love for her: for had not this love been granted me like a grace, capricious as inspiration?

'My dear young Werther,' said Christiansen, 'I find your dilemma interests me more than I had expected.'

'I don't intend to kill myself for love.'

He smiled.

'Not Werther, then. Perhaps you would rather be Guillaume de Lorris's dreamer? Or Ovid's amator? It's curious how we repeat our mistakes, don't you think? After all, it is two thousand years ago now that Ovid wrote *Arte regendus amor* – "Love is to be ruled by art."'

'If only,' I said.

'Or even our own Marotte. After all, he did face something of the same dilemma himself. How to declare his love in such a way that he would be loved in return. *Mademoiselle, je suis l'artiste!*'

I laughed at the image this conjured up.

'There now,' said Christiansen, gently guiding me. 'A little humour may be invaluable.'

Every morning at about nine o'clock in the December of 1889, Dr Paul Marotte set off from his house on the Keizersgracht to walk to the clinic in which he was then working, which was in Jacob Van Lennepkade, near what is now the Wilhelmina Gasthuis. His route there took him over the Leidsegracht, a canal that runs across the Keizersgracht and at right angles to it. At about the same time each morning, the English governess Kate Summer set off, with the little girl who was her charge, along the Keizersgracht from the opposite direction. Her route took her and the child up the busy shop-filled Leidsestraat to the Leidseplein, and so across a further broad canal into the park. The physician and the governess must have passed each other many times on or near the Leidsegracht bridge, before some unknown chance drew her to his attention; with all its dramatic results.

There was, it seems, a short sharp struggle in Marotte's conscience. He was a man of his times and of his class; he occupied a responsible professional position. There were things one did not do. For ten days his passion declared itself only through his art: in the first series of 'bridge' paintings, technically crude but emotionally powerful attempts to capture on canvas that moment crossing the Leidsegracht. Then it seems he accepted that what had happened was no passing fancy; that in effect his life was irrevocably changed.

As soon as he reached this conclusion he proceeded to make his love known to the English governess in a manner that was at once courteous and overwhelming. He transported the seven canvasses he had painted, by cab, to the Leidsegracht bridge, and there he lined them up along the iron railings. The governess approached, holding the hand of the little girl. She saw the paintings, and stopped to look at them. At first, it seemed, she did not recognise herself or the child in the repeated scene. Then the child spotted the blue ribbon. At this point the artist stepped forward, raised his hat, and said, 'Mademoiselle, I am the artist!'

Did she laugh when he said those words? I rather thought not. Even then there was a reverential air around the notion of art. A man who looked like a doctor and called himself an artist was to be treated with respect. I was not a painter, and could not replicate Marotte's striking display. But I was a writer. I could use words. I could write a letter.

I composed my letter with great care. It had to achieve two almost opposite effects: to convince Flora I was not in love with her, and to make her rather wish I was. Thus, as Christiansen said, a little humour would not come amiss.

Dear Flora

I shall be going back to London soon. You'll be relieved to hear that our meeting outside the theatre has had the necessary effect. I am of course embarrassed and apologetic, but my fault was a fault on the right side, I think. Better to speak and hit the rock of reality than to go about in a world of one's own cloudy imaginings. One short sharp shock, and I'm back in the human race.

I don't want to leave without returning our friendship to civilised terms. So I repeat my invitation to coffee —

tomorrow, at 10 am, at Berkhoff's? Since I'm broke and you'll have to pay, here as recompense (I am after all a writer) is a story:

Long ago and far away there lived a princess who had forgotten how to laugh. The princess's father, the king, said that whoever could make her laugh could marry her and inherit the kingdom. Suitors came from far and wide, all handsome and rich and well bred. They tried as hard as they could to make the princess laugh, but she never even smiled. Then one day there came to the palace a young man who was poor and ugly and of humble birth. This unlikely suitor said to the princess in front of the whole court: 'Princess, I love you, and I shall marry you.' The princess burst out laughing. 'Marry you?' she said. 'You must be joking!' But the king saw that the ugly young man had made the princess laugh, and he kept his word. They were married the very next day. Naturally, the marriage was a catastrophe. The princess ran away with a blond-haired officer in the guard. But the ugly young man inherited the kingdom, and he enjoyed that very much.

So there you are. The moral is there's always a happy ending, but it may not be the one you have in mind. See you at Berkhoff's.

I signed my letter 'B', and put it through the letterbox in the door of the house on Singel at about noon.

The next day, I made my way down the Keizersgracht towards Berkhoff's far too early, and so walked on past, and turned about and retraced my steps, like a sentry on patrol. Ten o'clock came, and no sign of Flora. Perhaps she hadn't received my letter. Perhaps her husband had found it and destroyed it. Perhaps they had both left town.

But she did come; about fifteen minutes late.

'Why aren't you inside? It's freezing out here.'

We went in and found a quiet table at the back. She talked a little too fast, as if we didn't have enough time for conversational courtesies, and avoided my eyes.

'You're going back to London? When do you leave?'

'A few more days. When I've finished my research on Marotte.'

'About the other night. You caught me by surprise.'

I took this to be an apology.

'It's nothing. I'm sorry, too.'

We both ordered cappuccinos. She seemed nervous. I hadn't expected that.

'Your husband looked very . . .'

'Very what?'

'Very blond.'

'Actually, his hair's grey. He dyes it.'

She smiled a rueful little smile. After that, things got easier.

'What are you doing, staying at Freddy's?'

'I'm broke. He's taken pity on me.'

'Are you really broke?'

'Utterly.'

'Nobody has to be broke.'

'Oh, it's a choice. Don't think I don't know it.'

'Well, it's a stupid choice. Get some money. Everyone needs money.'

'What do you suggest I do? Marry a rich husband?'

'No. I don't recommend that. On the whole.'

'Taking one thing with another.'

We smiled at the same time, but not together.

'But as you say, it's a choice.'

'And it does mean you can pay for your friends' breakfasts. That must give you a warm feeling inside.'

'Why don't you have any money? Everyone has some money. You're not a student. How old are you?'

'About to be thirty.'

'Are you really?' She seemed surprised. 'Then you should act like a grown-up. Men of thirty should be paying their own way.'

I wasn't paying close attention to her words, because I was absorbed in her nearness, her physical presence. Everything about her enchanted me. She was fiddling with a teaspoon on the table, turning it over and over between the thumb and forefinger of her right hand, so that it reflected the light above. It was her fingers I watched. I longed to touch her.

'Don't you think so?'

I returned to the moment. I should be paying my own way. I wasn't truly grown up. Not yet a man.

'It all depends on how you want to use your time. I could make money, yes. But that would use the time I have for writing. And if what I want to do is write, what's the point of making money instead?'

'That's all just talk. You don't use your time to write at all. Here you are having coffee with me, when you could be writing.'

'Yes, I know. But it's a funny thing, this writing. All the hours I spend doing nothing seem to be part of it.'

'Do they?' She looked unconvinced. 'I wish the hours I spent doing nothing felt like they were part of something.'

'Perhaps they are. Only it hasn't happened yet.'

'Do you think so?'

'Yes, I do. I think we all go through times when we're just waiting. Getting ready for the next chapter in our life.'

Her eyes were looking far away. 'I wish it would hurry up.'

'Ripeness is all.'

'What?'

'It's Shakespeare.'

'Oh. You read too much.'

And don't live enough. Yes, I've heard it before.

'Maybe you don't read enough.'

'Me? I never read. Not books. I'm not educated at all. Hadn't you noticed?'

'You must have gone to school.'

'Once. Long ago. They kicked me out. Who cares?'

She was both jumpy and bored, a strange unsettling combination. I kept trying to find a way in, to locate the door that would let me through the invisible wall she had built round herself. This was not the real Flora, I was sure. This was not her real way of being with me. Something was holding her back; or someone. I felt as if she was under orders to keep me at a distance, and that only if she saw her chance would she drop her pose and speak to me in an urgent whisper, saying, 'Act like we're still having a casual conversation. Don't make any sudden moves. I love you. Rescue me.'

However, the secret message did not come.

'Did you like my story?' I asked her.

'What story?'

'In my letter.'

'Oh, yes. Did you make it up?'

'Yes.'

That was all. A flicker of interest, and then nothing.

'Flora,' I said, speaking as you might to someone who doesn't look well. 'What's the matter?'

'Why should anything be the matter?'

'You seem so – so not here.'

'Do I?'

She looked at me then, her beautiful grey-blue eyes resting on me without seeing me.

'When do you go back?'

'In a week or so.'

'Come and visit me. Axel's away.'

'When shall I come?'

'Tomorrow evening. That Bogart movie's on TV. I saw it in the listings, and I thought of you.'

So there it was. The door at last. And it was Flora herself opening it.

11

She asked me what I wanted to drink and I said wine. She was drinking vodka, had been drinking before my arrival. The television was immense, a rich man's television, with a room all to itself. We sat in a deep leather sofa, hummocked in brown velvet cushions, and watched the old film. Flora wore jeans, red socks, her shoes discarded. She hardly spoke to me. It was strange, as if our agreement was that I was there to watch the film, and nothing else. Why then did she need to get herself drunk?

When Lauren Bacall came on screen, I saw how little like her Flora was after all. The resemblance was in the stance, and, of course, in the wave of golden hair; but in the movie Bacall has surrendered from the beginning, her every defiant line a front for submission. She had none of Flora's true distance.

There is a scene in the film in which Bacall, short of money and wanting a drink, sells herself to a French naval officer. She makes the pick-up in a bar called the Bar du Zombie, stalking between the tables, unlit cigarette raised. What she has sold remains unspecified, but the proceeds enable her to buy a bottle of wine. When later she turns up in Bogart's hotel room, the bottle of wine in one hand, he makes plain his dislike for what she has done.

She says, 'Alright, alright. I won't do it any more.'

He says, 'Look, I didn't ask you—'

She says, 'I know you didn't. Don't worry, I'm not giving up anything I care about. It's like shooting fish in a barrel, anyway, men like that.'

This drew a comment from Flora. She pointed one red-socked toe at the screen and said, 'You fucking stupid woman.'

'You think she shouldn't give way to him?'

'She thinks he's different. He's no different.'

At the end of the movie, Bogart is waiting to leave in the crowded lobby of the hotel. Bacall goes over to the piano to say goodbye to Hoagy Carmichael. As she makes her way back to Bogart's side, the piano plays, and she performs a little shimmy with her hips, her eyes on the admiring Bogart. Then arm in arm they stroll out into the street, followed by Walter Brennan carrying the suitcases and jigging to the piano's beat.

Flora jumped up from the sofa, saying, 'I can do that!'

Humming the tune that Hoagy Carmichael had played, she did her own shimmy, watching me as she moved. She was cool and controlled and extremely sexy.

'Am I good? Tell me I'm good.'

'You're good.'

She dropped back down on to the sofa beside me.

'Thank you for coming.'

Then she leaned closer, and suddenly we were kissing. She was very physical, pressed her body against me.

'So is this a vodka kiss?' I asked.

'Yes,' she said. 'The vodka thinks you're very sweet. The vodka wants you.'

Her hand between my legs, unambiguous.

'What if your husband comes back?'

'He's away. I told you. Do you want me?'

'You know I do.'

'Why?'

'You are so drunk.'

'No, tell me. Why?'

Kissing me. Stroking me.

'Doesn't everyone?'

'I want to know why.'

'You're beautiful, Flora.'

She rolled away from me.

'Oh, beautiful,' she said. 'Fuck beautiful.'

'Is that an offer?'

She jumped to her feet, and padded out of the room. Somehow the moment of intimacy had passed. What had I done wrong?

She returned with a small photograph: herself from a few years ago, in black and white.

'See?' she said. 'That's beautiful.'

There was writing scrawled across the picture. *You're the one! B.*

'Ten years ago.'

'David Bailey?'

'Bailey was crazy for me. He was insane. He had to have me. It was like being in a storm.'

The younger Flora was astonishingly lovely in the photograph.

'You're even more beautiful now,' I said.

'No, I'm not. That's a lie.'

Her voice changed. Suddenly she had gone hard, angry.

'It's not a lie—'

'It's a fucking lie to get me into bed. Don't lie to me. I've been lied to too much in my life. You're supposed to be my friend. Friends don't lie.'

She was talking fast, even a little hysterically.

'Give me a chance—'

'Just don't lie to me, okay?'

'I'm not lying. I mean it. In the photograph you're still half-formed. Now you've grown into your face. Then, you were pretty. Now, you're beautiful.'

'And later?'

'Later comes later. One day we'll all be dead. But we're not dead yet.'

She held my eyes with her suspicious gaze: the look of a child who suspects she's being comforted, but who craves the comfort. Then she gave in.

'That's true. One day we'll all be dead.'

'But now – we live.'

She threw herself down on the sofa beside me, but this time there was no roll into my arms, and no kiss.

'I'm out of it. I'm smashed. You're going to have to go.'

Her eyes were closed, her body limp.

'I don't want to go.'

No answer. I could have stayed. The flurry of anger had passed. It was as if she had surrendered, but not to me. She had stopped defending herself against the everlasting assaults of the world.

But I was a lover. More than my own gratification, I wanted to be chosen. I wanted to be wanted. I wanted to see the light in her eyes shining on me.

So I did as she asked.

'Let's meet up again before I leave.'

'Sure. Why not?'

She waved with one hand, not opening her eyes. No point in making any arrangements now. She wouldn't remember.

'Thanks for the movie.'

Freddy Christiansen took a paternal interest in my progress with Flora.

'She likes me,' I said. 'I'm sure of it. But there's some sort of block I can't get past.'

'Or she can't get past.'

'Yes.'

'What do you think it might be?'

'I wish I knew. I have so little to go on. Her father leaving. Some other betrayal. She must have been badly let down somewhere.'

'What makes you think that?'

'She hates lies. Being lied to really frightens her.'

'She told you that?'

'Yes. She was quite drunk.'

'She hates lies, and she gets drunk.'

He gazed at me with his cool, quizzical gaze.

'Yes,' I said.

'I wonder . . .' He seemed to have more to say, then to think better of it. 'Would you be very offended, my dear amator, if I told you how curious I am to see how she conducts herself with you?'

'What do you mean?'

'May I invite her to join us for an informal supper?'

'Yes. Please. I'd like that.' All I thought about was Flora, and my need to see her again. Not Christiansen. 'I'd like that very much.'

'Do you think she'd come?'

'I don't know. She's utterly unpredictable.'

'I can but ask.'

Flora came, the very next evening, bearing a big bunch of bright-red tulips. Christiansen's presence transformed our manner with each other. We were lighter and brighter, ready to laugh and to argue, as we drank Freddy's excellent wine. He stood at the stove, a blue striped apron over his shirt and tie, preparing a salad to accompany a Hungarian stew. Flora and I sat at the tiny kitchen table and picked at a dish of olives stuffed with anchovies, the tulips gaudy between us.

'Aren't tulips out of season?'

'Of course,' said Flora. 'They come from Gran Canaria. Axel has taught me only ever to give tulips out of season in Amsterdam.'

'Axel Jaeger is an interesting man,' said Christiansen, as if she had been disparaging him. 'You underestimate him.'

'He's not complaining,' said Flora with a shrug.

Christiansen then suggested that I entertain them with one of my stories of true love. This was his strategy to steer our talk on to more revealing themes. Flora seemed willing. So I went into the little spare bedroom and pulled out the page of my manuscript that recounts the first love of the composer Hector Berlioz.

I read it aloud.

'Berlioz fell in love, at the age of twelve, with a girl named Estelle, who wore pink slippers. Estelle was not the love of his life; nor does he tell us anything of her feelings in the matter; but the story stands as a little testament to the endurance of emotions commonly dismissed as immature.

'"Estelle was just eighteen – tall, graceful, with large grave questioning eyes that yet could smile – and feet – I will not say Andalusian, but pure Parisian, and on those little feet she wore – pink slippers. Do not smile; I have forgotten the colour of her hair (I fancy it was black) yet never do I recall Estelle but, in company with the flash of her large eyes, comes the twinkle of her dainty pink shoes. I had been struck by lightning. To say I loved her comprises everything. I hoped for, expected, knew nothing but that I was wretched, dumb, despairing. By night I suffered agonies, by day I wandered alone through the fields of Indian corn, or sought like a wounded bird the deepest recesses of my grandfather's orchard."

'Many years later, at the age of thirty, Berlioz writes of his emotions on finding himself in Saint Eynard again: "My eyes filled with tears at the sight of the little white house, the ruined tower. I loved her still."'

Flora said, 'I don't believe it.'

'What don't you believe?'

'That he loved her still.'

'Well, it's true he hadn't actually seen her again.'

'Let's do the sums,' said Freddy from the stove. 'He was twelve when he first saw her, and now he's thirty. So that's eighteen years later. She was eighteen. So now she's thirty-six.'

'And she's had six kids,' said Flora, 'and she's lost her figure, and her pink slippers don't fit her any more.'

We all laughed.

'And,' said Flora, pointing a finger at me as if I needed more convincing, 'he's spent the last ten years getting what he needs in brothels.'

'You don't know that.'

'I know he's not stayed struck by lightning for eighteen years.'

'Some people fall in love for life.'

'Some women. Not men.'

'I'm a man. I can imagine falling in love, and never wanting anyone else.'

'Liar! For the rest of your life? Never wanting another woman?'

I didn't want another outburst against lies, so I amended my claim.

'Alright, I expect I'd want other women. But I wouldn't do anything about it. Not if I'd fallen in love, and we were married, and all the rest of it.'

'Why not?'

'It's not that odd,' I said, reacting to her air of astonishment. 'Fidelity has been known to exist. There have been sightings.'

'Not by me. How about you, Freddy?'

'There are some well-authenticated reports,' said Christiansen. 'Our mutual friend Paul Marotte was clearly devoted to his mistress from the moment he set eyes on her to the day he died.'

'I don't believe it,' said Flora.

'He changed his whole life for her!' I said. 'How much more proof do you want?'

'Was she so very beautiful?'

'No, as a matter of fact. Not especially.' I turned to Christiansen. 'Wouldn't you agree?'

He shrugged.

'These things are so personal. To me, she is beautiful. To Flora – she must decide for herself. Go and visit her. One of Marotte's very best portraits of her hangs in the Rijksmuseum.'

'I don't do art galleries,' said Flora.

'That's because you don't know how to,' I said. 'You don't

know where to look, or why. You don't know what to feel about what you see. So you just feel overwhelmed. Which means you end up feeling nothing.'

Flora looked at me in surprise.

'That's right,' she said. 'That's how it is exactly.'

'You can't just wander in to an art gallery and hope for the best. Any more than you'd go to a big train station at rush hour and hope for a chance meeting with someone you know.'

'Very good,' murmured Christiansen, watching us, smiling.

'You have to prepare,' I said. 'You have to know what you're looking for, and why. It's a treasure hunt. You have to know what the treasure is, so you can spot it when you find it.'

'Will you take me?'

'Gladly.'

'Show me this woman. I want to see her. I want to see her with you.'

'I'd like that.'

I spoke lightly, but my heart was singing.

'Even so, I still don't believe it,' said Flora stubbornly. 'About never wanting another woman.'

'My dear amator,' said Christiansen, 'you had better explain to our friend why you value fidelity. I suspect she thinks you're being merely conventional.'

I was on my best form that evening, and more than happy to attempt an explanation. As Freddy well knew, everything I said was a form of love-making. Flora listened, frowning slightly, following me with close attention.

'It's all to do with what I mean by true love,' I said. 'I think the two are linked. Truth and love, I mean. You know how much you hate lies? You can't have lies and love together, can you? They'd cancel each other out.'

'Yes,' said Flora. 'I can see that.'

'So if I really loved someone, I'd want it to be true love. I'd want her to know the true me. That would make it real. I wouldn't want to hide anything from her. She'd be the one I was true with, and true to. If that makes sense.'

'Yes,' said Flora. 'Go on.'

'So if that's what I want with her, how could I possibly have an affair with another woman? I mean, I'd have to tell her all about it, if I did. She'd more or less have to have the affair with me. Otherwise she'd lose touch with my truth, wouldn't she? Then it wouldn't be true love any more. It would be love and lies.'

'You could always move on to true love with the new one,' said Flora. 'Especially if she's prettier and younger.'

'Come now, Flora,' chided Christiansen. 'Don't be bitchy. It'll give you lines round your mouth.'

She looked up at Christiansen and I caught her look. To my surprise I saw that she was dismayed by his gentle reprimand.

All she said aloud was, 'I've already got lines round my mouth.'

I looked at Christiansen. For the first time I found myself wondering if there was more between them than I had supposed.

'Our amator,' said Christiansen, 'challenges us with a bold hypothesis.'

'Why do you call him amator?' said Flora.

'Because of his great work. *Amator* is Latin for lover.'

'Oh. His book.'

'What hypothesis?' I asked Christiansen.

'That true love is possible between men and women.'

The spicy stew was ready. It was time to eat. But I knew, and Christiansen knew, that our conversation had only just begun.

*

That night, after Flora had left and Christiansen had retired to his bedroom, I stayed up late writing in my notebook. The evening's discussion had stimulated me to analyse my own feelings more closely. Flora had challenged my claims for true love not by denying its possibility, but by questioning its duration. Why not move on, and move on again? Why fidelity to one partner?

Because love is built out of memory.

So what of love at first sight?

I wrote in note form, for later use in my book.

Two kinds of love. First fast love, and later slow love. Distinct from each other in nature, linked to each other in time. The first, the being struck by lightning, very possibly based in illusion. But does this matter? What's important is the intensity of the energy released. Then the later love, the planted rooted love, formed out of shared experience. But there has to be the initial charge. What is that charge? Flora would say sex, but I've desired other women without falling in love with them. Must be something I've seen in her face, something that is also her beauty; but that's not all of it.

Could be that faces show more than we allow. She spoke of the lines round her mouth. I looked at her face after that. Hundreds of tiny lines, round her mouth, between her eyebrows, round her eyes. The more I looked, the more it seemed I saw what had made those lines. All the smiles she had ever smiled – all the frowns she had ever frowned – all the times she's listened the way she does, brow furrowing, attentive, unconvinced – all the times she's been hurt, and set her mouth into that expression that says, I don't care. It must be there, all of it, coded in those tiny lines, her life history, what it's made of her. Is this what I read in her face, in that first moment of meeting her?

Again and again I come back to this puzzle of love at first sight. I think it's this that she holds against me. That because it was so quick it was nothing to do with her. That I had picked her at random to be the screen on to which I projected my own needs. To this I reply: Why you? There was a choice. I made a choice. Why you?

I heard a movement behind me, and looking round saw Christiansen standing in the little hall, watching me through the half-open door. He was in a bathrobe, and held a glass of water in one hand. He smiled when I turned round.

'Still up?'

'My brain is buzzing.'

'Mine also. I am obliged to abase myself before the great god Mogadon.' He held up a sleeping pill. 'Would you like one?'

'No, thanks. I'm actually having some new ideas, for once.'

'For your book?'

'Yes.'

'May I know?'

'Oh, it's all very raw. I've been puzzling over what happens when you see someone and know they're the one. Trying to analyse what it is you've seen.'

'That does seem to be the question.'

'I've been wondering about faces. Whether faces actually communicate much more than we think. Personality, character, life history, cultural prejudices – everything. Everything you need to make an informed choice.'

'My word!' Christiansen opened his eyes very wide. 'That's quite a claim.'

'Some sort of recognition must be going on. Unless you believe in past lives.'

'No. I don't think I believe in past lives.'

He was looking at me with that quizzical gaze of his. I recalled how he had looked at Flora.

'Were you ever in love with her?'

'Me?' A flicker of confusion in his eyes. Then the cool control returned. 'With Flora? No. I must be twice her age.'

'That needn't stop you.'

'No? Then let me say that for me to be in love with Flora would be − a breach of trust. I am her friend, at times her confessor, almost her father. But her lover, no.'

'Here we are, talking about love all the time. You've got needs too.'

'Of course. But not all our needs are met. As I think you are finding.'

He then gave me a sweetly old-fashioned bow, standing there in the doorway with his glass of water and his sleeping pill, and retired to his bedroom.

I went back to my notebook. I re-read what I had written so far, and then added:

Does it make sense to go on loving if you're not loved in return? Yes, if loving is giving. Yes, if loving is an act of generosity. Yes, if the person loved is the richer for it. But is this so?

Is true love possible between men and women?

12

I saw her some way off, sitting on a bench outside the Rijksmuseum in the morning sunshine, waiting for me. As I crossed the museum bridge towards her, I saw that she was reading Christiansen's collection of Marotte's letters and journals.

'Am I late?'

'No. I'm early.'

She had just come upon the word 'Synthetism', and asked me what it meant. I told her about the exhibition at the Café Volpini, on the site of the Paris World's Fair, in 1889, where Gauguin exhibited seventeen paintings, not one of which sold; and how he and Emile Bernard issued the Synthetist Manifesto that so impressed Marotte on his visit to Paris.

'It was an attack on the Impressionists, really. The Synthetists' idea was to paint from memory rather than by eye. They thought that memory selected the essential characteristics of an image, and so the painting would be more than an impression of reality, it would be a synthesis of what the artist saw and what he felt. Emile Bernard said that the Synthetist paints "from the mysterious midriff of the mind".'

'What did he look like, this Marotte? There's no picture of him in the book.'

'There's no picture of him anywhere. He wouldn't sit for photographs, or paintings. His friends called him the Invisible Man.'

'There must be something, somewhere.'

'Maybe so, but nothing's been found. He painted one self-portrait that we know about, for his mistress, but it was destroyed in a fire.'

We entered the museum and wound our way through room after room, down corridors and across halls, asking our way of the blue-uniformed guards.

'The secret is to be one-track-minded,' I told Flora. 'Don't be distracted. We're here to see the Marottes. We want Room 149 and nothing else.'

We passed rooms full of ornate silver teapots, and Delft porcelain, and fine lace. Briefly breaking my rule, we stopped by an eighteenth-century doll's house and peered in at its windows, to see laundry hanging over rafters in the attic, and the master and mistress at cards, and the cook in the basement kitchen. We seemed to be alone in the museum but for the guards, and our footsteps clicked loud on the parquet floors. There were Meissen apes taking snuff, and paintings of men in long white wigs; and then the grass-green landscapes of Van Os, and the snow-white landscapes of Koekkoek; and so we reached Room 149.

The room was an elongated octagon, with pale-grey walls and a barrel-vaulted window-light in the ceiling. In the centre of the room was a double-seated bench, upholstered in black leatherette. Apart from that there was nothing but the dozen or so paintings hanging on the walls in their florid gold frames.

Most of the paintings were Amsterdam street scenes by Marotte's contemporary, George Hendrik Breitner; among them his view of the bridge over the Singel, so often compared to Marotte's Leidsegracht bridge. The two hung side by side: Breitner's *Singelbrug* with its busy random crowd of passers-by and its air of arrested time, Marotte's *Woman and Child on a Bridge* by comparison almost deserted, almost outside time altogether.

The only other Marotte was on the facing wall: one of the Pont-Aven portraits of his mistress, Kate Summer. The style of the painting was immediately recognisable: areas of strong simple colour overlapped to create an elusive, almost blurred effect, as if the subject had not sat to be painted at all, but had paused while passing through the room. There was a window to one side of her head, through which could be seen the sea, a dark threatening mass like a rain cloud. The surrounding wall was similarly dark. But the woman's fleeting face was pale, almost delicate, and filled with light. She looked older than in the Courtauld portrait: grave, and not quite beautiful. From the tilt and turn of her head she seemed tired, even resigned, her eyes directed down and to one side, as if her thoughts were elsewhere.

As I studied her face, I found myself thinking how much of a struggle life must have been for her: an educated woman from, presumably, a poor family. What chance had led her to Amsterdam? And what can it have been like to have been assaulted, on a canal bridge, with so much love?

I said, 'I wonder what she's thinking.'

'She's just day-dreaming,' said Flora. 'When you have your portrait painted, that's all you can do.'

'Have you had your portrait painted?'

'Once.'

'Who painted you?'

'Oh, some protégé of Freddy's.'

'Not the vegetarian, I hope.'

'Not him, no.' She laughed at the thought of herself in one of Bakker's glossy canvasses. 'You know that was all Freddy's idea?'

'What was?'

'The raid on the restaurant. Burying the steaks. Even not paying the fine. Freddy's very clever.'

She turned back to the portrait of Kate Summer.

'So what do you think?'

'I don't really know. Yes, I do. I find it hard to believe that she had such an effect on him.'

'Other people's obsessions always seem ridiculous. You think, why her? What's so special about her?'

'I'd thought she'd come across stronger, somehow.'

'Christiansen says he has a better portrait of her in his house in Switzerland.'

As we left the museum we visited the hall where souvenirs were sold, and I bought postcards of both the Marottes.

Outside the museum the sun was still shining, and we set off into the narrow herringbone streets back to the centre of town. As we made our way past the antiquarian shops and art galleries of Spiegelgracht, it was easy to imagine that we were in the Amsterdam of the 1880s, and that at any minute Paul Marotte would come hurrying towards us, with his black hat and his leather bag; or the doll-like governess, wearing a straw boater with a pink satin band.

This was the first time I had been out in public with Flora, and what I noticed at once was the way that every man who passed us looked at her. Sometimes it was no more than a quick flick of the eyes; others stared openly, as if unaware that

133

their longing was visible. Because I was walking beside her, and might be thought to be her lover, I took a guilty pleasure in these attentions. Flora herself did not.

'I had no idea people stared so much,' I said.

'Not people. Men.'

'How strange it must be,' I said. 'Like being royalty.'

'Sure,' she said. 'The princess who didn't know how to laugh.'

'How old were you when you first knew you were beautiful?'

'I've never felt beautiful.'

'When you first knew other people thought you were beautiful, then.'

'Oh, that.' She thought back down the years. 'When I was fourteen. My mother took me to a party. I was admired.'

'Don't sound so glum about it.'

'You have no idea.'

'Alright, I have no idea. Give me an idea.'

We turned the corner of the Petit Bordeaux into the Keizersgracht, and there ahead, on the far side of the canal, was the Marotte Huis. A woman was walking along the canal with a small dog on a long lead. A much larger dog, with no visible owner, was trotting behind the small dog, sniffing its bottom.

'You see that little dog,' said Flora. 'Do you think she feels proud when the other dogs run after her? Do you think she believes it's something special and unique to her that attracts so much attention? Or do you think she knows it's just the way she smells, which she never planned and can't help, and is the same way every bitch smells, on every street of every city in the world?'

I caught her eyes. She gave me a jumpy smile, to take the edge off the bitterness in her words.

'I suppose you think I'm ungrateful.'

'It can't really be that bad.'

'I know. I must be wrong, mustn't I? Everyone wants to be beautiful. Just like everyone wants to be rich. And if you're beautiful and rich and still not happy, well, you must be either very sick, or very bad.'

We turned off the Keizersgracht at the corner by a lampshade shop, and passed a sweet-smelling bakery and a shop with a gaping head above its door. I wanted to tell her that she was wrong, that beauty was a free gift to be enjoyed, like sunlight.

'You don't have to look the way you look. You could wear baggy clothes, and no make-up, and let yourself get fat.'

Flora smiled, but so sadly I could hardly bear to see it.

'Don't you see? That's what's so cruel. Beauty's just another drug. Once you've started using it, you have to go on using it. At first the drug makes you feel fantastic. Then you stop feeling fantastic, but you have to keep taking it to feel good. Then you stop feeling good, but you have to keep taking it not to feel like hell. Then you feel like hell, but you have to keep taking it not to die. Then you die.'

13

'Remember,' said Christiansen to me across the restaurant table, 'that I lived through the war. Do you have any idea how many people simply disappeared during the war? For example, when Holland was occupied by the Germans, in 1940, there were almost 150,000 Dutch Jews. On 8 May 1945, when the Canadian First Army marched into Amsterdam, 110,000 of those Jews were dead.'

We ate in the Keyzer, next to the Concertgebouw. The wide bustling restaurant with its clusters of amber lamp-shades and its gilded walls was too prosperous, too kindly a setting for tales of the war; though without doubt during those years of occupation German officers had sat here, and had eaten well, and had asked the meaning of the Dutch words painted over the hatch to the kitchen: *Hetgeen de Smulpaap verschilt van der Gastronoom is de Geest*. 'What distinguishes the glutton from the gourmet is the spirit.' On every plate, beneath a tiny picture of the restaurant, was the proud boast: *Sinds 1905*.

This handsome dinner was yet another of Christiansen's kindnesses to me. I had asked only for some of his time, to talk about Paul Marotte. I was interested to know what had drawn him to Marotte in the first place, given that he did not share my own fascination with Marotte's love life. Christiansen had offered to take me out to his favourite restaurant; and over dinner, chose to lead me indirectly towards the main subject, at first by talking of his experiences in the war.

'I was seventeen when the occupation began. Only a boy. But of course, an adult by the time the war was over. My family – shall we say I had no family? I lived as we all did then, on my wits. I came to the attention of a German officer called Krause, who had the same first name as myself: Friedrich. He called himself Big Freddy and I was Little Freddy, though I was the taller of the two. Big Freddy was a senior aide to Ostkommandant Schröder, so he was an important man. He was also a lover of art. It is the done thing, you know, to deride Nazi taste in art because Hitler had such poor taste, and Goering was so rapacious. But Krause had a good eye. He collected paintings for his own delight, not in vulgar ostentation. And I, as a very young man, was employed by Krause in the building up of his art collection. You can see where my story is going, I think.

'There was a law passed, one of many against the Jewish population, I remember it well, it was called Regulation 58/42. The Jews were known to possess many fine paintings. Under this regulation, all works of art owned by Jews were to be handed over for storage at the Lippman-Rosenthal warehouse. The owners were given receipts, it was all to be official. The receipts said the works of art were on loan.

'Then the deportations began. There were the empty houses. Well, we know all about that now. The Dutch plundered the empty houses as much as the Germans. And I, I was Big Freddy's emissary, he trusted my judgement. I went from house to house, examining the paintings. Some I sent back to the collection, others not. You see what an excellent grounding I received in the art of Amsterdam.

'Big Freddy had an especial fondness for the work of Paul Marotte. I might say, this was much to his credit, since Marotte was not at all the fashion at that time. After the liberation, when the Krause collection was examined, there was much laughter over the Marottes, which were seen as evidence of bad German taste. There were thirty-nine canvasses by then, but even all together they had little value in 1945. Only I, it seemed, had any liking for them.

'The general view was that I had saved the Krause collection for the nation. I had used a little ingenuity, there had been a little risk; but at that time, as the Allies were advancing and the Germans retreating, mere survival demanded ingenuity and brought risks. Big Freddy went to Berlin; the paintings did not. I received the credit. This was the time of the Schermerhoorn-Drees coalition, June 1945. There was talk of some recognition for my services to the nation. I asked that since no one wanted them, I might be allowed to keep the thirty-nine Marottes.

'Today it looks as if I was possessed of a crystal ball. Marotte has proved to be a sound investment. But at the time it seemed only the immature taste of a very young man. Krause's collection included works by Rembrandt, Van de Velde, Jongkind, Lucas van Leyden, Honthorst. A treasure trove of Dutch art. Nobody was interested in the work of a minor French follower of Gauguin, and Gauguin before his Tahiti period at that.

'So there you have my story of how I came to Paul Marotte. My road leads through war. Yours, my dear young Werther, leads through love. That is, I think, the more direct route of the two.'

We ordered our meal. The menu handed to me was printed in English, and had on its cover a photograph of the Tower of London. Inside, the translation was unpretentiously direct: 'Brussels foliage', I saw, and 'Fluffy pudding'. I chose the *cassoulet carcassonne*, described as 'stewed lambs with pieces of garlic sausages'. The restaurant was full, with a constant coming and going of diners, and a pulling about of tables. Beyond the two arches, where the big room became a café, people sat reading newspapers at tables covered in carpet-cloth.

I asked Christiansen what he made of the biographical side of Marotte's fame: the story of love at first sight.

He said, 'It's very charming.'

'Nothing more?'

'What more do you want? But of course, I know. You want true love. Truth, and love.'

'If possible.'

'If possible. But is it possible?'

He was holding his wine glass before him as he spoke, looking through the glass at the flame of the candle, then flicking his sharp eyes up to meet mine; his articulation precise, speculative, creating a context for the more personal questions to come.

'A man can feel love for a woman, of course. Who can deny that? But can a man give love to a woman? Is the gift acceptable? Let me ask this: is it possible that what a man wants to give is not what a woman wants to receive?'

I said, 'It's possible.'

'In such a case, a man must disguise his true intentions. A little make-up round the eyes? A mint, to sweeten the breath? No, I see that you disapprove of the cosmetic arts. You would rather be loved as you really are.'

He gave these last words a light mocking emphasis, so that they sounded like vanity.

I said, 'Truth lasts longer.'

'Truth lasts longer.' He considered this observation, his head on one side. At a neighbouring table a large and convivial group burst into a roar of laughter. Beside our table there stood a copper pan-warmer, shallow and rectangular, pierced along its low sides with star-shaped holes. Inside I could see two winking flames, like nursery night-lights. These little flames kept warm my cassoulet, should I want more.

Christiansen said, 'I wonder what it is you mean. Moral truth? Intellectual truth? You believe, I suspect, that truth somehow procures love.'

This was his method: erosion by definition. He had the mind of a lawyer. But I too colluded in the game, wanting to draw him into confidences.

'I believe that truth makes love possible.'

'Come now, amator. Your truth is a more active element than that.'

'What do you mean?'

'Would you not claim that the telling of truth itself creates love?'

'I don't claim that, no. But I think that sometimes it might be so.'

'Why so cautious tonight?' He held my eyes in his, and read my mind. 'Perhaps you have tried, and failed.'

'Perhaps.'

'You have seen Flora again?'

'Yes.'

'And does love live on?'

I nodded. Christiansen sighed and refilled my glass, and the waiter put more food on our plates.

I said, 'So you think men and women want different things from each other.'

'I think men's and women's interests are opposed.'

'You don't believe in the possibility of love?'

'Not what you call love. Alliances, yes. Treaties. Exchange of hostages. Also, invasion, conquest, annexation.'

'Love as war.'

'Life as war.'

'I don't feel as if I'm fighting anyone. I don't feel as if I want to fight anyone.'

'You are a romantic pacifist. You are neutral territory.'

'Like Switzerland? I'm not sure I want to be that.'

'I have a house in Switzerland, by the shores of a lake. It's beautiful in winter; you must come. The lake freezes over, and the snow lies on the ice.'

'Thank you.'

'I confess I'm curious about your feelings for Flora. I would like to understand them better.'

There was nothing I wished to conceal. Freddy was curious as I wanted Flora to be curious. I told him the truth as I would tell her the truth: rehearsing all that I had to say to her one day.

'Ask away.'

Christiansen's questions took the form of statements.

'You are in love. You have an impulse of fidelity. You wish to be free no more.'

'That's true. I'm not free any more.'

'Not free by choice. You've become weary of freedom.'

'Not in general. But until I met Flora, there was nobody for whom I was willing to surrender my freedom.'

'You wish to surrender yourself into her power.'

'Something like that. It sounds bad, I know.'

'Nevertheless, you like it. The powerlessness.'

'I like it, yes.' Because in my mind I was speaking to Flora, I tried to be honest. 'I feel in danger. That's partly what I like. Not being safe any more.'

'The sensation of risk excites you.'

'The being exposed.'

Christiansen listened, nodding his head, as if all I said had been predicted. He was a magician pretending to be a mechanic. He too sought exactitude.

'As one might say, undressed. The bare skin sensitive to the motion of the air.'

He smiled as he spoke, at his own exaggerated image.

'Yes.'

'We're talking about sensations that are, despite my modest attempts, incommunicable. Private.'

'Another person can have the same feelings.'

'But it is not necessary that they should do so.'

'No.'

'So this love you feel for Flora, it is not determined by her feelings for you. It is, in fact, an independent entity; independent of Flora, I mean. An entity constructed out of elements of yourself.'

I could not deny it. My love for Flora was part of me, not part of her. But had she not awoken it?

Freddy said, 'Flora is the occasion for your adventure.'

So it seemed. So she believed. How could I show her that they were the same, the reaching out of my arms to her, and the unfolding of herself? For example, her smile. When she smiled at me, as I had seen her smile, not at something I had said or done that amused her, but from an impulse of affection, her mouth wide and her eyes tender, that smile which melted me was also a melting within her. It pleased her to smile; and one can't smile well alone. So it was true to say, I was the occasion for her smile. I came into being for her smile.

Freddy said, 'You create Flora for your love.'

But she was not of my making. She was the familiar stranger. When I saw her I recognised her. Every day that passed we came closer. I wanted only for her to believe in our chance of kindness.

Freddy listened to all I said, and was content. This was as he would have it. He said to me, 'I live by other rules.'

He told me a story, which purported to come from his past. Perhaps it did.

'I, too, used to believe in true love.'

His soft, courteous voice lulled me into acceptance. Because Freddy was supremely rational, he had no faith in reason. He compiled his arguments like tarot cards, image laid on image.

'I was just twenty-one years old. She was very beautiful, very rich. There was a husband, but in this story there is no part for a husband. He was, shall we say, away on business?'

He sketched in the background for me: a country house, a high drawing-room with a balcony, a view of pasture land running down to a river. A young man rode up to the house on an American motorbike. He climbed the stairs to the room with the balcony, where the beautiful woman was waiting.

'She wore a kimono. That is how I remember her. A black-and-grey kimono, and in its folds, as in the wing feathers of a bird, hidden streaks of colour: orpiment, madder, aqua-marine. All the time I was talking to her she would sit with a magazine on her lap, turning its pages slowly; but she did not read it. Her eyes were on me. Can you imagine it? The pages turn, turn, and she smiles. Every day I asked her, Do you love me? Every day she gave me the same answer. How am I to know? My sweet boy, how am I to know?'

Every day, in Freddy's story, the young man rode his motorbike along the river road to the house with the high balcony. There was a fork in the road. The turning to the right led to the house, the turning to the left, which narrowed into a path, led to the river. There it met a footbridge, made of the trunk of a single tree, laid from bank to bank.

'She admired my motorbike. It was a four-cylinder Harley-Davidson, magnificent, wide as a horse. She used to sit on its warm leather seat and stroke the gasoline tank and ask me how fast it could go. I said, Do you love me? Always, Do you love me? And she replied, My sweet boy, how am I to know?

'When she said these words, sometimes she looked at me in a certain way. It was like a challenge. It was as if she said, Make me love you. Then one day she told me about the old Provençal tests of love. A test of love! The very words excited me. But what test? How to arrange it? I was eager for some difficult and dangerous task, the doing of which wins love. Very well, then, she said, we'll have a test of love. But first we have to decide who is to do the test. Am I to test you, she said, or are you to test me? I never hesitated for an instant. There was nothing she could do that would make me love her more. She was the one who was unsure. So I said, You must test me.

'I was in love. I wanted to prove my love. Would you not have done the same in my place?'

Freddy's story was a cautionary tale, a moral fable. There was a fork in it, a point at which the hero must choose between two paths, in the knowledge that one led to happiness, the other to despair. This was Freddy's sentimentality: a fondness for the irrevocable. He did not like to live with second chances, changes of heart, sliding possibilities.

'This was the test she gave me. I was to ride my motorbike across the footbridge over the river. I was happy with the test. There was some skill in it, some danger. The tree trunk that formed the bridge might not take the weight of the machine. I risked losing my bike, perhaps injuring myself. But she wanted more. She wanted to ride with me. I pleaded with her, I was afraid she would be hurt, I begged for another test. But she was adamant. This was my test.'

So the beautiful woman climbed on to the Harley-Davidson, and leaning forward, pressed her breasts against the young man's back. The motorbike roared slowly down the road, and turned on to the path that led to the river. As it lurched over the rutted track it picked up speed: its weight and power were such that the tyres cut a wide groove down the path. The woman held the young man tight, her hair streaming free in the wind. The river came in sight. The young man opened the throttle and they charged the bridge, bucking the land crests like a power boat. The bridge passed under them in a moment of sudden stillness, as if they had leapt the river. On the far bank the racing wheels bit into loose earth, and spun out of control. The great motorbike stumbled like a shot deer, throwing its riders clear to one side. The young man struggled to his feet, dazed and breathless. He stood in long grass, in sunshine. The machine's engine had cut. There was no noise. He searched for the woman, and found her lying in the long grass, unharmed, smiling up at the blue sky. Now do you love me? he said. Now do you love me?

Freddy spread his long fingers before me like a conjuror at the climax of his trick.

'What does she answer? Have you guessed my story's ending?'

'She still doesn't know?'

'Of course. She says, My sweet boy, how do I know? Now, my friend – can you tell me why?'

I shake my head.

'I had chosen the wrong test.'

'How was it wrong?'

'She was testing me. What could that prove? That I loved her? We both knew that already. No, I should have tested her.'

'Did she want to be tested?'

'Of course. But I did not know it. Just as you do not know it now. Ah, amator, I see in you so much of myself. In those days I believed, as you believe, that love could be given. Whereas, of course, it can only be taken.'

The black-coated waiter brought coffee, and with the coffee, on a little dish, chocolates in the shape of crustaceans: shrimps and scallops. The restaurant was full of cigarette smoke. The concert was over in the concert hall next door, and the café beyond the arches was now crowded. I had drunk too much wine to be able to disagree with Freddy's pronouncements.

'Did you find my story instructive?' he said. 'I mean you to.'

He bit on a chocolate shrimp. The Keyzer's curtains were now being drawn to warn latecomers that the establishment was closing.

This was Freddy's advice to me.

'You must learn to make demands.'

14

My research in the chaotic Marotte archive proved to be a waste of time. The truth was, my mind was not on my work. It was on Flora. By now I had confided in Camille. It had proved impossible not to: every time I began to speak, the matter that filled my mind came crowding forward, demanding expression.

Camille's advice mirrored Christiansen's, but was more specific.

'You must do it with her.'

Her plain round face lit up as she spoke. Clearly this was a source of vicarious excitement.

'Think of it as a kind of electrical build-up,' she said. 'Sexual arousal has charged your nervous system to peak capacity. You must discharge the energy. You must do it with her.'

'I'd be glad to,' I said. 'But I don't think she'd agree.'

'Have you asked her?'

'No.'

'So ask her.'

'I can't just ask her out of nowhere. That sort of thing needs the right setting.'

'So make the right setting. Make it a special occasion. Tell her it's your birthday. Then ask for a birthday present.'

As it happened, my actual birthday, my thirtieth birthday no less, was only three weeks away. All it would take was a small adjustment. Christiansen had left Amsterdam and was in New York, meeting wealthy art-collectors. I had the apartment on Spiegelstraat to myself. Something in my relations with Flora had to change; and that change needed a catalyst.

I bought a cake. I bought a bottle of vodka. I raided Christiansen's wine cooler for champagne. For this imaginary birthday, I named a day and a time of day that made no overt demands: six thirty on a Tuesday evening. I invited Flora, and she came.

'Is it just me?'

'Freddy's away. Who else do I know?'

She brought the inevitable flowers, and also a more costly gift: a Mont Blanc fountain pen.

'Because you're a writer.'

I felt grateful and fraudulent.

'Isn't this birthday your thirtieth?'

'Yes.'

'That's a bad one.'

'Just another year,' I said. 'Just another excuse for a drink. Vodka or champagne?'

'Oh, Bron. What a decision. Can I have both?'

'Of course you can.'

'I shall get drunk.'

'So shall I.'

I poured for both of us, joining her in excess.

'Here's to the last thirty years,' I said, raising my vodka glass. 'May they never return!'

148

I drank and she drank, straight down in one. Now for the champagne.

'Here's to the next thirty years,' I said. 'And transformation!'

We drank together again. I refilled both glasses.

'Don't let me drink too much, Bron. I'm no good when I'm drunk.'

'I disagree.'

'You want me to get drunk?'

'Of course. How else can I get what I want from you?'

'What do you want from me?'

'Your story.'

'My story!' She laughed. I could hear the relief. 'What story is that?'

'For my book. That I shall be writing with my new pen. The Book of True Love.'

'But I don't know anything about true love.'

'Have you never fallen in love at first sight?'

'No. Never.'

'I have.'

I refilled our glasses.

'With you.'

I raised my glass, my words hurrying on, denying her the chance to object.

'So what I want to know is—'

Back went the glass. Down went the vodka. Fire in the belly.

'—why you won't love me back.'

She burst into laughter.

'Oh, Bron!'

'All I want is a reason.'

'Maybe I don't find you attractive.'

'I don't believe you.'

'What!'

'I have evidence. You kissed me.'

'Kisses mean nothing.'

'Don't believe you.'

'Alright, then. You're a good-looking boy. You've been sweet to me. I may kiss you from time to time. But that doesn't mean it goes any further.'

'Why not?'

'I don't know. How should I know? These things are mysterious.'

'No, they're not. Something's not right about me. I want to know what.'

'Maybe something's not right about me.'

'Alright. I still want to know what.'

'I don't want to tell you.'

'Alright. You don't have to.'

More vodka. More champagne.

'But just tell me this. Does the secret that stops you loving me stop you loving other men, too?'

'Yes.'

'All of them?'

'Yes.'

'So it's not just me?'

'No.'

'Let's drink to that.'

We drank.

'Now, Flora, we come to it. You can't love, because of this secret. But you can make love.'

'Where exactly is this going?'

'It is my birthday. My thirtieth birthday.'

'I don't believe this.'

'It could be a birthday present.'

'I've given you a present already.'

'And I've thanked you.'

She thought for a moment. She didn't seem offended. Then she said, 'I don't really think it's a very good idea.'

'I do. I think it's a very good idea.'

'I'd much rather be friends. Too many lovers, not enough friends.'

'Even so.'

'Amsterdam's full of women you can have that with. It doesn't have to be me, does it?'

'No. But I'd like it to be you.'

'What would happen afterwards? We wouldn't be able to go on like this.'

'I don't think I want to go on like this.'

'Oh, Lord. It's always sex that fucks things up.'

'As a matter of fact, that's not true. My best friend used to be my girlfriend. We used to sleep together. Then that finished, and the friendship began.'

'Really?'

'It's like we moved beyond sex.'

'Beyond sex?' Then she saw where this was heading. 'Oh, I get it. I have to sleep with you so I can be your friend.'

'Why say it like that? It's not a trick.'

'Maybe it's not a trick. It's just so depressing, the way it always comes back to sex. Sex isn't so important. It doesn't take long, and nobody has anything to say afterwards. Men who want sex are all the same, all as boring as each other. Why don't you do what Axel does? Go to one of the clubs and have your sex, and then come back to me and we can do something more interesting together.'

'Your husband goes to brothels?'

'Everyone's husband goes to brothels. It's what men do.'

151

'I don't.'

'You can't afford it.'

'Don't you mind your husband having sex with other women?'

'Not at all. It saves me having to do it.'

'So you don't like sex?'

She thought about that for a moment.

'I don't like what everyone makes of sex. They make it so important, and it's not so important. Did you mean what you said? Have you and your friend really moved beyond sex?'

'Yes. Really.'

'And you're best friends?'

'Yes. Anna tells me everything. All about her frightful boyfriends.'

'And do you tell her all about your frightful girlfriends?'

'Of course.'

This was not entirely true. I had not yet told Anna about Flora. But then, Flora wasn't my girlfriend. I'd not talked about her to Anna so far because I'd not been sure exactly what to say. Or so I told myself.

'I've never had that with a man,' said Flora.

'You've never had a man who was just a friend?'

'No, never.'

'They've always been lovers?'

'Not necessarily lovers. But they've always been playing games.'

'Games to get sex?'

'Oh, sex. Fuck sex. Sex isn't the only game.'

Fuck sex. That was vintage Flora.

'Isn't your husband your friend?'

'Husbands aren't friends. They're husbands.'

'But you must like him.'

'Must I?'

'For God's sake, Flora! What's going on? Why stay married to the man?'

'There has to be somebody. Why not him?'

'Because it can be better than that.'

'True love?'

'Laugh if you like. But I do believe people can tell each other the truth and still love each other.'

'Well, that's the question, isn't it? How much truth can anyone bear?'

I filled our glasses again.

'How much vodka can anyone drink? How much champagne?'

'No limits,' she said.

'I'll drink to that.'

We drank.

'No limits.'

I put down my glass.

'Now, Flora,' I said. 'It's my birthday, and I'm going to kiss you.'

'I don't think—'

I kissed her. She let me kiss her, and then after a few moments she kissed me back.

I lifted her up and carried her into Christiansen's bedroom, where there was a big bed. We lay kissing on the bed, and I undid her blouse, and kissed her body. She lay still, unresisting, as I unbuckled the belt of her jeans. I moved back up to kiss her lips.

She was crying.

'What is it?'

'I'm sorry,' she said. 'I'm sorry.'

'You don't want to?'

'I'm sorry. I'm sorry.'

Gently, I buckled up her belt again, and button by button fastened up her blouse. Then I kissed her very softly on the lips, and wiped the tears from her cheeks.

'I'm sorry,' she said again.

It was all she could say.

'Doesn't matter,' I said. 'There's no rush. We have all the time in the world.'

I expected Flora to call the next day, but there was no call. Nor the day after. I phoned, but no one answered. By the third day I was frantic. Unable to stop myself, I went to her house on the Singel, and knocked on the front door. Axel Jaeger answered the door himself.

'The English friend!' he said. 'Come in.'

I entered the shadowy, elegant hallway, long and narrow, at the far end of which, in the well created by the rising curve of the staircase, hung a painting in a soft pool of light. It showed a smiling plump-cheeked man in a red cap and coat, sitting with his legs crossed, plucking at the strings of a lute. Jaeger seemed to have been expecting me. He beckoned me in to the front room.

'I didn't know how to find you, or I would have sent this on earlier.'

It was a letter, to me.

'I've been staying with Freddy Christiansen.'

'I don't like that man.'

Jaeger stood with his legs apart, his hands clasped behind his back, smiling at me.

'So she's gone,' he said, watching my reaction.

'Gone where?'

The arms reached out and up.

'I thought perhaps to you. But it seems not.'

I opened the letter and read it quickly, looking for clues. There were none.

'There was a letter for me too, of course. It's what she wants.'

'Why? I don't understand. Do you understand?'

'She's a woman. Women are crazy.'

I frowned. To my surprise, he was sympathetic. It was as if he felt we shared a common cause, being men.

'You had it bad, huh?'

'Quite bad.'

'She's a looker, alright. That's how you say it? A looker?'

'Yes. A looker.'

'Listen, my friend. There's always another fish in the sea.'

She the fish in the sea, I the fish in the barrel. I was bewildered by the letter.

'Flora said you were some kind of artist?'

'I'm a writer.'

'A writer. Okay. How does that pay?'

'Hardly at all.'

'Hardly at all. Okay. So not much spare money, yes? So how about I treat you.'

'I'm sorry?'

'Forget your troubles. Console yourself. I know a very lovely young lady. The bill comes to me.'

I looked back at him without speaking, unable to formulate a response. Absurdly, I found myself afraid of appearing priggish. After all, by his own terms, he was behaving with generosity.

He understood me better than I gave him credit for.

'You don't like to pay for women?'

'I'm not used to it,' I said.

'It's not so hard. But then, I am not an artist. I am a dealer. I should show you the flower auction at Aalsmeer. Perhaps you have seen it?'

I stood there with Flora's letter in my hand, feeling that my life had run out of control. The husband of the woman I loved wanted to tell me about flower auctions.

'The auction house in Aalsmeer is the largest trade building in the world. Every morning little trains roll through the building, pulling carts of flowers. Twenty million flowers a day. More than one thousand dealers. Everything must be done fast! fast! because the blooms will fade. There are giant clocks on the wall, marked with the prices for each cart of flowers, and the price is falling, falling. The first bid to stop the clock buys the cart. On with the next! You see? A Dutch auction! You make your bid, you win your prize. Bid too soon, you pay too high a price. Bid too late, you get nothing. So you learn the exact moment, when the blooms are perfect and the price is right.'

He rocked back and forth on his expensive heels, and grinned at me as he delivered his conclusion.

'It is the same with women.'

He gave me his business card.

'Call me if you change your mind.'

'Thank you.' I took the card. 'I don't want you to think – I mean, Flora and I are just friends.'

'That's okay. That's okay.' He waved the issue aside, as if I had said that I had been his wife's lover. 'Women are crazy. But men are crazy too, yes?'

Dear – who? – I don't even know how to start a letter to you. Dear John? That is your name. So now you know what's coming. It's half past ten in the evening. I was drunk

156

when I left you, but not any more. You think you know me, but you don't.

I do love you in my way, which is a very limited way. We said no limits, but there are limits, and if you don't know it then it's no good. Do you remember telling me about your raft floating down the river? Everyone's on a raft. We each have our own raft. It suits us all that way.

Dear Bron you have to believe me. I know what sort of person I am and what I need. I've worked out my own way of not going under. It's not so solid so don't go leaning on it. I'm not going to tell you what it's all about because part of not going under is not thinking about it and not talking about it. You want words for everything but I don't. That's another reason why I can't see you any more.

I'm going away tomorrow. Not just because of you. Don't think I'm ungrateful, just not grateful enough. People never are grateful for being loved, only for loving. That's what you said once anyway. Perhaps you were quoting someone else.

Darling if you want me to be happy or at any rate not to go under then let me go. Dear friend. Anyway I've gone now.

15

The Breton town of Pont-Aven is not much changed from the days of Gauguin and his artist friends, except that the artists themselves, their works, their histories and their heritage have now taken possession. There is a Place Paul Gauguin and a Rue Emile Bernard. The triangular Place de l'Hôtel de Ville contains a Café des Arts and a Café du Commerce, and to evidence this happy collaboration, every other shop has become an art gallery. The Pension Gloanec, where the artists stayed, now sells postcards and guidebooks and magazines, and a plaque on its wall proudly informs visitors that here in this house, in 1888, the school of Pont-Aven was founded.

The owner of the pension, Madame Marie Jeanne Gloanec, 'la mère des peintres', did well enough out of the connection to build a rather grander hotel in the town square itself, which opened in July 1892 as the Hôtel Gloanec. Gauguin stayed here in 1894, on his final visit to Pont-Aven, which turned out to be longer than he had planned, because he broke his ankle in a brawl involving a monkey. Here too came Anna and I in January 1978.

The hotel had changed hands down the years, and was now called the Ajoncs d'Or; but the memory of the artists had not been allowed to fade. Each bedroom was named after a member of the group. Our room, which looked over the main square and its single pollarded oak, was called 'Maurice Denis'.

The little room was almost entirely filled by a double bed. Anna saw this with dismay.

'I told them twin beds,' she said. 'I made a point of it.'

'It doesn't matter,' I said.

'We could ask for a different room. I bet the one called Gauguin is bigger.'

'We'll be fine.'

Ridiculous to admit, but I did not want the hotel staff, who presumed us to be a couple, to learn otherwise. I did not want to be on the receiving end of pitying looks.

These three days in Brittany were Anna's present to me for my actual thirtieth birthday, which was now imminent: also to herself, because her birthday falls five days after mine. This was one of those coincidences that had briefly persuaded us, ten years earlier, that we were destined for each other. Anna's plan now was to break herself in gently to the shock of being thirty by sharing my birthday, which was due on the third and last day of our short trip.

As for me: Flora's disappearance had returned me unceremoniously to what I knew as the waiting room. This was my private image for the life I had been leading for some time. Here I sat, surrounded by empty chairs, before an array of outdated magazines, waiting for the door to open and my life to begin. To a neutral observer, the frustration and the monotony must appear self-inflicted. Why not get up and open the door and go outside? The waiting room is not a prison. But I cannot leave. I have come to believe that it is here that it will happen. It is through this door that the longed-for person will come, the one who alone makes the waiting worthwhile.

However, this was no more than an image of my inner state. My outer self must at least simulate activity. So I was getting on with my much-delayed book.

On the ferry from Portsmouth to St Malo I had at last told Anna about Flora, adopting the ironic and self-mocking tone with which we speak of unsuccessful love, in order not to sound too humiliated. Anna was not fooled.

'It sounds as if you're totally pop-eyed about her.'

'Yes. A bit.'

'I wonder why.'

'So do I, rather.'

'I expect it's because she's so very beautiful.'

'Maybe.'

'And unavailable.'

'Maybe.'

With that her patience gave out.

'Honestly. Listen to you. You'll start sighing in a minute. It can't be that bad. I mean, I know you flatter yourself that this is a grand passion, but as far as I can tell, you haven't even got to first base.'

'You sound jealous.'

'Of course I'm jealous. You get the bolt of lightning, the mysterious beauty, the whole roller coaster of romance. I get a few weeks of lukewarm attention, and then he's gone to the bourne from which no phone call is returned. It's not fair.'

This was Harry, the promising boyfriend no more.

'I'm sorry. I wasn't going to tell you.'

'Oh, what the hell. We've both ended up in the same boat for now. It's good to get away.'

My work in progress had now evolved a sub-section called The Transformative Moment: Love at First Sight. Its principal exemplar was Marotte. His stay in Pont-Aven had not been long – no more than nine weeks in the summer of 1890 – but it was here that his new personality, that of the artist-lover, had invaded and replaced the old, the analytical physician. The change is evident in his letters. In Amsterdam he writes with controlled objectivity, the sentences properly shaped. In Brittany he writes as if only forming the thoughts as the pen touches the paper, as if he no longer knows what's happening to him, and is intoxicated by the adventure of it. This recklessness, this hurling of an ordered life into jeopardy, was what seemed to me to lie at the heart of the love-shock. This was the transformative moment. It had struck Marotte on a bridge in Amsterdam, but he had only come to embrace it and live it here in Brittany.

I had no expectation that I'd make discoveries over these three winter days. But I would walk where Marotte had walked, and make notes, and so collect material for some descriptive passages. In particular I had in mind an imaginative reconstruction of the artist painting his lost self-portrait, watched by his mistress, in the Bois d'Amour: the transformation achieved.

The drive from St Malo brought us into Pont-Aven on the Bannalec road, which runs as it approaches the town along the south bank of the Aven. The river is screened by a series of long ugly sheds, the remains of the mills and the canneries that were the source of the town's wealth before the artists came. Beyond the river rises the steep wooded bank that is the Bois d'Amour. On this drizzling January day the bare trees had a dank and cheerless air about them; and the town beyond appeared to be entirely grey.

'I hope this is going to be fun,' said Anna, not sounding convinced.

There was no information office for visitors. We were assured that a lady issued leaflets from a room in the Syndicat d'Initiative, but only from June to September. There was no town museum. However, in the modest lobby of our hotel there hung a black-and-white photograph of the artists of the school of Pont-Aven, all sitting in a line on the parapet of the bridge.

'Goodness!' exclaimed Anna. 'What a lot of them there were!'

We asked if Paul Marotte was among them, but the hotel receptionist was unable to say.

'I'm sure this was taken before Marotte came here,' I said. 'And anyway, if there was a photograph of him, I'd know about it.'

'How?'

'Because there aren't any photographs of him.'

'No photographs at all?'

'No photographs. No portraits.'

'I can't believe that.' Anna took it as a challenge to her professionalism, as a one-time art historian. 'There's always something.'

'He didn't like it. He hated being looked at.'

'There must have at least been a self-portrait.'

'He did one. But it was destroyed in a fire.'

We asked the receptionist where we should go for information about the artists. She said that she herself was not a native of the town. She recommended a Monsieur Satre, who had a shop on the far side of the bridge. Monsieur Satre had been born in Pont-Aven.

We made our way beneath umbrellas past the Maison de la

Presse with its plaque, and found we had crossed the bridge without being aware of it. This was partly because umbrellas limit the view; but the bridge that gives the town its name is not imposing.

'I expect it looks better in summer,' said Anna. 'With artists sitting on it.'

We seemed to be the only people on the streets.

'Are we having fun yet?' said Anna. 'Tell me when we start to have fun.'

Monsieur Satre turned out to be a jeweller. His shop was about to close, but he was happy to talk to us, even when it became clear that we were not there to buy jewels.

'You come for the artists? In January? Even the artists did not come in January.'

He had heard of Paul Marotte, but was eager to talk about Gauguin.

'You know *La Belle Angèle*?'

'No,' I said.

'Yes,' said Anna. 'It's a famous painting by Gauguin.'

'La Belle Angèle,' said Monsieur Satre with pride, 'my cousin!'

'Your cousin? The woman in the painting?'

'From the past. My cousin.'

I explained that I was writing about Paul Marotte, who had come to Pont-Aven in the summer of 1890. He shook his head. He had nothing to offer on Marotte. So I tried the name of Marotte's patron, Medellin.

'Medellin? Yes, of course. La Maison Medellin is just over the bridge.'

Maison Medellin turned out to be a *biscuiterie*. We had walked right past it without seeing it: a shop that made and sold galettes, the thin butter biscuits which are a local speciality. We thanked Monsieur Satre and made our way back over the bridge, to find that the *biscuiterie* too was on the point of closing. The elderly woman in the shop did not speak English, so Anna, whose French was far better than mine, explained our interest in Paul Marotte.

The name produced an immediate reaction, but not a favourable one. The woman pressed her lips together and shook her head, and spoke in a rapid stream, none of which I caught.

Anna translated for me as best as she could.

'The grandfather of the present owner favoured this artist. Madame his wife did not. Madame was a good Christian, may she rest in peace. The artist did not have good morals.'

'What does she mean?'

Anna asked, and the shop lady looked away as she gave her answer, to show that she did not wish to associate herself with such matters.

Anna translated once more, keeping a very straight face.

'The ladies this artist painted were naked.'

At this point there came a rattling of keys, and it was clear that the shop must be shut. We thanked our informant and left.

We contained our laughter until we were out in the street.

'Naked ladies! *Quelle horreur!*'

'Mind you,' said Anna, 'she does have a point. Artists don't just paint their models. They screw them too.'

'Marotte was in love.'

'Did you know he painted nudes? I didn't.'

'I think that woman's got him muddled up with one of the others.'

'We're not doing very well, are we?'

We ate an early dinner in our hotel. Outside, the drizzle of rain never ceased.

'I don't think the fun has started yet, do you?' said Anna. 'I expect it'll come on your birthday. Birthdays have to be fun, by law.'

'I can't wait.'

We grinned at each other. I liked being with Anna. There was no effort involved.

'What do you want to do tomorrow?' she asked.

'Follow in the footsteps of Paul Marotte. A stroll in the Bois d'Amour.'

'In the rain?'

'I'll just have to imagine the romance.'

'That's rather your thing, isn't it? Oh God, I'm sounding bitter.'

'Just a little.'

'Seriously, what are you going to do about your romance? You can't just leave it there.'

'I take it we've moved on from Marotte.'

'Yes. We're on to fascinating Flora.'

'I don't know. What can I do?'

'You could just forget about her.'

'If only.'

'Well, this is no good, is it? You're like someone who's stuck in a door, and won't come in or go out.'

'I expect I'll move on eventually.'

'But if she were to reappear and click her fingers, you'd come running.'

'I expect so.'

'Honestly, Bron. You're a disaster.'

'I know.'

'There's only one thing for it. We'll have to kill her.'

'Isn't that a bit extreme?'

'Extreme cases call for extreme measures. Do you really

want to sit around pining until she gets old and wrinkly?'

'No, not really.'

'We could do it so no one ever knew. Cut her car's brake cables or something. Do you know about brake cables?'

'You don't think you're enjoying this a bit too much, do you?'

'Yes, maybe. We'd better go back to Marotte.'

'I was just thinking, he must have walked down the street outside. He might even have sat and had a drink in the café opposite.'

'While the governess stayed home and washed his smocks. Have you ever wondered about that?'

'About his smocks?'

'After all, he was a painter, so he painted all day. What did she do?'

'She was his subject.'

In my mind the echo of Flora, saying: *I'm the subject. I'm the one you write about.*

When we got to our room we were confronted by the double bed. It was late and we were tired, so we agreed to sleep like married people: which is to say, side by side, in the same bed, and without intimate contact. In the event, it turned out to be more like a school dormitory, in that once the lights were out what we did was talk. Why is it that talking in the dark is so much easier? Perhaps it's because the words we speak seem to slip away from us into the shadows, and not to belong to us any more, so that we need fear no aftermath. Words spoken in the light are clear and sharp and inescapable. Words spoken in the darkness are halfway to dreams, and forgotten by morning.

Anna's voice was a sleepy whisper by my ear.

'So here's a question, Bron. Now that you're such an expert. What is it that men want?'

'Oh, God. I don't know.'

'I mean, really and truly. I mean, as well as sex. We all know about that. But what else?'

'It's too late for this. We're going to sleep. And anyway, everyone's different.'

'Do you really think that? Or is it that you're just too tired to give me a real answer?'

'I'm too tired.'

'Alright. We'll go to sleep, then.'

But how could I sleep now? Her question scratched about inside my head like a restless dog. Various answers presented themselves to me, but they all seemed to contradict each other. What is it that men want? To feel loved. To feel it's not too easy. Challenge. Safety.

Anna could tell I wasn't asleep.

'It's all about beauty, isn't it? This Flora of yours is beautiful. That's really and truly the only thing that matters.'

'No. It isn't.'

'Yes it is. You just don't like to admit it. All the famous love stories, he sees her, and she's beautiful, and that's it. I mean, what's Juliet got? Nothing. She's just a pretty girl.'

'Alright. Beauty comes into it.'

I said this to make her stop talking about it, but it only moved her on to the next question.

'How? How does a woman's beauty give you something you want so much more than all the other things?'

A strange question. I'd never even considered it a question before. Beauty is desirable: end of discussion. But Anna had a point. Why?

'I expect it's biological. Or chemical.' I was remembering Camille. 'Or something to do with evolution.'

'You mean sex.'

'Do I?'

'But why should sex be better or more evolutionary with a beautiful woman than a plain woman?'

'I don't know.'

'Suppose you were in bed, in total darkness, and an unknown woman got into bed with you. Suppose you made love with her, and she was a wonderful lover, and the sex was terrific.'

I supposed. This was no burden. It was a fantasy I had had on my own behalf more than once.

'Now suppose you turn on the light, and she's ugly.'

'Oh.'

'I've spoiled it, haven't I?'

'You have rather.'

'But the sex was good. So what's changed?'

I had no answer. Something had changed, something so obvious that it had no name. But what?

'Shall I tell you what I think?' said Anna.

'Go on.'

'I think men want their women to be beautiful so they can show off to other men.'

Again I was silent, lying beside her in the dark.

'Well?'

'That may be part of it.'

'I know it's not subtle. And it's depressing. But none of that stops it being true.'

'Or part of the truth.'

'The other part being sex.'

'You really want to be unromantic, don't you?'

168

'No. I just want to know what's going on.'

'Alright.' I caricatured Anna's theories, in part to test them more harshly, because they weren't feeling as off-target as I might wish. 'You're saying all men want from women is sex and the envy of other men.'

'Not just envy. Respect. The respect of other men. I know women want that from other women.'

'But women don't only want good-looking men.'

'No, but women do want something to show off. We want to be able to say, Look, I've brought home a winner. Nobody wants to be seen going round with a loser.'

Was I a loser? Could you be a loser to one woman and a winner to another?

'But,' went on Anna, 'men just want beauty. All other forms of achievement need not apply. Or am I over-reacting here? You can tell me I'm wrong. I'd quite appreciate it, actually.'

More silence from me.

'Bron? Have you gone to sleep?'

'No. I'm thinking about it.'

I was thinking about respect. I had always assumed that my love life was essentially a search for the right partner, and that when I found her I would recognise her, and be happy with her. I was not foolish enough to suppose there was only one twin soul for me, among all the women of the world; but I did act on the assumption that there were not many, and that if I were to come upon one, I would be well advised to act decisively. Hence my persistence with Flora, in the face of all her evasions. But now I found myself exploring a new possibility. What if the fundamental drive of my love life was not the discovery of some other person, but the securing of myself? At once, as soon as this notion came into focus in my mind, I heard a voice proclaim:

Love overcomes fear.

Of course, there was no voice. There were no words printed in isolated italics. But something very like this did come to me: the revelatory suggestion that I sought love because I was afraid, and that the task of love was to ease my fears. At first there was no theoretical underpinning to this, just a kind of recognition. Yes, I said within myself, that's how it is. The unpacking, the comprehending, would have to come later.

I spoke my thoughts aloud for Anna's benefit, and for my own. Truth spoken in darkness.

'Here's what I'm thinking,' I said. 'I'm thinking that maybe all the things we want are the same thing. Love, money, success. All ways of getting the same thing. Like you said – respect.'

It sounded weak. I expanded.

'Not being a loser. Being someone who's worth something. Being able to feel good about yourself.'

Anna listened and did not speak. She wanted it to come from me uncontaminated by her views. I heard myself, and knew I had not yet named names.

Loves overcomes fear.

'Maybe it's all about fear. Maybe that's what we want love for. And money. And success. To overcome fear.'

Still Anna said nothing. But I could hear her listening; listening hard. She didn't need to speak. I was asking my own questions.

'Fear of rejection. Fear of failure. Fear of being left behind. Fear of being inadequate. Fear of being laughed at. Fear of being shamed in the eyes of other people. Fear of being alone.'

Now Anna spoke, her voice small and awed.

'Love has to overcome all that?'

'Maybe.'

'That's very heavy-duty, Bron. Are you sure?'

'No. I'm not sure at all. I've only just thought it.'

I fell silent.

'Golly,' said Anna. Then, 'It's depressing enough to be true.'

'But what if it works?' I said. 'What if the love does overcome the fears? Then it could be good, couldn't it?'

We seek beauty as a trophy, to win the admiration of our peers. We choose partners who raise our status, even if the choice makes us anxious, because we crave status more than peace of mind. We fall in love to feel better about ourselves. Could it be true?

'Oh God, oh God, oh God,' said Anna. 'Why did I start this? What am I supposed to do now? Am I supposed to be all cosy and lovable because men are full of fears, or cool and unavailable because they want to feel proud of winning? Am I supposed to jump into bed with them right away so they don't feel rejected, or make them wait so they'll feel rewarded? And when do I just give up on the whole stupid game and say yes to the next man who wants me?'

What could I say to that? My turn to be silent.

'I don't think I'm like you,' said Anna sorrowfully. 'I don't get a buzz out of chasing someone who keeps running away. The bottom line for me is I don't want to grow old alone. One day quite soon now I'm going to settle for whoever's available. Which probably means Bernard.'

That woke me up.

'Bernard! My Bernard?'

'Your Bernard.'

'I didn't know there was anything between you and Bernard.'

'There isn't. I just get the feeling there could be, if I were to let it.'

'But he's not at all your type.'

'There's only two types of men. Men who are available, and men who aren't.'

'You don't really think that.'

'Maybe I don't. I don't know what I think any more. It's all so fucking hard.'

'Yes. It is that.'

Silence. Quite a long one. Then:

'Bron?'

'Yes.'

'Do you think we take all this stuff a bit too seriously?'

'Probably.'

'Do you think maybe we're living in a long-running television show for an audience of aliens on another planet, and the aliens are all sitting about watching and pissing themselves with laughter?'

'That would explain quite a lot.'

She reached out one hand under the bedclothes and found my hand and squeezed it. After that we went to sleep.

16

The next day the rain had passed, and a pale white sun rose in the sky. The air was sharp and cold. The sound of the rushing river filled the town, and the grey roofs glistened. We stood on the bridge and I told Anna the anecdotes I had picked up from the time of the artists: how they wore striped sailor jerseys and wooden clogs to blend in with the native population, and fed brandy-soaked cherries to the geese to make them drunk, and thought it was a great joke to switch the signs outside the shops in the night.

'Artists really are the pits, aren't they?' said Anna.

We went in to one of the art galleries, where a man sat quietly reading a newspaper. The paintings on display were all original works, but not one of them was original in style.

'It's like meeting people you know you've met before,' I said, 'only you can't remember where. Then you realise you met them on holiday, and now they're wearing less colourful clothes.'

Anna, in her perverse way, was more tolerant of the pastiche work than I.

'Some of this is quite good. If only they had the guts to go all the way and do outright fakes, they'd be making real money. I mean, look at that one. If you were told that was Van Gogh on an off-day, you might believe it.'

She had not anticipated that the gallery owner would understand English; but he heard her, and his torpor fell away. He folded his newspaper and rose from his chair.

'The lady is a connoisseur,' he said.

'She sells art,' I said. 'It's her business.'

'She sells art? My card.'

He pressed his card into her hand.

'You would like to see some art in the Pont-Aven style?'

He steered Anna to the back of the gallery, and drew back a curtain. There in the space beyond there were more canvasses.

'You are familiar with Gauguin's *Vision of the Sermon*, of course? Jacob wrestling with the angel? Look at this.'

The largest of the canvasses showed a group of Breton women in nineteenth-century peasant costume standing on a red beach. Beyond them, in one corner of the composition, a small and distant figure hovered on a yellow sea.

'*Christ Walking on the Water*. Not so bad, eh? Five thousand francs. No signature. If you want to tell your friends it's a Gauguin, that's your business.'

Anna laughed. 'Except it's not in any catalogue of his works, and doesn't have a provenance.'

The gallery owner shrugged.

'You are a wealthy collector. You hang this painting in your apartment. You tell your friends it's a Gauguin. Do they ask to see the provenance?'

Anna studied the painting.

'Five thousand francs?'

'Anna!' I exclaimed. 'You can't buy a fake.'

174

'Not a fake, no. A homage. Don't you think it would add class to a hotel lobby? And if the doorman in his ignorance says he's heard it's a Gauguin, what's the harm in that?'

'You do not have good morals. You'll be selling naked ladies next.'

'Oh, well. Maybe you're right.'

The gallery owner drew back the curtain.

'You have only to call me,' he said. 'Since you are in the business, I can offer you a ten per cent discount on the price.'

As we were leaving, it occurred to me to ask about Paul Marotte. The gallery owner wrinkled his eyes.

'Marotte? Was he the one who was the lover of – I forget her name – the one they all wanted.'

'Kate Summer?'

'No, no. The sister. The sister of Emile Bernard. Madeleine, yes. That's it. Madeleine Bernard.'

'Marotte's lover was an Englishwoman called Kate Summer.'

'Was she? If you say so. There were so many of them.'

When we came back out on to the street we found that the sunshine had strengthened, and the sky was clear.

'If we're ever going to manage that walk in the woods,' I said, 'now's the time. Can you bear it?'

'Yes, of course. Let's take a picnic.'

'A picnic? We'll freeze.'

'No, we won't. We're well wrapped up.'

So we bought ourselves a picnic of bread, saucisson, tomatoes and a bottle of red wine. We returned to the Maison Medellin, in tribute to Marotte's patron, and bought a tin of galettes. The picture on the tin interested Anna. It showed three fishermen in a row, eating giant biscuits, against a back-drop of yellow sea, mauve hills and red sky.

'It's pure Synthetism,' she said. 'Do you think Marotte himself did it?'

'Maybe,' I said.

'I'd like that. But somehow I don't think so. He was far too self-conscious.'

'The Synthetists claimed they were painting from the mysterious midriff of the mind.'

Anna was impressed.

'Who said that?'

'Emile Bernard.'

'Well, this comes from the mysterious midriff of the sales department. That's what makes it so perfect.'

The hotel provided us with a rug, a corkscrew and two plastic beakers. Thus laden, we set off on foot across the bridge once more, following the Rive Gauche, which was the north bank of the Aven, to the Rue du Bois d'Amour. This street climbed away from the river, ever higher, and so the grey roofs and granite walls of the town came into view below us. We passed the great hulk of a flour mill, and arrived, beyond the mill, at the trees. Here the path forked. To the left, a sign pointed to the Chapelle de Tremalo. To the right, to the Bois d'Amour.

'Somehow it's not quite so romantic having it proclaimed on a signpost,' said Anna. 'It's like those signs by roads saying Picnic Area. It makes me feel got at.'

'I think the *amour* is seasonal,' I said. 'This is the off-season.'

The path ran down from here between bare beech trees, past darker clumps of yew and holly, back to the riverside. Beechmast squelched underfoot, and the branches dripped. There were large moss-covered rocks strewn at random on either side of the path, and rocks in the river too, as if long ago a party of giants had stood at the top of the high wooded bank and rolled boulders down the hill, to splash to rest in the water.

The river was narrow and fast-flowing. The water churned its way past the great rocks, and round little tree-crowned islands. Beneath its gleaming surface streamed long strands of green weed, combed smooth by the racing torrent. The whole effect was undeniably picturesque, and might even have been romantic, but for the factory buildings lining the far bank.

There was no way of knowing where Marotte had set up his easel to paint, so we chose a spot at random. We spread our rug at the foot of a rock that was roughly the size and shape of a table, and laid out our picnic on the rock's surface. Pale patches of winter sunlight filtered through the bare branches. I took out my notebook and made notes on the scene, while Anna uncorked the wine and filled the plastic beakers.

'Here's to Paul Marotte,' she said.

We drank to Marotte, and felt the wine deliver its customary charge of inner heat.

'I think maybe this is the fun,' I said.

'Maybe it is,' said Anna. 'It is really rather alright.'

'It is rather.'

'I mean, in its way, it couldn't get much better, could it? I mean, this is what people do things for.'

'Like strive and suffer?'

'Exactly.'

Suddenly it all seemed perfect. Because of this un-anticipated perfection, Anna proposed that we made the picnic into my birthday celebration, one day early.

'It won't be half as good tomorrow. It's bound to be raining.'

'Okay. This can be it. And yours too, if you want.'

'Happy birthday, Bron.'

'Happy birthday, Anna.'

We touched plastic cups.

'Do you feel like you're thirty?' she said.

'Not at all. I feel like I'm thirteen.'

'Me too.' She pulled a face. 'I don't want to be thirty. There should be a law that nobody's thirty until they're married.'

'You're not thirty yet, anyway. Not as thirty as I am.'

'But you don't mind as much as me. You're a man. And you've got fascinating Flora.'

'Except I haven't got her.'

'Why can't I pull off that forever-out-of-reach trick? It's so corny, but it goes on working. Actually, don't answer. I know the answer. You have to be gorgeous. That's the bit they don't tell you. They tell you, treat 'em mean, keep 'em keen, but they don't say you have to be gorgeous. If you're not gorgeous and you treat 'em mean, they just bugger off.'

'You are gorgeous, Anna.'

'Yeah. Like hell. Am I as gorgeous as fascinating Flora?'

I floundered for words.

'So that's it, isn't it? There's gorgeous, and there's everyone else. I'm everyone else.'

'It doesn't seem to have done Flora much good.'

'It's got her a husband. It's got her you trotting after her like a little dog.'

I said nothing to this.

'Sorry. I'm being bitchy. Not fair on your birthday.'

'That's okay. You're quite right.'

'No, I'm not. You're not a little dog. You're a man in love. That's very noble and romantic.'

'Much good may it do me.'

'I've thought of a birthday present for you. This is me being noble and romantic now. You have to appreciate this. I'm going to tell you how to get her.'

'You've never met her. You know nothing about her.'

'Oh, we're all the same underneath. One size fits all. Do you want to hear this or don't you?'

'I'm listening.'

'Okay. This is what you say to her. You can say it in a letter or to her face, it doesn't matter. A letter's best, because then she can take it out and re-read it any time she wants.'

She reached for my notebook.

'I'm going to write it down for you, otherwise you'll get it wrong.'

Dear Fascinating Flora,

she wrote.

There are three things I'm sure of: that we are right for each other, that I can make you happy, and that one day we'll be together. So please know that I'm waiting for you. When you wake one morning thinking of me, all you have to do is call me, and I'll come to you, and I won't leave you ever again.

I read over her shoulder as she wrote, and I marvelled.

'Where did you get that from?'

'Where do you think? From my rich fantasy life. It's what every woman wants to hear.'

'Are you sure?'

'It's irresistible. Love without demands. Love that's strong and faithful. Love that waits till you're ready. It's perfect.'

'Yes, but doesn't it take all the pressure off? I mean, if she knows I'm always there, waiting, then what's the rush? She can have all the affairs she wants. And one of them may work out, before she ever gets back to me.'

'No.' Anna shook her head. 'Not after you've sent this letter. This is a time bomb. This fucks up all other affairs. Think about it. You've turned yourself into the final destination, after all the others have failed her along the way. And the others always do fail. Nothing's perfect. So with every wobble she's thinking, "He's still there. One day we'll be together." I'm telling you, it's a sure thing.'

At the bottom of her time-bomb letter Anna wrote *Happy 30th birthday*, and her name and the date, and *Bois d'Amour, Pont-Aven, Brittany*.

The next day, my actual birthday, we headed home. I felt a sense of anticlimax. We had learned next to nothing about Marotte, and I found I didn't like being thirty after all.

'Can we not mention it?' I said to Anna. 'We did the celebrating yesterday, anyway.'

'Okay with me,' she said.

We argued about self-portraits as we drove. I liked Marotte being the Invisible Man and not wanting to see himself in mirrors. Anna said it was vanity and he should grow up. She said all the great artists painted self-portraits and it was about self-knowledge, and that proved Marotte wasn't a great artist. I told her this was an example of the logical fallacy called the Undistributed Middle.

All pigs eat acorns.

My pig eats apples.

My pig is not a pig.

She said she wasn't talking about pigs, and what had pigs to do with self-portraits? I said Marotte had done a self-portrait anyway. She said she'd like to see it, because she bet he looked like a weasel, and that it would show in his face that he didn't have good morals.

So the journey passed.

In Cross Street there was a letter waiting for me from Freddy Christiansen. It was an invitation to see his collection of Marottes in his house in Switzerland, together with a pre-paid air ticket.

17

Alpine firs walled the winding mountain road for miles. The descent was slow, accompanied by the constant sounding of the taxi's horn. Then, by an outcrop of rock on which there stood a cross marking a fatal accident from some years back, there came the sharpest bend of all, and a break in the wall of trees, and a sudden cascade of light. The taxi driver stopped the car, and indicated that I should look out of the window to my right.

Here the forest which had pressed so close dropped away, falling steeply down the mountainside to the valley far below. In the valley glittered a little frozen lake. The snow-covered forest rolled from horizon to horizon like clouds; the lake a hole in the sky.

The taxi engine idled. Condensation formed inside the windows. Somewhere down there, still out of sight, was Christiansen's house. I was grateful for this brief view. The little lake is so much a world of its own that it is necessary also to see it from the high forest road, in its true proportion, a crack of ice between the mountain ranges.

The day was coming to an end when the taxi deposited me before high iron gates. Beyond the gates, a snow-covered avenue ran to an unseen house. Evidently cars were not allowed past these gates. There was a small side gate, which was unlocked. Through this, bag in hand, I stepped into what revealed itself as a formal park.

The paths and hedges and lawns were all under snow, which smoothed out the variations in colour and texture, leaving only the pure forms, like a giant plan outlined on white paper. At first the park seemed to be made of geometric arrangements of straight lines; but as I walked up the avenue to the house, which was no great distance, I saw how the designer had played tricks with perspective and visual expectation, so that down curious paths and through arches of evergreen there was the illusion of limitlessness.

The house presented itself quite suddenly: a long steep-roofed timber building, its upper rooms built into the pitch of the roof, a deep balcony all round its first floor. A flight of steps descended from this balcony to the ground. Lights were on in some windows.

I walked round the building, looking for a main entrance, so that I could make my arrival known. Behind the house, or rather before it, since it was at once obvious that this was the house's front, there was a terrace bounded by a low wall. Beyond the terrace lay the full length of the frozen lake.

The view was striking. I stood for a few moments by the wall, gazing at the flat snow-covered expanse, and up over the forest-clad mountains to the high fading sky. I meant then to turn and knock on the door to the house, but before I could do so my attention was attracted by distant sharp sounds: voices, and the snapping of trees. On the far side of the lake, perhaps half a mile away across the ice, there was a village. The sounds came from the forest to one side of the village. All at once, as I watched, there came a clatter and crash, and a deer broke out from the trees on to the ice-bound shore of the lake. There it stood, nervous on the ice, turning its head from side to side. One by one, dark figures stepped out of the trees, forming a line along the lake shore that cut off the deer's retreat. Each man had in his hands a pair of wooden sticks, and they now began to strike these sticks together, to frighten the deer. It was an eerie sound, that clack-clacking, carried to me clear across the level snow-covered surface.

I thought the hunters would shoot the beast, now that it was in the open. But they carried no guns. Instead they advanced in an orderly line on to the ice, and struck their sticks once more. The deer started away from them, ran a short distance across the lake, then stopped and stood still. All this was sufficiently far away from me to be taking place beyond my control, as if on the other side of some unopenable window. And yet I could see and hear everything.

The hunters advanced with a terrible deliberateness. They made no unnecessary noise, only striking their sticks together if the deer made a move towards them. The beast backed away, moving carefully, becoming more and more afraid of the ice. Once its hooves lost their grip and it fell to its knees, only to be up again, in a flurry of kicks that caused the ice to creak and groan. I saw now what it was the hunters meant to do.

The day was ending, and the light was failing fast. Men and beast were become silhouettes against the white snow. I heard some words spoken, a low laugh. I heard the small frightened steps of the deer, and saw how its head turned this way and that, seeking a direction of escape. Then, at some prearranged signal, all the men raised their sticks in unison, and struck them twice: crack-crack, like gunshots. The deer bolted over the lake. There came a series of snapping sounds, one after the other, all overlapping, and the seemingly solid white expanse gave way. It was such a strange sight. The deer stood very still at the end, no longer jerking its head, and it made no cry as it sank. The line of hunters lowered their silent sticks. There was a thrashing in the freezing water. Then all was still again. The entire incident had lasted no more than three or four minutes.

When I turned back towards the house, I found the door had been opened, and a man stood in the lighted doorway. He too had been watching the hunt.

'Why do they do that?' I said.

'Deer hunt,' he replied.

He was an old man, with a vigorous and alert air about him. He had a shock of white hair, and a white beard, but no moustache, which made him look like an eccentric professor; an impression that was reinforced by the fact that he wore, on the lower half of his skinny frame, yellow plastic over-trousers.

'The taxi dropped me off at the gate,' I said.

He nodded, and gestured at the open door.

'Go on in.'

Then, without further explanation, he raised his eyebrows, gave a jerky shrug of his shoulders, and set off across the terrace into the park.

Left to myself, I found a bell and rang it. Christiansen himself answered it.

'My good friend! Where is your taxi? Did he make you walk? The rogues, they pretend they don't know the way. You came through the park?'

'Yes. It was beautiful.'

'It is the best way to come. Still! To make you carry your bag!'

He ushered me in, and was all that a host should be. I was provided with a comfortable room which looked on to the lake, and which had its own adjoining bathroom. After I had bathed and changed I found him waiting for me downstairs before a fine log fire.

I asked about the deer hunt. He chuckled.

'The ingenuity of the human mind. Hunting is forbidden at this time of year, but deer found dead of natural causes — well, why let good meat go to waste?'

'How do they get it out of the ice?'

'You didn't see the ice boat? They have a light craft that rides on the ice, and when the ice breaks, it floats. They rope the carcass and drag it in.'

'And who was the old man who was leaving as I arrived?'

'Ah, that must have been William Gandy. He is what you might call a charitable dependent. I let him use the old stable block. He's a painter.'

'Not much of a talker.'

'No. The best of men, but not a social creature. Now tell me about yourself, my friend. How is the great work on true love? Does my poor Marotte still have a part in it?'

'Marotte has become my star.'

'Excellent! Later I will show you my collection.'

Dinner that evening was served in an almost formal fashion by a stout housekeeper called Maria. The old painter joined us at table. He was very shy, and I felt my presence made him nervous. Over dinner I told Christiansen about my trip to Pont-Aven, and how the old lady in the Maison Medellin had said that Marotte painted naked women, and did not have good morals. 'And those, presumably, were the paintings lost in the fire.'

As I was speaking, Gandy managed to get some food stuck

in his throat, and coughed on and off for a long time, apologising for each cough with little looks from his watery eyes. When at last the coughing stopped, he murmured, 'I'm so sorry. I'm so very sorry.'

We returned to Pont-Aven.

'Naked women?' said Christiansen, greatly amused. 'Did she mean they were pornographic?'

'We did rather appreciate the irony. The nude as pornography, in France of all places.'

'The French are one of the most philistine races on earth,' said Christiansen. 'Don't make the mistake of confusing Paris with France. But may I ask – you said "we" – you travelled with a companion?'

'An old friend. A former girlfriend.'

'Ah. Not—'

'No. Not Flora.'

'But your visit to Pont-Aven was of some value?'

'A little. I took some notes in the Bois d'Amour. There's not much trace of Marotte left.'

'He was only there for nine weeks, one summer.'

As soon as dinner was over, Gandy got up and left, with a mumble that I took to be a goodnight.

'Now,' said Christiansen to me, 'if you are not too tired by your journey, I will show you what you have come to see.'

He drew out a key and unlocked the door of an adjoining room.

'Forgive the security. A requirement of the insurance company. Also, I have an obligation to posterity, perhaps?'

There were a large number of canvasses, but by clever placing they did not dominate the comfortably furnished room. A timber partition had been built into one end, to create a corner for quiet reading, and this increased the hanging space. Also there stood in the centre of the room two double-backed easels, each carrying two canvasses, as if the artist himself had recently finished working on them.

I walked about among the paintings, filled with admiration.

'How many are there?'

'Seventeen,' Christiansen replied. 'The number goes up and down. I still buy, when I can; and of course I sell, if the price is right. This is not a museum.'

There were three portraits of Kate Summer, placed together, though clearly painted at different times. Below them, in a plain frame, was a facsimile of the letter she wrote in London in 1901, immediately before killing herself. The handwriting was bold, and unexpectedly florid.

> For the Future:
> May you who are not yet born read this when you are old and pray for me, because at the End of Time there is no Time, and all things happen within the same moment. I do what I do because I have become tired, but I shall not die. Look on my face and see how we have loved. My eternity is in his art.
> I sign myself
> True wife of Paul Marotte
> Proclaimer of his genius
> In scorn of the world
> Katharine Summer

After reading the letter I looked again at the portraits.

'She's right, don't you think? "Look on my face and see how we have loved."'

'Do you know,' said Christiansen, 'there have been times

when I've looked at these portraits and seen quite different emotions. For example, pity; or even indifference. I find the expression fits just as well.'

'That's because you choose not to believe in the possibility of love.'

'You see it as a matter of choice on my part. I take that as a compliment.'

I looked for some little time at the patient face in the portraits, the same face seen over and over again. It seemed to me that the artist was doing what I too tried to do, which was to penetrate the mystery of the face. For all of us who have fallen in love at first sight, it is this that holds like a bud all the love that will unfold over a lifetime.

Christiansen's thoughts on Kate Summer were less romantic.

'It has always disappointed me,' he said, 'that she killed herself by putting her head in a gas oven. Such a bourgeois method. Though there is an attempt at style discernible in the timing. You know she died on the day of Queen Victoria's funeral? I like to think that she turned the gas-tap just as the funeral cortège was processing past her lodging-house windows; but I doubt if the route took in the Battersea Bridge Road.'

My gaze returned to that last letter. I found it both moving and brave.

'"All things happen within the same moment." That's quite a claim. That's a slap in the face of death.'

'A slap in the face of death. Yes, you're quite right.'

He seemed preoccupied with some private thoughts. I turned my attention back to the paintings. One of the canvasses on the easels was yet another version of the Leidesgracht bridge, that encounter which had transformed the artist's life, and to which he had returned, so obsessively, over and over again.

'Why do you think he felt so compelled to repaint that same scene?'

'Why did Cézanne return so many times to Mont St Victoire? Artists don't paint a scene merely to record it.'

'They seek transformation.'

I was thinking of my book. Christiansen was struck by my choice of word.

'Transformation! Just so.'

'It's my new idea for my book. Love at first sight as the transformative moment.'

'Excellent. Highly provocative.'

'This scene' – I was indicating the Leidsegracht bridge view – 'is a visual attempt to grasp, to possess, that moment of transformation. Which is why he kept returning to it. Or so I'm guessing.'

'You try to put yourself in his place? You try to feel what he felt?'

'Yes, I do.'

'You even identify yourself, a little, with Paul Marotte?'

'Yes, a little.'

'And you like him, you would say? You believe you would enjoy his company?'

'I don't really know. What I do like is the way he let himself be swept away. I like the risks he took, and the happiness he found, for a while at least. I like – oh, I like the way he loved. He was so open-hearted.'

Christiansen listened, smiling. I could tell my enthusiasm pleased him. It was as if Marotte was his protégé.

'I shall never understand,' I said, 'how a man as unromantic as you can have ended up as the guardian of Paul Marotte.'

'Perhaps by the time you leave you will understand better.'

'I think all your mockery is just a pose. I think secretly you find their love as moving as I do.'

'Perhaps.' He smiled. 'But I am far more interested in you than in me. Tell me, does the flame of love still flicker in your own breast?'

To my embarrassment, I blushed.

'Faintly.'

'I hope so. I have acted on that assumption. I have invited Flora to join our little party. She comes tomorrow.'

I was astonished. However, responding to a sudden instinct, I concealed my surprise.

'I hope my news pleases you.'

'Yes. It does.'

Of course I wanted to see Flora again. Our story was not over. But how had Christiansen known where to find her after she fled from Amsterdam? And what hold did he have over her that he could command her presence at the time of his choosing?

'Does she know I'm here?'

'No. I thought it best not to tell her.'

'Because she might not have come if she'd known?'

He bowed his head in acquiescence.

'But she would come for you alone?'

'We are old friends.'

'Just old friends?'

'Ah, amator. You think because you're a lover that all men must be lovers. But I have told you before. Flora trusts me.'

I however now began not to trust Christiansen. He was playing some sort of game with me, that much was clear. I did not resent this. On the contrary, I found it exciting. But because he concealed his motives from me, I learned to be suspicious; and once the suspicions began, they multiplied.

For example: Gandy's coughing fit at dinner. When it began I caught a sharp look from Christiansen to the old man that seemed to be warning him to stay silent. I had been talking about Marotte's paintings, the ones that had been destroyed in the stable fire. I had simply discounted the old woman's description of them as dirty pictures, because Marotte is not known to have painted any nudes. But why then would Christiansen warn Gandy not to speak? For the first time I asked myself if it might be true. It was not beyond possibility that the mill owner had commissioned Marotte to paint nudes. Marotte had no money. Artists must take their commissions where they find them. But if it were so, the collection would hardly have included the self-portrait; in which case, the self-portrait would not have been destroyed in the fire.

So perhaps it was still in existence.

This thought excited me.

'I wonder,' I said aloud, 'if the self-portrait has survived after all.'

Christiansen closed his eyes, as if the discussion was wearisome to him.

'Why do you say that?'

'Just wishful thinking,' I said. 'I would like very much to see what he looked like.'

'If it has survived,' said Christiansen slowly, still with his eyes closed, 'why would its owner not show it?'

'It may be stored in some attic somewhere. A younger generation, with no awareness of what they've got, and what it might be worth.'

'It would be worth a very great deal.'

I recalled Christiansen's words to me: *My collection is my capital, my security*.

An odd notion then jumped into my head, prompted by this sense I had that Christiansen was playing some kind of game. What if he himself owned the self-portrait, and had owned it all along? He had nurtured Marotte's reputation for years, and had seen it grow and his prices rise. Was it possible – was it conceivable – that he was holding back this jewel of his collection until he could achieve the maximum impact by revealing it? And the maximum price?

Even as I framed this suspicion, I saw that it could not be true. Christiansen was an art historian as well as a collector. He would not feel permitted to hide so major a work from the public eye. The temptation to show it, to boast of it, would be too great. I sensed how pleased he was by my interest in Marotte. He would, I was sure, have shared such a secret with me.

Then I thought: perhaps that's exactly what he's going to do. Perhaps that's why I'm here. Even the most secretive of men feel the need of a witness.

18

I spent the next morning alone in the room known as the Lake Room, where two wide windows looked east over the lake. The understanding was that I was at work, perhaps even writing my book; but I never so much as opened the briefcase I had brought with me. I sat instead in a deep armchair and looked out at the glittering snow and waited for Flora.

All my puzzling over Marotte was now displaced by thoughts of Flora. We had come so close in Amsterdam, and then she had run away. Just as she had fled from Tawhead. The pattern was clear: I must expect it to repeat itself. She had told me, in as many words, that it was not my love she rejected, but all love. Why?

Just before noon I heard a taxi roll up to the main door. I came out of the Lake Room into the empty front hall. I heard the taxi door close outside. Then the front door opened, and there she was. She came in and dropped her bag to the floor, and let the door swing shut behind her: and suddenly we were alone together.

She was staring at me, shocked and bewildered.

'What's going on?' She spoke rapidly, her voice full of suspicion. 'What are you doing here?'

I said, 'Freddy invited me.'

'What for? What's going on?'

'Nothing's going on.'

'Freddy didn't tell me.'

'He didn't tell me either. He meant it to be a surprise.'

'It's a surprise.'

She was looking at me so fearfully that it began to alarm me.

'Wouldn't you have come if you'd known?'

'No.'

'Would you like me to go?'

'Yes.'

'Alright, then. I'll go.'

She looked intently into my face, wanting to believe me. 'Will you?'

'If that's what you want.'

She took hold of my arms just below the shoulders with both her hands and squeezed me and shook me a little: like an embrace, but without closeness.

'You really will go?'

'If that's what you want.'

'You shouldn't have come.' Then, with a jumpy little smile, 'But it is good to see you again, Bron.'

'Good to see you, Flora.'

'You're a fool. You know that?'

'I know.'

Without releasing her grip she bent her head and lightly butted my chest. I put my arms on hers and she leaned against me.

'Whatever I say to you later,' she said, 'I want you to go. Even if I seem to change my mind, I want you to go.'

'What is it you're so afraid of? Is it Freddy?'

195

She shook her head against my chest.

'I don't want to make things harder for you,' I said. 'I want to help.'

'All you have to do is go. That's all.'

'You know why that's hard for me.'

'Dear Bron. If you love me, leave me. Okay?'

With that she broke away from me, and the door from the gallery opened, and Christiansen entered the hall.

'My dear Flora! I see you have met your fellow guest.'

He greeted her with a kiss on either cheek. Her manner changed immediately. She unbuttoned her coat, letting it lie where it fell on the floor, and said, 'Get me a drink, Freddy darling. I'm wrecked.'

Her voice had become light and bantering. She lit an inevitable cigarette. 'What a surprise to find Bron here.'

She followed him into the drawing-room.

'He's been looking at my Marottes.'

'He must know as much about Marotte by now as you do.'

Christiansen poured a drink, and put a glass into her hand.

'And Humphrey Bogart,' she said. 'And Richard Burton. And the one who cried.'

'Berlioz,' I said.

'I expect you know all about love by now.'

I responded in the same flippant manner, since that seemed to be what she wanted.

'Of course. You feel it, I'll name it.'

'He has to go soon,' she said to Christiansen. 'He was telling me. He has to finish his book.'

'Oh, not too soon, I hope,' said Freddy. 'He's only just arrived. The forecast is for more snow. He must see the snow falling over the lake.'

'Do you want to see the snow falling over the lake, Bron?'

'Also,' said Freddy, 'I have plans that include our friend. I would like him to stay a little longer.'

Flora shrugged and turned away.

I said, 'What plans are these?'

'I had in mind a party game. A little home-made entertainment.'

Flora said, 'I shouldn't get involved in one of Freddy's games, if I were you.'

'You're quite wrong, my dear. This is a game our amator will enjoy.'

She put down her drink, not yet empty.

'I'm off to see the Mahatma. You two do what you like.'

With that, she left us.

I said to Christiansen, 'You like people to have surprises.'

'If I had told Flora you were here, she would not have come.'

'That's what Flora wants.'

'Perhaps. On the other hand, might it not be better for her to be made to face the truth? One can't hide for ever.'

'Face what truth?'

'That is what we have to find out.'

'You think Flora is hiding from some truth?'

'Don't you?'

'I know there's something she won't tell me.'

'Don't you think it would be better if she did tell you? Better for her, as well as for you? After all, you are the one who believes in the therapeutic properties of truth. Yes?'

'Yes.'

'That is the object of my game.'

This was the manner in which Christiansen introduced me to the 'trial of love'; never pretending that it was mere amusement, and holding before me the bait he knew I could not resist. As a preamble, he told me of his fascination with the medieval 'courts of love'; a subject on which I too had done a little research. As he spoke, I listened with half my mind; the other half was with Flora.

'I picture them in the court at Troyes,' said Christiansen. 'The bored nobles, the clever clerics, the Countess of Champagne herself, in a dress of such complicated stitchery that she can hardly move. The sexual gossip refined by ever more elaborate rules of debate into moral theology. You've read Andreas Capellanus? You remember the dispute on the upper and lower halves of a woman's body: which should the true lover choose? He called them the Upper and the Lower Consolations. The language is a large part of the charm. The Upper and the Lower Consolations.'

I remarked that modern scholarship took the view that the courts of love were a literary invention.

'Civilisation is a literary invention,' said Christiansen, unmoved. 'Does it matter, one way or the other? The concept of love on trial has a peculiar fascination that is quite independent of what happened or did not happen in twelfth-century Champagne. We think of love as being opposed to law, or beyond the writ of law; but there's no reason why the truths of love should not be elucidated in the courts, by legal processes, in just the same way as the truths of crime. And when it comes to the establishing of points of principle, the form of a properly conducted trial seems to me to be ideally suited. Speeches for and against, summing up, judgement. I would have thought it could be most revealing.'

In short, he proposed that we should ourselves convene a 'court', and conduct a 'trial of love'.

'You and I could dispute, could we not? We hold different views on most matters, as far as I can tell. We could sharpen our wits on each other, and possibly even learn something in the process. At the very least it would help us to understand our own convictions more clearly.'

'What would Flora do in all this?'

'Flora shall be the judge. There must be a judgement.'

'She won't agree. She'd hate it.'

'But if she were to agree? Would you find it entertaining?'

I had seen at once, of course, that Christiansen's game would give me the chance to speak openly to Flora in a way I had not so far been able to do; and possibly even to overcome the fears that kept her from me. But I did not believe she would go along with the scheme.

'What would we dispute about?'

'I have given that a little thought.'

He went over to a bureau and took out a black marker pen. 'We should choose an issue of significance, to encourage us to our best efforts, don't you think? And of course, we must be sure to disagree. Here is my suggestion.'

He then wrote across the mirror over the fireplace:

Is true love possible between men and women?

'What do you say? You would argue for, I against. You the protagonist, I the antagonist.'

I looked at the black-inked words, beyond which I myself stood, in reflected thought.

'I don't think we agree on what we mean by true love.'

'You shall define it, since you are to defend it.'

I thought for a moment.

'What I mean by true love is, the more truth, the more love. The kind of love that's made bigger by truth and smaller by lies.'

'Ah! The fruit of many hours of thought.'

'Yes. I've thought about it.'

'I accept your definition. I shall argue accordingly.'

Freddy's game was beginning to interest me.

'So what do you say?'

'If Flora agrees, I'll do it. But she won't.'

He raised his glass, looking pleased.

'Here's to our trial of love.'

I saw nothing of Flora until that evening. Christiansen and I were in the Lake Room drinking martinis, a drink that even then was old-fashioned. However, a martini delivers a powerful jolt to an empty stomach, and I was tingling with its impact when the door opened and Flora joined us.

She was looking so beautiful I could not speak. She had changed, into a pencil-slim black skirt and a silvery-grey jersey, a fine knit that hung gracefully over her body. Her hair was brushed to silkiness. Through the curtain of gold glinted tiny silver studs in her ears. She wore a perfume I had smelled on her before, but could not name. I was entranced.

'Flora, my dear. A martini.'

'Thank you, Freddy.'

She didn't exactly ignore me, but she behaved as if there was nothing special between us. I found this disconcerting.

'Isn't it a beautiful spot? You should see the view across the lake in summer. Shouldn't he, Freddy?'

'I hope he will return in the summer.'

'Dear old Mahatma still won't show me his paintings.' This to Christiansen. She had done her duty by me. 'He says my beauty would eclipse them.'

'Flora calls my old friend William Gandy the Mahatma, for obvious reasons.'

Christiansen seemed embarrassed by Flora's casual

treatment of me. As for me, I didn't know how to respond at all. What had I done wrong?

Over dinner Christiansen announced that he had told Flora about his game, and that she was in favour, and that therefore he planned to go ahead with it the following day.

'Do you really want to do this?' I asked her.

She looked me directly in the eyes for the first time since she had joined us. It was a cool, even a hostile, look.

'Why not?'

So it seemed I wasn't to leave in the morning after all.

'It's a game we haven't played before,' said Christiansen. 'We've never had a trial of love before.'

Flora said, 'Freddy will win. Freddy always wins.'

19

When Flora came down in the morning, I was waiting. I came directly to the point.

'I don't know why you're angry with me, but I want you to know that none of this is my idea.'

'I know that,' she said.

She seemed subdued.

'This game of Freddy's,' I said. 'We don't have to do it.'

'Freddy wants it. You want it. So why not?'

'I think it's not what you want.'

She looked at me, but I didn't feel she was seeing me at all.

'Honestly, Bron, it doesn't matter to me one way or the other.'

It was this remoteness, this indifference, that I found hardest to take. I wanted her to respond to me or to reject me, I wanted to believe that my love for her had power, even that it threatened her. But here were her eyes slipping away from me, and already I was forgotten.

I said, 'You know it'll be all about you.'

'Will it?'

She responded with a tiny shrug of her shoulders. Either she didn't believe me, or she didn't care. She moved off towards the room where breakfast was laid, saying as she went, 'Have you had breakfast? The coffee's always good here.'

'Yes. I've been up a while.'

I followed her into the breakfast room. I guessed this would be my last chance to speak to her alone.

'I met your husband. I got your letter.'

She poured coffee and didn't speak.

'Have you left your husband?'

For a fraction of a second she was still. Then the indifferent actions resumed.

'It seems so. Are you sure you don't want any more coffee?'

I pressed on, hoping to widen the door that had opened a crack.

'Are you having an affair with Christiansen?'

'No.'

Once again, the small shrug of the shoulders. No real hesitation. It was convincing. But I was no nearer understanding her.

'Please tell me, Flora. Something's wrong. What is it?'

'Why should anything be wrong?'

She drank her coffee. It maddened me, that unseeing gaze, that detached manner.

'Are you on something?'

'What do you mean?'

'Some drug.'

'Oh, that. No, I don't do that.'

'It's like you're not fully here.'

'Is it? I'm sorry about that. I expect I'm tired.'

'You don't even look at me.'

She looked at me. I searched deep into those wide grey eyes, but she gave me nothing.

'We're not strangers. Don't look at me like this. Please.'

In a very low voice she replied, 'I never meant to see you again.'

At last.

'Flora. I beg you. Tell me what this is all about.'

Very low: 'I can't.'

I recalled her letter to me: *I'm not going to tell you what it's all about*.

'Make me understand why you don't want to see me again. I need to know. Then if that's really the way it has to be, I'll do my best to forget you.'

She looked back at me and I thought I saw something stir in her eyes: a faraway sadness, a long-ago loss.

'Freddy will make you understand,' she said.

The trial of love took place in the Lake Room. I sat in one armchair, Flora in another. Flora smoked, and stared out of the windows, and showed no signs that she was listening. Gandy came in from time to time, and then wandered away again. Maria, the housekeeper, brought in coffee and sandwiches, and later slices of cake and mint tea. I had no sensation of time passing at all. I was entirely absorbed.

Christiansen spoke first, pacing up and down the long room as he delivered what he called his speech for the prosecution. It amused me to discover that he had prepared a small sheaf of written notes. Clearly this game mattered more to him than he had so far admitted.

Our subject was still lettered on the mirror before me. Christiansen read it aloud.

'Is true love possible between men and women?'

He shuffled his sheaf of notes, and began his speech.

'Two thousand years ago, Ovid wrote *Amor vincit omnia*,

which, by one of the many ironies that have followed the flight from classical education, has become the legend on the banner of romantic love. "Love conquers all!" But of course Ovid was writing in the context of his dominant metaphor: *Militiae species amor est*. "Love is a kind of warfare." I maintain that what was true of Augustan Rome is true today. The interests of men and women are opposed. We are, as we always have been, at war.

'Truth, as always, is the first casualty of war. The hostilities are concealed by an edifice of lies that teach us to see what-ought-to-be in place of what-is. The most convenient and therefore the most widespread of these lies is the presumption that men and women want the same thing. In modern times this has been elevated into a meta-lie, which is that men and women are designed to fulfil each other's needs. Of course, for a few moments of biological collaboration there is a coincidence of interests; but note how it is achieved. The natural antipathy between men and women is overwhelmed by an intoxication of the nervous system that lasts only as long as is necessary for the sperm to be deposited in the mouth of the cervix. Long before the sperm has reached the ovum, the man will have pulled his trousers on and laced up his shoes and gone on his way. The moment of conception belongs to the woman alone.

'Strip away the lies, and what do we see? We see that men are unblushingly promiscuous, and pursue sexual pleasure without concern for the consequences. Note the bewildering brevity of men's sexual attention, so suddenly aroused and so suddenly forgotten. The emotional detachment, the separation of feeling from touching. Men can desire and not care. They can yield up their naked bodies in an embrace of utter trust, with someone they do not care for, and whose name they don't even know.

'Now look at it from the women's point of view. Women conceive, bear and nurse children. It's in their interests to have husbands. This is as much as anything a matter of practical necessity. Women need partners to provide food, shelter and protection. I'm aware that this is now considered to be an outmoded view. But what have thirty years of contraceptives and social welfare done to alter the single inescapable reality that sets women apart from men, which is that women carry the baby?

'There used to be a bargain between men and women, of a rough and ready sort. The man paid for sexual satisfaction by becoming a husband. The woman paid for economic security by selling her body. It was a sensible deal to strike, there were customs to enforce it, and on the whole it worked. A language evolved, the language of love, to dignify the bargain; and so that men's needs and women's needs would appear to be the same, everyone collaborated in calling them by the same names.

'Today, that bargain no longer holds. Men have found that they can obtain their sexual satisfaction without having to pay for it; without involvement and without responsibility. For women this has meant a catastrophic loss of bargaining power. But how are women, brought up on the language of love, to admit to themselves that sex is a biological bait? How can they learn to think of men as wild animals that must be trapped and broken in and hobbled? Such attitudes are a denial of everything they have been taught to recognise as their heart's desire. But they have been lied to; and now they are paying the price for their credulity. The love of men is not as the love of women. I know that in this sentimental democratising age such discriminations have been outlawed. But so it is: the love of men is not as the love of women.'

Again and again, as Christiansen spoke, I looked towards Flora for a reaction, a sign of how she took all this: not just the spoken arguments, but the strange concept of the trial of love itself. She smoked, and looked at the lake, and was silent. And yet, she was our subject. A new emotion stirred within me, an irritation that was growing towards anger.

'Please don't suppose I mean to suggest that there is no reality in the emotion of love.' Christiansen spoke on. 'It is as real as any other feeling. It will endure as long as any other feeling. Which is to say, for a little while. But if we may picture the lovers as setting out down a road together, there comes in time a fork in that road, and at that fork truth goes one way and love another. They may follow the path of love if they wish, but they will have to learn to lie to each other; or they can follow the path of truth, and say no more about love.

'That is the path I speak for, the path of truth. Is it so very terrible a road? I don't see that it is. Some comforts are not to be found there, but there are others, in compensation. Let men and women only deal truthfully with each other, and there will be mutual respect, and they will recognise their need of one another, and they will know how to measure one another's real worth. Marriage will no longer be the pretty fragile toy we have made of it, but will become once again a sustainable practical arrangement. Our society will no longer be obsessed with sexuality, because that obsession derives its energy from the tension between what we are and what we pretend to be. Men and women will live together in friendship and security. And true love? True love will once again become a delightful story, about other creatures in other lands, where there are also angels and dragons, and winter never comes.'

He was done. I clapped. Flora turned at the sound of my clapping, and stared, and lit another cigarette.

'Quite a performance,' I said. 'I'm impressed.'

'But are you convinced?'

'Not in the slightest.'

'Excellent. I yield the floor.'

He poured himself a cup of coffee and settled himself down in a chair. Not once had he looked at Flora to assess her reaction to his speech. It seemed it had indeed all been for my benefit.

I rose to my feet. I spoke without notes. Every word was aimed at Flora, of course. All three of us knew that.

'I've been reading about love for months now,' I began. 'I've been writing about love. I've been thinking about love. But I'm still no nearer to understanding it. So I'm not going to try to put forward a theory of love. I'm just going to tell you what's true for me.'

'Bravo, amator,' murmured Christiansen.

'Your lovers reach a fork in the road, you say, and they follow the path of truth, and they say no more about love. I say that if they follow that path of truth far enough, it will lead to love.'

My eyes on Flora, who so hated lies.

'You've said a lot about lies. I don't deny it. I too have lied. Why do we lie so much? I can only answer for myself. I have lied because I've been afraid.'

This was the fruit of my night talk with Anna. Now, with nothing left to lose, I spoke my secrets in front of Flora.

'I've just turned thirty. Not so far from my youth that I've forgotten how it was. People say, Enjoy your youth, the best years of your life. I think they forget how afraid they were. But I've not forgotten. I was afraid of parties, because I couldn't dance. I was afraid of clothes, because they didn't look good on me. I was afraid of conversation, in case what I said was naïve. I was afraid of dates, because I didn't know what was expected of me. I was afraid of sex, afraid of not knowing how to do it, afraid of turning out to be no good at it. Fear upon fear upon fear. And all the time, afraid of people finding out I was afraid.

'So what did I do? I lied, and faked it, and bluffed, and concealed what was really going on inside me. What kind of love can you give when you're living a lie? Not much. You can't afford to let her see the truth. What you want from her is evidence that she's bought the lie, so that you can feel a little less afraid. But of course, all that happens if she does buy the lie is that you have to keep her at a distance. Let her come too close and she'll see how afraid you really are. So every love affair goes nowhere. It has to go nowhere, because that's how you've set it up. That's what you want. Love as a defence against fear.

'This kind of thing can go on for years. I think it would have done for me, if something hadn't happened to me that was stronger than my fear. What happened to me was that I fell in love.'

I looked towards Flora again. She sat by the window, cigarette between her fingers, acrid smoke rising. She was very still, her left hand clasped her right upper arm, a defensive barrier against the world. But she was listening. She heard me.

'At first, I didn't believe it had happened. Maybe I should say, I didn't believe that what had happened was important, or lasting. I didn't trust my own feelings. But something had happened. As the days went by, it didn't go away. It grew. It filled my thoughts. It felt as if a change had taken place in me. It was exciting and frightening. Most of all, it was beyond my control.'

'I think,' said Christiansen softly, 'that we should name names. Since all concerned are here present.'

'Yes, I'm talking about Flora.'

'You don't mind, do you?' Christiansen asked her.

'No,' she replied. 'Say what you like.'

In this way she granted me permission to make my defence of love be about her and to her. More than this, by her air of indifference, she goaded me into directness. I needed a reaction.

'So – I fell in love – with Flora. I make no great claims for this. At first I didn't take it any more seriously than she did, or does still. After all, why her? That I don't know. I'm not even sure that it matters. What matters is how it has changed me. It has made me hungry for truth.'

Now I was speaking directly to Flora. Surely she must answer me now?

'I wanted to know everything about you. I wanted to tell you everything about me. Just as I'm doing now. Regardless of the consequences. I said to myself: This time there are no limits. This time I go all the way. And ever since that day, the more truth I've told, the more I've loved you. Maybe I've made a terrible mistake. Maybe it will all come to nothing. But even if it does, I know, I know for certain, I feel it in every fibre of my being, that I can only love and be loved if I tell the truth about myself; and that it's the same for you. That's why I've begged you to trust me, and tell me what you're so afraid of, because that's the only way you'll ever defeat it, and love anybody. Not just me, anybody. But it could be me. Truly, I believe it could be me.'

She bowed her head and did not speak.

I turned to Christiansen.

'That's what I mean when I say that truth and love are the same thing.'

I had no more to say. He clapped, as I had done.

'A worthy riposte. You put me on my mettle.'

'What about Flora?'

'She is our judge.'

'Maybe she's had enough.'

'You haven't had enough, have you, my dear?'

She said nothing; but she gave a slight shake of her head. The fingers of her left hand made tiny stroking movements on her arm, the kind of unthinking caress a mother gives the child on her lap.

'She must hear the cross-examination.'

I was now in a strange state of controlled excitement: both angry and elated. Nothing could be the same between Flora and myself after this. Before night fell, I was sure the nameless barriers between us would crumble. Christiansen had planned it so, and I now willed it. No limits. We were to go all the way.

20

Christiansen proposed the order of the next phase in the trial of love. First, I was to put questions to him; later, he was to put questions to me. Why not? At least it perpetuated the moment. I knew that when the trial of love ended, Flora would go.

So I began my cross-examination of Christiansen.

'You describe the dealings between men and women as war,' I said. 'What are we fighting over?'

'It's a power struggle,' he said. 'Like any war.'

'Is anybody winning?'

'Of course. Men are winning. Men have always won.'

'Then the war is over.'

'Not at all. Women must fight on, even though defeated, for their very survival. They fight a guerrilla war. A bush war.'

'For their very survival? Do men not want women to survive?'

'Not as women, no. Not as they really are. Women's demands are too great, too enduring. What men want is a different sort of creature, the body of a woman with the mind of a man. A willing sexual partner who makes no demands.

Such a creature doesn't exist, so in trying to force women into becoming what they are not, men mount an attack that women must repel. This is the fundamental position of all women, and always has been.'

'So you think that all men want from women is sex?'

'If a man finds a woman desirable, then all he wants from her is sex. If he does not find her desirable, then he will want service.'

'So women are either sex objects or servants.'

'Preferably both.'

'Most men would not agree with you.'

'Most men are liars.'

'Nor would most women.'

'Some women would not agree with me.'

'I don't see why women would tolerate the position you say they're in.'

'Why does anyone tolerate any position that isn't to their liking? Why do the poor starve in Calcutta? They lack power.'

'Men have all the power?'

'And the money. And the physical strength. And the social position.'

'It seems to me that all you're doing is describing the relationship between men and women in its crudest, most basic form. It may be true as far as it goes, but it doesn't go far enough.'

'What more would you propose?'

'Friendship. Trust. Or can't men and women be friends? Can't they trust each other?'

'Men and women can be friends so long as they are not lovers, and so long as there is no prospect of them becoming lovers.'

'You sound so detached, so reasonable, as if nothing that you say affects you personally. You deny tenderness and respect between men and women, and honour and fidelity and ordinary kindness. You describe a world where all human dealings are brutal and self-interested. Yet you don't sound as if this affects you at all.'

'People don't conduct their lives according to my likes and dislikes. What would you have me do? Rend my garments? Sprinkle ashes in my hair? I'm sorry I can't sound more distressed about it. It's not exactly news to me.'

'You seem almost complacent about it. Does it please you to think of love this way?'

'What has my pleasure to do with it? It doesn't please me to think of malnutrition, or cancer, or growing old. The world is as it is.'

'Do you feel lonely?'

'Ah, yes. You can't have me wrong, so you'd have me sad. Well, why not? I am alone. I will grant you that much.'

'Will you always be alone?'

'I think so, yes.'

'You don't believe that another person could ever come to know you really well?'

'No.'

'Do you love yourself?'

'I am myself. What else can I say?'

'You told me once of a youthful love affair.'

'A fantasy of my own fabrication.'

'So you have no experience of love. For yourself, or for anyone else.'

'Possibly not.'

'Why should you be so different from everyone else in the world?'

'I'm not so very different. I think everyone else is much like me. Only, they tell themselves lies.'

'Me included?'

'Of course.'

'What lies do I tell myself?'

'You have persuaded yourself that a fantasy of your own fabrication is true love.'

'Will I come to see that it's no more than a fantasy?'

'I think so.'

I looked at Flora. There she sat, silent, her fingers stroking her arm. This gesture fascinated me. It made her vulnerable, therefore more attainable.

'Will you be the means of my enlightenment?'

'Indirectly.'

'Who else?'

'Flora herself. Naturally.'

'So Flora will play a part in this game?'

'She will.'

At that, Flora got up from her chair. I thought she was going to leave the room, but she only went to the window and stood there, looking out.

'Is that true?' I asked her.

'If that's what you want,' she said, not turning round.

'I want to know everything,' I said.

Flora's passivity was a cloak for some pain she chose not to reveal. I was sure of it. If she had no interest in our so-called trial, why stay? But if she too was part of our game, why not speak? Somehow I knew I must break through Flora's defensive indifference. Somehow I must force her to become involved.

To Christiansen I said, 'You could prove to me that everything I feel is an illusion, but when you're done here I'll still be feeling it.'

'Ah, my friend,' said Christiansen with a sigh. 'You deploy your heavy artillery against me. Feelings, feelings. You feel it, therefore it's real. You're like a man who's had his right leg amputated, and still feels discomfort in the phantom limb. The itching in your right foot is real. But you have no right foot.'

'If that's your notion of love,' I replied, 'I'd rather be me, believing what I believe, than you, believing what you believe.'

He bowed his head, acknowledging what we both understood to be an impasse. I turned to Flora.

'Do you want Freddy's war? Do you want to believe men and women must always be enemies?'

'Please,' said Christiansen. 'Flora's judgement is to come later.'

'I don't want a judgement. I want to know what Flora's making of all this.' Without intending to, I had raised my voice. 'You're part of this, Flora. You can't say nothing.'

She shook her head. She said, 'None of this has anything to do with me.'

'Yes. It has. Even if you don't believe me, or my love, you must believe that somewhere, some time, somehow, people can love each other.'

She looked at me with that unfathomable faraway look.

'I don't know what you want from me, Bron.'

'I want the chance to know you. To come close to you.'

Her smoke-blue eyes on me, not seeing me. She was like a sleep-walker. They say you must never wake a sleep-walker, but what if she's walking towards the edge of a cliff?

I clapped my hands.

'Wake up!'

She gave a little jump of surprise, very much as if she was indeed waking up. Her eyes flicked across to Christiansen, seeking guidance. He said nothing. She looked back at me.

'Why should I wake up?' she said in a low voice.

'Please, Flora!' This was my chance. 'Tell me what it is you're so afraid of.'

She shrugged, and once more she stepped back from the moment of revelation.

'Oh, you know. All the usual things.'

Safety. Love. Not to grow old. The usual bag of tricks.

She returned to the window, to her cigarettes, to her silent detachment. But for a moment, she had been real.

'Do I take it,' came Christiansen's courteous voice, 'that you have finished?'

'I think we've all finished,' I said.

'Not quite. I am to have my turn to ask the questions.'

'I don't think Flora is enjoying this any more.'

'Flora, my dear? Would you like us to stop?'

'Do as you please,' she replied.

'Then I think we should complete our trial.'

He indicated the words inked on the mirror.

'The trial of true love.' To me: 'I would like to bring us back to what I believe you have defined as the transformative moment.'

I shrugged. I didn't want to go on; but nor did I want to stop here. I too had not finished.

'I am particularly interested,' he said, 'in understanding just what it was that took place when you first met Flora. In the early morning, I think you said. By a river?'

I nodded.

'By a river. In a mist. It must have been ghostly. Unreal.'

'Yes.'

'You have a clear memory of it?'

'Yes.'

'Can you describe it?'

I glanced at Flora. She was listening, alright. I decided I would describe it for her.

'I was walking by the river. It was about seven in the morning, quite cold. The mist lay all down the valley. I had never met anyone there before, not that early in the morning. It never occurred to me there'd be someone else there. I suppose my mind was full of my own thoughts. I don't know what, the coming day's work, I expect. Then there she was. It gave me quite a shock. Except I wasn't surprised. What I mean is, I was taken by surprise, because suddenly there she was, very close; but I wasn't surprised that it was her. I thought at first that I must have met her somewhere before. Then as I stared at her, rudely, I suppose, I knew that I hadn't met her before, ever in my life – but it seemed to me that I knew her. That was all that happened.'

'Were there any sensations?' asked Christiansen. 'Or was it more like an idea that entered your head?'

'All the things people say. My heart started to pound. My mouth went dry. I felt light-headed. Time seemed to slow down. And most of all, there was this strange certainty, that had come from nowhere. I felt as if I knew her already. I felt as if I'd known her for a very long time.'

'You didn't speak?'

'Neither of us spoke.'

'So how long did the encounter last?'

'Oh, no time at all. Ten seconds, maybe. It was very brief.'

'Ten seconds. Very well. Now tell me more about how, in those ten seconds, you apprehended the experience of love.'

'I'm sorry. I don't understand.'

'Did you see it? Smell it? Hear it? Did it reach out and touch you? Some combination of the senses must have been involved.'

It was an unexpected question: so specific that it seemed hardly relevant. Yet as I pondered that brief meeting by the island in the mist, I was surprised to discover how very little I had had to go on. Flora had made no sound. She did not touch me. I had no recollection of her scent. My memory of her impact on me was all emotional, as if my heart were a part of the apparatus of the senses. But in plain truth, all I did was see her.

I said as much to Christiansen.

'Ah, the golden arrows,' he said. 'You remember the *Roman de la Rose*? Love enters through the eyes.'

The God of Love shoots five arrows at the Dreamer, which pass through his eyes and lodge in his heart. The five arrows are Beauty, Simplicity, Courtesy, Company and Fair Appearance.

'Now we must try to find out what it was you saw.'

'Why? What are you trying to prove?'

'At this moment I'm not trying to prove anything. I'm trying to discover the secret of love.'

'The secret of love? Why should there be a secret?'

'Perhaps I should say, the secret ingredient. The magic key. There must be a magic key.'

'I don't see why. It does happen all the time, after all.'

'Does it happen all the time to you?'

'No. Not at all.'

'You're not in the habit of looking at beautiful women for ten seconds and then falling in love with them?'

'Absolutely not.'

'So in this case, there must be something extra present. A

secret ingredient. A magic key. Of course, it may be that the secret ingredient is not to do with the persons concerned, but with the timing. Have you ever heard of imprinting?'

'No.'

'It happens to ducklings. When ducklings are newly hatched, they attach themselves to the mother duck, and follow her wherever she goes. Very natural behaviour, you might think. But how do the ducklings know which duck is their mother? The simple answer is, they attach themselves to the first duck they see when they come out of the egg. Sometimes they get the wrong duck. If the first sizeable moving object they see is a wheelbarrow, or the poultryman's boots, they attach themselves to that. Whatever it is they see in that first critical moment they will love like a mother. That is what naturalists call imprinting. If we could ask a duckling why it was so fond of that particular wheelbarrow, it might tell us that it had fallen in love at first sight, don't you think? Whereas, of course, the secret ingredient is all in the timing.'

I shook my head, irritated.

Christiansen added, 'Your mind had been filled with notions of love for weeks. You tell me you were thinking of your coming day's work even as you walked by the river.'

'I'd been researching my book for months. I'd met lots of women in that time.'

'So you don't like imprinting. Do you have any suggestions? It's a simple question, really. Why Flora?'

'I don't know. Does it matter?'

'I believe so. As it happens, I also believe that we can locate this magic key to true love. After all, we do know some things about it. We know that it doesn't require much time to operate. A matter of seconds, in fact. We presume that, as far as you are concerned, it's a female attribute. We know that it's perceived through the eyes. And we know that it accelerates the heartbeat.'

He extended his fingers one by one as he recapitulated the list. 'It's superficial. It's female. You see it. It arouses you.' He stared at his fingers, and then at me. 'Do you know what I think it is?' He smiled a frank, friendly smile. 'I think it's sexual attraction.'

Flora burst into laughter.

Christiansen turned to her. 'You find that amusing?'

'Poor Bron!' she said. 'True love turns out to be just sex, after all.'

'I don't think so,' I said.

Flora laughed again. It was the wrong sort of laugh. She seemed to be rejoicing in the defeat of my claims.

'Just sex!' she said. 'Poor old sex!'

'If it was just sex I wanted,' I said, 'why would I hang around you?'

She stopped laughing.

I said, 'It's not as if we've ever actually got that far.'

She stared at me. 'But you're still hanging around.'

'Looks like it.'

'Well, now you know, don't you?'

'Not yet,' I said.

'You and your true love.'

So much hurt. But when, where, how had I hurt her?

'I told you Freddy always wins,' she said.

'It's not over yet.'

'Why isn't it over? What more do you want?'

'The chance to know you.'

I heard the door open, and saw Gandy come into the room. Christiansen was watching us with silent attention, like a spectator at a play.

'This is all there is,' said Flora. She was speaking more rapidly now, a flush forming on her pale cheeks. 'What you see. There's no more.'

'I know there's more.'

'How do you know there's more? What right do you have to ask for more? Why should there be more?'

'Flora—'

But she was too agitated now to listen to me.

'You want more? I'll show you more!'

She kicked off her shoes. Unbuckled her belt.

'You want to see more?'

She started to pull off her jeans. She staggered a little as she tugged her foot out of the crumple of denim.

'Stop this,' I said.

But she did not stop. With jerky feverish movements, she stripped before me. She pulled her jersey over her head. Then the shirt she wore beneath. Then her bra. Her breasts were small and white. She pushed off her panties, exposing a soft brown bush of pubic hair. And so she was naked.

I could not speak.

'There,' she said, staring at me, almost crying. 'That's all. There's no more to see. You can go now. There's no more. No more . . .'

The explosion of anger ended as abruptly as it had begun. She fell silent. She stood there awkwardly, one knee bent a little forward, arms by her side, golden hair tangled across her face. She looked at me with the sullen eyes of a child caught in some transgression, expecting my reprimand.

But after all, she was beautiful.

Then her left arm came up and crossed protectively over those naked breasts, and her left hand clasped her right arm,

222

and the fingers began to make those little movements, those almost imperceptible self-comforting strokes.

I picked up her clothes from the floor and gave them back to her. She took them and held them but made no move to get dressed again.

'I'm sorry,' I said. 'I never meant to hurt you.'

I left the room.

21

The snow had started to fall as forecast. There was no wind. The large flakes descended slowly, in straight lines, out of a featureless white sky. In a long coat and boots, with a wool hat on my head, I walked down the avenue and followed random paths, escaping the confusion of my thoughts. Already the snow had laid a carpet of untouched whiteness over the park. It was as if I was the first to set foot there; as if the world was new, and just as I saw it, with none to see it otherwise. My own footsteps were smoothed out behind me, and soon gone, the snow fell so thickly. I stood still between high hedges and felt the heavy flakes settle on my head and shoulders, and thought how if I stood still long enough I too would vanish, and how that would be a relief of a kind.

I walked on. The path curved, the hedges parted, and there lay a sudden opening, a planned prospect across the lake to the white mountains, now veiled in falling snow. The unexpected view reminded me of the way the woods at Tawhead came to an end by the two gates. I thought then of how I had stood with my hand on the latch of the wicket gate, looking up at the red-and-gold sky, and had been overwhelmed with love.

What reasons had I had then? Yet the feelings had been real enough.

As I stood there I heard footsteps approaching me from behind. I turned to see the old painter, William Gandy, without hat or outer coat. His wild white hair was thick with snow.

'You should have a coat,' I said.

'Coat? I don't need a coat!' He spoke sharply, evidently annoyed at being the object of my concern. 'You,' he said. 'You'll hurt her. Why do you go on with it? You'll kill her.'

'What are you talking about?'

'You should go away. It's not you she needs. It's him.'

'Christiansen?'

'You know,' he said angrily. 'You know you know.'

He fanned his hands at me, as if to shoo me away. Then he stomped off through the snow to his studio.

Now more disturbed than ever, I returned to the house by another way; and here I came upon Flora, standing alone on the terrace, looking out over the frozen lake. She was dressed once more; like me, she was well wrapped up, and had her hands deep in her coat pockets.

She gave no sign that she was aware of my presence.

'That was quite a show you put on,' I said.

'Was it?'

'Is that one of your party tricks? Strip for the guests?'

'You know why I did it.'

You know you know. But they were both right, the old man and Flora. I did know.

'Too much talk,' I said.

'Yes.'

'Gandy thinks it's all my fault. He's just been shouting at me. He told me I should go.'

'He's right.'

'He said I'll kill you.'

She shrugged: not at all surprised.

'If I go,' I said, 'will you come with me?'

'Freddy isn't finished yet.'

'For God's sake! Haven't we gone far enough? We have to stop this thing right now.'

'You can stop any time you want.'

'Why do you let him do it to you?'

'Why do you let him do it to you?'

'I'm trying to get through to you. That's why I'm doing it.'

'There you are, then.'

She was as she had been in the house earlier: detached, not fully present even in her own voice.

'Please, Flora. Tell me what's the matter.'

'I can't.'

The snow fell and fell, trapping us in a dream.

'Come inside. We'll freeze to death out here.'

'I'm cold, Bron.'

I put my arms round her. She was shivering.

'I tried not to be nice to you,' she said.

'Why? Why shouldn't you be nice to me?'

'Because it's never enough. Everyone always wants more. And I can't give more.'

'Why?'

Her answer came in a voice so low I could barely hear her.

'It's not fair. Why do I have to be so alone?'

'You don't have to be alone.'

I kissed her, on the cheeks, on the eyes. Another shift of mood. Now she was hungry for affection.

'Come inside. You need warmth.'

She let me take her into the house. I drew off her coat and

shook the snow on to the mat. The fire was burning in the Lake Room. No sign of Christiansen.

'Stand here by the fire. Get warm.'

She obeyed like a child. I poured us both a brandy from the sideboard.

'There. Brandy. That's what they give people when they rescue them.'

'Have you rescued me?'

'Drink up.'

She drank.

'I can't stop shivering.'

'You've let yourself get chilled.'

Little by little she was returning from that faraway place where she went to hide.

'Your game with Freddy,' she said. 'None of it matters. It's all just talk.'

'Yes, I know. All just talk.'

'People talk. It doesn't mean anything. All that matters is what they do.'

'Yes, I know. It doesn't mean anything.'

'I'm so cold, Bron.'

I put my arms round her to warm her. She made no objection.

The door opened. Christiansen was standing in the doorway, taking in the scene. His face was expressionless, his voice neutral.

'What are you doing, my dear?'

She moved away from me.

'Nothing. I was cold.'

'Have you let him pity you?'

'It's alright. I'm alright now.'

So there it was, before my eyes: Christiansen in control. The puppet master.

'Don't listen to Freddy,' I said. 'You don't need him.'

Christiansen closed the door behind him and crossed the room.

'Come, my dear.'

Flora went to him. He took her in his arms, folding them round her in a manner that was both protective and possessive.

'Tell our young friend. There's no need for him to pity you.'

'Stop this!' My own voice, shouting. Something had snapped inside me. 'Stop telling her what to do!'

They were both looking at me now: he with his arms round her, she diminished by his embrace. Freddy the protective wall between Flora and love.

'Look at you!' I cried. 'You're her jailer!'

Christiansen parted his enclosing arms.

'Flora is free to do as she pleases.'

But she stayed there, head on his shoulder, body huddled against his chest.

'Flora, please!' I begged her. 'You must break free from him!'

'Free?' she said.

'You don't need him!'

'Then who do I need? You?'

She was speaking in a small shivery voice.

'At least I don't treat you like a child.'

'No. Not like a child. You're the one with the true love.'

It had all become a nonsense; Christiansen's trial had sucked the meaning from the words. I wanted to be rid of it all.

'Fuck true love,' I said.

'Yes,' she replied. 'Freddy was right. It's only sex. It's all just sex in the end.'

I felt trapped. I felt as if the walls were closing in on me. Sex, always sex. Every impulse of joy and wonder stripped naked, reduced to animal need.

'Alright! It's sex!'

'Ah!' said Christiansen. 'Judgement.'

Freddy was claiming victory. Flora was in his arms, and he was the victor, and there was no true love, only sex. This was not a trial of love after all: it was a sexual contest, male against male, for possession of the female.

So I had got it the wrong way round from the very start. I had chosen the wrong transformative moment. First the fuck, then true love. I must learn to make demands.

'It's not over yet,' I said. 'Flora must choose.'

'What must Flora choose?'

'You or I.'

'We're not in competition. I'm not Flora's lover.'

'Then get out of my way.'

I went to her and took her hand. I held her hand gently but firmly.

'Come with me.'

She looked to Christiansen to know what she should do, but he said nothing. He gave her no sign. For a moment, she hesitated. Then her eyes turned to me.

She looked so lost. So helpless. And I, I was filled with a new certainty that was sufficient for both of us. I knew what must be done. This prison wall must be burst asunder. This spell must be broken.

Her hand was ice-cold in mine. But she came with me, and Christiansen watched her go.

I took her upstairs to her bedroom, and she undressed. Her hands were shaking so much I had to help her with her buttons. When she was down to her shirt she slipped into bed, and lay there shivering.

'Cold. So cold.'

'I'm going to warm you.'

'Yes. Warm me.'

I kicked off my shoes and got into bed with her. She huddled up close to me, and I put my arms round her. She was so cold. I could feel it everywhere our bodies touched. But slowly she became warm, and the shivering stopped. She pressed against me, and her face nuzzled my face. We kissed.

The time had come. My caresses became more intimate. She made no objection. I felt the awakening of desire.

Such a simple thing. If only we could do this, and she could see that the world went on turning—

Love overcomes fear.

'No, Bron.'

'Hush. Don't talk.'

'Don't—'

No energy in her protests. Kissing me even as her hands felt for me to push me away. She wanted not to bear responsibility. She wanted not to have to blame herself later. But this was the necessary beginning of our journey. All it took was the act of will, and so the consummation.

'No, Bron. Please.'

'Don't talk. Don't think.'

'Please —'

She twisted away from me, but I held her tight, I drew her back. Finding she couldn't escape my embrace, she went limp in my arms. She was telling me, this thing that you do is yours alone. I'm not part of this.

Not so long ago that would have been enough to dismiss me. Why stay when I'm not wanted? But this was one time too many. Again and again she had shown me she wanted me, only to rebuff me at the last minute. She had enticed me to pursue her, only to flee me as I came near. Enough. This game would now end.

This that I was about to do had ceased to be an act of love alone. It was an act of awakening. This limpness of her body, this retreat from me into unreachable distance, made me want to smack her back into consciousness, strike her until she saw me again, and knew me. Love is also invasion, conquest, annexation. Desire is also anger.

'Please stop—'

But I did not stop. It did not please me to stop. It pleased me to be pleased. It pleased me to drive on, and on.

A sudden frenzy. Her feet, her hands, convulsing in spasms of attack. Choking cries, alternating with the pitiful whimper of an animal in pain. Her body juddering, thrashing. Her face contorted, blotched with terror.

Not like this.

I let her go. Our sweat-gummed bodies peeled apart. The air cold where she had been. I left the bed; ungainly, half-dressed, defeated. Fumbling, I forced buttons into buttonholes.

Her eyes on me. Her faraway voice. 'I'm sorry.'

'Yes.'

I'd heard it too many times. Didn't want to hear it any more. What use was it to me if she was sorry?

'Don't go.'

'Why not?'

'Sit here by me. Don't look at me. I'll tell you.'

So I sat once more on the bed. I waited in silence. And she told me.

'I can't do it. Not with anyone.'

It came out in fragments, like a puzzle I must fit together for myself: but one familiar enough for the outline to be discernible from the beginning. A fourteen-year-old girl growing into beauty. A man who was her mother's friend, almost her stepfather. Flattering attentions that became a seduction. A seduction that became a rape. She wept as she told me.

'I thought it was my fault. I must have made him think I wanted it. Must have made him want it. So it was my fault. So I couldn't stop him. Couldn't ask him. Couldn't speak—'

There followed a pregnancy, and an abortion, and complications. What should have been routine was not routine. So this first experience of physical love ended in evisceration. And ever since, what is known as *hysterical closure*.

'I can't do it. Not with anyone. My body won't let me.'

Deep down in me, far off, I felt the sadness gathering for her, the reluctant pity.

'You've never made love?'

'Only that one time. If that's what it was.'

'Jagger? Bailey?'

'No.'

'Did you even know them?'

'Yes, I knew them. Not for long. Never for long.'

'Like with me.'

'Yes.'

'You want love. But not—'

'I'd want that too, if I could. But I can't.'

'So you run away.'

Hysterical closure.

'There's nothing I can do. It's just no good.'

So here was the final judgement in our trial of love. I was the loser. And Flora, too.

'Does Freddy know about this?'

'Yes.'

'Then why did he put you through this whole charade?'

A new anger rose up in me. I thought back over the day's debate in the light of what I now knew, and it seemed to me we had been engaged in an obscenity. Our judge and our trophy nothing more than a deeply damaged child.

'Freddy likes games,' she said. 'And he likes you.'

'He shouldn't have done it. If I'd known—'

'I'm sorry.'

So much churning within me. I wanted to go. I wanted space, and cold air.

'I'm going out.'

'Bron? Are we still friends?'

'Yes, of course.'

But it was a lie. We had never been friends. We had been lovers, lovers in waiting. And now there was nothing to wait for. So why pretend?

'But it's different,' I said.

'It always is.'

'I need to take it all in.'

'You do that.'

Silent tears rolled down her cheeks. She was curled up in bed, her knees to her chest, to make herself safe, to make herself small, to make herself not be there at all. She knew what was happening in me. She had seen it before.

'I'm sorry,' she said.

'So am I.'

22

I needed time alone. I was in shock. I needed to discover my own feelings.

I left the house by the terrace door, and turned off the terrace into the park. The snow was no longer falling. The short winter day had ended. I wanted only to walk, and grow cold, and forget. Some way away I could see a light burning in the window of the former stable building where Gandy lived and worked. It threw a faint glow down the path, and so gave me a safe route to follow in the darkness. I tramped down the path towards the light.

There must have been a dense layer of low cloud over the lake that night, and no moon, for there was no light at all in the world, it seemed to me, but for that one bright rectangle. I approached the window like a spaceship sailing towards a sunlit planet. Here alone was life.

I was still fifty paces and more away when I began to interpret the shapes and colours within its glowing frame. There was Gandy himself, moving back and forth, back and forth. There was the flue of an iron stove, rising up to the ceiling. There was a long-legged lamp, its light turned so that it shone on a rectangle within the rectangle, which seemed to float in shadowy space.

So I came nearer, moving more slowly now, guessing that even now, long after sunset, the old man was at work on a painting. Back and forth he went, as if only by this oscillation, this shifting of his angle of view, could he determine what he must do next. And there before him, resolving now into focus, was the canvas on which he had been working, supported by an easel. No surprises here: the painter scrutinising his own half-finished work. No doubt he would wait for daylight to take up brush and palette. Electric light is deceiving.

And then I saw the painting. I came to a stop about ten feet from the window. Gandy showed no signs of being aware that I was watching. I no longer cared. I was taking in something I should have guessed long ago.

The unfinished painting on the easel was of the Leidsegracht bridge in Amsterdam. There was the woman in grey, the child with the blue ribbon in her hair. The figures, and part of a tree behind, were fully worked. The rest of the scene, the canal, the lines of houses, were outlined in blue paint.

Gandy was painting a Marotte.

I returned to the house, slammed the door shut behind me, shouted, 'Christiansen! Where are you?'

He was in the Lake Room, standing before the bookcase with a book in one hand, hunting along the lower shelves for a second book. He spoke to me without turning round.

'I had not expected the pleasure of your company so soon.'

'Liar,' I said.

He was quite unmoved.

'Flora is in her room?'

'I suppose so. I don't really know.'

'So am I to take it that Flora has made you her confession?'

'Why didn't you tell me?'

'It was for her to tell you, not me.'

'I don't understand you. Why put her through it? Why put me through it? Do you have no feelings at all?'

'I'm sorry you see it that way,' he murmured.

'Is everything just a game to you? Even your precious Marottes? Oh, yes, I know about that too.'

'Yes,' he said. 'I saw you, from the window.'

He found the second book he was looking for, and drew it out. It was a handsomely bound volume of reproductions of seventeenth-century Dutch paintings.

'I do have a defence of my conduct. If you'll allow me.'

He opened the book and laid it on the low table, turning over the crisp shining pages, on each of which lay a sheet of translucent protective paper. His calm demeanour was unwarranted, but I found it hard to maintain my outrage in the face of it. Too much had happened to me too quickly. I felt confused and unsure of my own responses.

'So you admit that Gandy forges Marottes for you.'

'Yes,' he said. 'He's very good.'

'Is that all you can say?'

'By no means. Look at this.'

The reproduction he wished me to look at showed a dark interior with three figures: to the right, a man in soldier's dress, seated on a chair, with one hand raised; in the centre, a middle-aged woman, also seated, with a glass in her hand, apparently listening; and to the left, standing with her back to us and her head turned slightly away from the other two, a young woman with braided hair.

'This is a painting by Gerard ter Borch. The original is in

Berlin. Isn't the girl's gown fine? He was famous for his skill at painting drapery. Do you like it?'

'What has this to do with Gandy?'

'You'll see. Now I am going to read you a passage of Goethe, Goethe who created young Werther, the paradigm of the romantic and sorrowful young lover. Goethe knew and admired this painting. This is how he describes it, in his novel *Die Wahlverwandtschaften*.'

He read from the first and smaller volume, translating from the German. What was I to do? Dash the book from his hands? I sat and listened.

'A noble knightly father sits with one leg over the other and seems to be admonishing the daughter who stands before him. His daughter, a magnificent figure in a white satin dress, which hangs in full folds, is seen only from behind, but her whole attitude seems to indicate that she is restraining herself. That the admonition is not violent or shaming can be seen from the father's expression and bearing. And as for the mother, she seems to be concealing a slight embarrassment by looking down into a glass of wine, which she is in the act of drinking.'

I followed these details in the painting itself, and struggled with the sensation that I had tumbled into a hall of mirrors. Everything reflected everything else, and everything was distorted.

'You see them all? The noble father. The embarrassed mother. The humble daughter.'

'Yes. I see them.'

'At the time Goethe was writing, this painting was known as *Instruction Paternelle*. But that was not ter Borch's title.

Please observe the raised hand of the man in the picture. Look at it very carefully. Do you see anything?'

I bent down close to the shiny paper of the book. I observed as instructed. The thing began to have a fascination in itself. I saw that the man in the picture was holding something between his thumb and forefinger.

'It's not easy to see, but it's there if you look for it. He's holding a coin. Goethe did not see that. Possibly he knew the painting through a copy, or an engraving, and the coin had been eliminated. Because of this, and because of the title, Goethe failed to see what was there, and saw what was not there. Perception dictated reality.'

Oh yes, that I knew all about. Perception dictating reality.

'Gerard ter Borch never painted an *Instruction Paternelle*. He painted a brothel scene. That is his original title. There is no father, no mother, no daughter. This is a client, and a procuress, and a whore.'

I looked again at the reproduction. I turned to the list of plates at the front and saw it numbered there: *Brothel Scene, circa 1654–5*.

'Goethe was an acute observer, with a fine appreciation for the subtleties of human relationships. Was he deceived? Was he wrong? You saw nothing amiss in his description. Had the original title not been recovered, perhaps we would still be seeing what Goethe saw, to this day: the kindly father, not the lecher; the dutiful daughter, not the whore.'

What could I do? I laughed. 'So there's no objective reality. The world is whatever you choose to make it.'

'No, no. You're such an extremist. I mean only to show you that truth is a compound, that it is compounded of the perceiver and the thing perceived. This is so in matters of common perception, and more so in the visual arts, and most so when we talk of love.'

'I'm not talking about love any more.'

'Aren't you? That's a shame. I had more to tell you.'

As ever, his imperturbable manner goaded me. What right had he to behave as if everything was under his control, and nothing had changed?

'For God's sake! I've found you out! Do you really think I'm going to keep what I know to myself?'

'I couldn't say. What do you know?'

'That you deal in forged Marottes.'

'Some are forged. Others are authentic. Do you know which are which?'

'I don't. But there are others who will know.'

'I doubt it. But even if there were, why should they speak up? Ours is an uncertain and fallible business.'

'Forgery's not a matter of uncertainty. Forgery is forgery.'

'How limpid the world must look to you! Let me tell you some true stories, to muddy the water a little. At around the time when you were born, a Parisian art dealer called Jacques Marisse was tried on the charge of selling forged Utrillos. Maurice Utrillo himself was called as a witness in the trial, and shown some of the paintings in question. He was quite unable to tell the court which were his own work and which were forgeries.

'Then there's the case of Giorgio de Chirico and the dealer Dario Sabatello. Sabatello had a de Chirico painting that he said was authentic, and therefore valuable, but de Chirico himself said it was a forgery, and therefore valueless. Sabatello took de Chirico to court, and the judge found in the dealer's favour, and de Chirico had to pay a large fine for the damage he had done to the dealer's reputation. Poor de Chirico went on insisting that he was the victim of forgers, but he had made something of a habit of disowning his own earlier work, so no one took him seriously.'

He spread his arms, as if to offer me an entire forged world.

'It's no good, Freddy,' I said. 'Something somewhere has to be real. The whole point of a fake is that it pretends to be something real. However many fakes there are, they all depend in the end on the existence of what's authentic, and valuable, and good. The forger may deceive everyone else, but he himself knows the truth.'

'You are right,' said Christiansen. 'Perhaps it is only the forger who knows the truth.'

He looked at me intently, as if uncertain whether I understood the implications of this paradox. Then he began to walk about, not with his usual measured tread, but in a more restless fashion, stopping here and there and staring into space.

'I'm glad that you've discovered my little secret,' he said. 'It pleases me to talk with you in this way.'

'You have quite a nerve. I'll give you that.'

He ran one finger over the surface of the fireplace mirror, as if meaning to rub off the words he had written there. The ink was hard, and did not even smear.

'Granted that there exists an intimate relationship,' he said, 'between the forgery and the original, do you think it matters which is which? Suppose there was no way of knowing, just by looking at them, which works were by the original artist and which were by another artist, working in his style. Would it matter? There are over three thousand works by Rubens, for example, but nobody knows which ones were actually painted by Rubens, and which were painted by his pupils. He signed them all.'

'That's different. That's not forgery.'

'What is the difference?'

'The intention of the painter. A forger sets out with the intention to deceive.'

'And does that show on the canvas? Are the colours more gaudy? Do the brush-strokes reveal the duplicity? Is the varnish suspiciously smooth?'

'I don't know. But I'm sure the artist's intention is there in the picture.'

'You may be right.'

Again he stopped in his pacing, and stared at nothing.

'Shall I go a little nearer to the edge of the cliff?'

He turned to me with a smile. 'Come. Let's try an experiment.'

He led me across the hall to the locked gallery. Taking his bunch of keys from his pocket, he switched off the alarm system and unlocked the door.

'This is an experiment I have had in mind for years,' he said.

He directed my attention to the wall where there hung the three portraits of Kate Summer, all in a row. 'One of them is by Gandy. Can you tell which one?'

'This isn't fair.'

'I don't mean it to prove anything. I'd just be interested to know if it's obvious.'

It was not obvious. I looked from portrait to portrait. Each was different in its own way, but none in a way that identified itself to me as a fake.

'I've no idea.'

'Make a guess.'

I guessed at the portrait on the left. It was a little more hastily done than the others, and did not seem to have been fully finished.

Christiansen shook his head.

'Here's your fake.' He indicated the middle one. 'Gandy painted this in 1952. I've kept it ever since.'

I looked round the room.

'How many of these are Gandys?'

'See if you can tell.'

I tried to identify the other fakes, but it proved impossible. Christiansen would not enlighten me.

'Now you know that the portrait in the middle isn't the real thing,' he said, 'can you see a difference?'

'It doesn't look any different,' I said. 'It feels different.'

'In what way?'

'He never knew her. He never loved her. That makes it feel different.'

'Do you value it the less for that?'

'Of course.'

'For example, to be mercenary about it, now that you know it to be a forgery, you would pay less for it than for the portrait on the right, though they are very similar?'

'Yes.'

'I wonder. Should I make you a gift of it? I can sell that forged portrait for over a hundred thousand dollars. Would you like it?'

I shook my head.

'Why not? You're interested in Marotte.'

'The gift would be too big,' I said. 'Also, too small.'

'You would prefer the portrait on the right. I understand. That one feels different. The artist's intention is in the picture.'

'It has to be.'

'What do you think of my experiment?'

'It proves I can't tell a forgery from an original. I knew that already. I'm no art expert.'

'Ah, amator. It proves a little more than that. I have not been entirely candid with you. For the purposes of the experiment only, of course.'

'That isn't the forgery?'

'It isn't.'

'The one on the right is the forgery?'

'It is.'

'What difference does that make?'

'To me, none. But surely you will have to transfer your feelings. It is this one that feels different now, is it not?'

I felt annoyed with myself for not having guessed that he would play some such trick on me.

'Do you never stop playing games?'

'We all play games. Some games matter more than others.'

'Everyone can't play games. Everyone can't be forgers. Everyone can't tell lies.' The anger began to mount within me, fuelled by hurt vanity; but what I said I believed to be true none the less. 'There have to be some people who mean what they say. There have to be some people who have real feelings. What about Marotte?' I gestured at the paintings that hung all around us. 'He had real feelings. He painted real paintings. Without that, you'd have nothing to forge. You're a parasite on his art. What's more, you're a parasite on his love.'

'A parasite on his love!' For some reason, this struck Christiansen as amusing. 'Ah, amator, how you tempt me.'

'If Paul Marotte had never loved Kate Summer, do you think you'd be able to sell a forged portrait for a hundred thousand dollars?'

'I would not. You are right.'

He took out his keyring and selected one small key. With this, he unlocked the door of what seemed to be a cupboard, built flush into the wall between the windows.

'Take care before passing judgement on me,' he said. 'You do not know the whole story.'

A clatter of running feet, and in burst Gandy, white hair flying.

'The ice! She's on the ice!' And to me, venomously, 'I told you!'

Christiansen and I ran out on to the terrace. There, on the new snow lying on the lake, we saw a line of footprints leading out into the darkness. The lights from the house reached so far and no further.

'Flora!' I shouted. 'Flora!'

There was no answer. Christiansen went back into the house, moving fast, and I could hear him making a brisk telephone call.

I turned to Gandy. 'You're sure it's her?'

'Of course it's her! I saw her.'

'Will the ice bear my weight?'

'No! There are currents. Where the currents run, the ice is thin.'

I remembered the deer. How it had stood still. How the ice had buckled beneath it.

Christiansen came back out.

'Why now?' he said bitterly. 'After so long, why now?'

'I'm willing to go after her,' I said.

'No!' He barked the word with fierce contempt. 'For what? One death is enough.'

'Death!'

'Five minutes in the water and she'll be past saving.'

'I have to go after her!'

'I've called the ice boat. There's nothing else we can do.'

As he spoke, a light came on across the lake, and we heard the distant whirr of an engine. The beam of the boat's searchlight swept the darkness until it found her: a tiny figure on the great expanse of ice. The beam then held her in its grip as the craft began its careful journey towards her.

'Won't the boat break the ice?'

'Very likely,' said Christiansen curtly. 'They'll have to work fast.'

She stood there, unmoving, as if willing to accept whatever fate had in store for her.

'Why now?' said Christiansen again, speaking to himself.

The light crept towards her, the boat itself invisible to us. The sound of its engine grew louder as it drew further away from its home shore and nearer to us. There was no sound of breaking ice.

We heard voices. The men on the ice boat were urging her to walk towards them, but she didn't move. Now that the light was closer I could see that she was dressed only in her shirt. She must have gone from her bed to the lake, seeking no protection from the cold, seeking the anaesthetic of the ice.

The light was almost upon her when she dropped to her knees. This slight impact was enough. The ice, already stressed by the weight of the nearing boat, sighed and snapped beneath her. She slipped silently into the black water, and out of sight.

We cried out, all of us. The light dipped and rocked, as the boat too settled through the ice on to its floats. Voices on the boat shouted, weighted ropes snaked across the light's beam. I could make no sense of the dance of shadows on the distant water.

'They have her,' said Christiansen softly.

Now the engine was roaring again. The craft was crossing the lake towards us. As it came within reach of the house lights, now riding on the ice once more, I saw its outreached spidery arms, which spread its weight on to long runners, and the high caged propeller mounted at the back, which drove it forward. There were three men on board. One operated the craft, while the other two held a limp blanketed form in their arms, chafing heat back into the frozen body.

Christiansen said to me, 'I'll get the car out. I'm taking her to the hospital.'

Gandy and I went to the lakeside, and the men on the boat lifted her out into my arms. She was alive, but torpid, as if drugged. I could hear Gandy making a clicking sound with his mouth, an expression of his dismay.

'Adrenalin,' said the boatman to me. He mimed injecting a needle into her arm. 'Adrenalin. She'll be okay.'

I nodded. I carried her quickly across the terrace and down to the front drive. Christiansen's car was just pulling up. Together, without a word, we laid her on the back seat, the boat blanket still wrapped round her.

'Shall I come too?'

'No.'

He gave no reason. But already he was in the driving seat, and engaging the gears. I watched as his car drew away down the drive and picked up speed on the level road beyond.

I returned to the house. Gandy was gone. The ice boat was heading back to the far shore. I went to the Lake Room and poured myself a brandy. The turmoil of feelings in me began slowly to resolve.

Flora had wanted to die. 'Why now?' Christiansen had asked. I knew. Because of me. Because of what had passed between us in her bedroom. Out of it, unknown to me, for whom it was the beginning of understanding, had come for her an ending. One loss too far. So somehow I was to blame. Gandy had said, 'You'll hurt her. You'll kill her.' I must bear that guilt. I had almost killed her. Only now she would not die.

'She'll be okay,' the boatman had said, with all the authority of one who knew how long it took a deer to die.

No, Flora would not die. It was something else that was dead.

I no longer loved her.

This shamed me. Had it all been about sex, after all? But it wasn't that. In a sense, it was worse. My passion had been fed, not by sex, but by mystery. Now that I knew her secret, all her power had drained away, to be replaced by pity. And pity is the death of love.

23

Christiansen's private art gallery was still unlocked. He and I had run from the house without stopping to close any doors. I returned to the collection of paintings, some of which were real and some of which were forged, and it no longer seemed to matter any more. What harm did it do, to add to the world's small store of Marottes? If the buyer believed them to be real, as I had done, he would get as much benefit from them as if they were from the hand of the master.

My eyes then fell on the cupboard door that Christiansen had been about to open when Gandy burst in. The key was still in the lock.

I opened the little door.

A light came on automatically, illuminating a painting that hung within. It was a portrait of a young man wearing spectacles. It was painted in the bold heightened manner with which I had become familiar, but there was more detail, and more character, than usual. Grave eyes gazed out at me from beneath a high brow. He seemed amused to be discovered, head a little tilted down, eyes raised. He looked younger than I had expected. I liked him at once, as I had known I would.

I was looking at the lost self-portrait. I was sure of it. This was Paul Marotte.

I heard footsteps behind me. It was Gandy.

'I told you!' he said, his voice shaking with grief and rage. 'I told you!'

'She's going to be alright.'

'No! She will not be alright!'

Then he registered the illuminated portrait, and his cheeks went pale, and the anger in him died. He looked from the portrait to me, and back to the portrait.

'So you know,' he said, his voice very low.

'Yes.'

'What will you do?'

'I don't know.'

He went to one of the chairs, and gripping its arms with his own trembling hands, he sat down.

'Will you send us to prison?' he said. His voice too was shaking.

'This is the lost self-portrait, isn't it? This is Marotte.'

He nodded.

'How many Marottes have you painted?'

'Who knows?'

'Are any of them in the major museums?'

'Of course. Many.'

I shook my head in amazement.

'Please,' he said. 'I'm not important. My life is almost over. But he is a good man. A fine man. I am the guilty one. I was the one who first copied a Marotte. If I had not done so, he would not have done what he has done.'

'But have you painted nothing else? Nothing of your own?'

'Of course. This is all my own work.'

He gestured round the walls.

'My own work!' He said it again, with more emphasis, regaining some pride.

'But even so,' I persisted gently, 'it's work signed with another man's name.'

'What other man?'

'Paul Marotte.'

He pulled himself up from the chair to stand defiantly before me, his eyes flashing, his beard twitching.

'I am Paul Marotte!'

He looked so absurd I almost laughed out loud. He blushed a deep brick-red.

'You think I delude myself?'

'All I mean to say is – you may well have painted more canvasses than Marotte himself, for all I know—'

'I have!'

'But it wasn't you who met the governess on the bridge. And it wasn't you who wrote the letters.'

He stared at me. Then he sank back slowly into the chair. 'You said you knew. But you know nothing! No wonder you look on me as a pitiful old fool.'

Now I was lost.

'There was another Paul Marotte before me,' he said. He waved his hands before his face, as he had done to me earlier. 'Woo-woo! Forget him! He is unworthy of the name! He is not the real Paul Marotte!'

By now I was beginning to think the old man was mad. But I had questions that needed answering, so I chose not to challenge him directly.

'If you are the real Paul Marotte,' I said gently, 'then who was the other one?'

Gandy responded with venom, as if the historical Paul Marotte was the impostor who denied him his own authenticity.

'Who was he? He was a vain lecherous Frenchman! He forced the female patients in his asylum to strip naked for him. He drew pornographic sketches of them in their nakedness. He satisfied his lust on them. There were pregnancies – he terminated them. He was a *medical practitioner*.' He spat out these words in his disgust. 'There was the English woman. Another abortion. He was discovered, and disgraced. He ran away. He thought he could make a living as a painter. Woo-woo! Not so easy! But pornographic pictures, oh yes! Those he could sell!'

I listened in stunned silence. When he was done, all I could do was stare.

'You don't believe me? Ask Freddy Christiansen.'

'I don't understand. Everything you say – it's impossible.'

'Very well. It's impossible. You are the expert. Who am I? An old fool.'

He stood up to go. I could see that already he was regretting his outburst.

'No, please,' I said. 'Help me to understand.'

'But it's impossible. You said so. Marotte is a great artist. He had a famous love affair.'

'Did he not love her, then?'

'Oh, love. For a few weeks, perhaps. In the way such men love.'

'But he did paint? He was an artist?'

'He had an eye. He had a gift. But he never knew how to develop it. Only I have understood that.'

At this point I had still not grasped the full extent of the deception. I believed Gandy was no more than an envious copyist.

'But your work – it follows after Marotte. He is the original. He was the first to paint the meeting on the bridge.'

'The meeting on the bridge!' He looked at me and broke into a curious barking laugh. 'Young man, there was no meeting on the bridge.'

'But that's where he fell in love! That's what changed his life.'

Gandy shook his head, and went on cackling with laughter. 'No, no, no!'

Was it possible? I felt the entire edifice crumbling about me. No love at first sight. No transformation. Now at last I began to comprehend the enormity of the project that Christiansen and Gandy had undertaken thirty years ago.

'The journals?' I said. 'The letters?'

'Freddy.'

'Freddy!'

'In the beginning, six Marottes. No more. Six canvasses – and me. That's how we began. We had nothing! No money at all. But Freddy said to me, a romantic life sells pictures.'

'Freddy wrote the letters? But – they're love letters!'

'What of that?' Again the pride flashed in his eyes. 'Has Freddy never loved? The paintings are love paintings. Have I never loved?'

I looked round the room, at all the works I had believed were images of true love.

'Is there a single painting here by the real Marotte?'

'Not one.'

I turned to the self-portrait.

'This is your work?'

'Of course!'

'Then who is it?'

He gave me no answer. But he changed the angle of his head to mirror the young man in the painting, and he lifted his eyes to mine. I looked from the painting to the old man, with his halo of white hair and straggle of white beard. Then I looked at his eyes. The eyes had not changed.

'It's you.'

'Of course. The self-portrait. I am Paul Marotte.'

His mad self-belief was beginning to erode my doubts. Why not? If his story was to be credited, he had painted all Marotte's paintings.

'Freddy was going to – discover it – one day?'

'It was our pension. It was to pay for our old age. So that I could go on, to the end.'

'And you feel no – no guilt – at this lifelong deception? This thirty years of forgery?'

He gave his high cackle of a laugh once more, angrily amused by the sight of my perplexity.

'Why should you understand?' he said. 'The signature in the corner – that's nothing! The life of the artist, all this gossip about love and poverty and death – that's nothing. All that matters is the work. This has been my life! This! You can call it forgery. I call it reincarnation!'

With that, his final dramatic flourish, he left me.

I remained in Christiansen's gallery, absorbing all that I had heard that day, knowing I would not sleep. The words I had believed were written by Marotte came tumbling out of my memory. *I need only a warm room, a still mind, and you . . .*

I stood before the facsimile letter written by Kate Summer, that I must now suppose was written by Christiansen.

Look on my face and see how we have loved.

All this gossip about love and poverty and death.

A romantic life sells pictures.

They had made fools of all the world, these two old men, forging love. They had made a fool of me. But I found I was

253

not angry, after all. This was unexpected. I had discovered an audacious fraud, the forging not only of works of art but of an entire life, and I felt no urge to expose the forgers. More curious yet, I began to realise that I liked them for it. Perhaps this was to do with Gandy himself. The old man had been so proud, and so indifferent to fame. It was almost as if he had laboured for the pure love of the work, like the anonymous artists who built the great cathedrals. We live in an age where art is the supreme expression of the self, the ego enthroned in glory. And here was a lonely old man whose work hung in the art galleries of the world, and whose name would never be known.

As for the money: for all Christiansen's talk of capital and security, I did not believe that either of them had pursued their fraud in order to get rich. Surely it was the other way about. They had sought only that their mad enterprise generate enough income to pay for its own perpetuation. The house by the lake was no doubt a valuable asset. But the life they lived here was not extravagant. They lived like two monks who were the keepers of a holy icon. It must have been a lonely life, walled as it was by the massive edifice of their secret.

And now their secret was discovered. I had forced the guardian doors, and entered the tabernacle, and held the holy icon in my infidel hands.

No – there had been no need to force the doors. The locks had been turned as I approached. The doors had been opened to admit me.

Now why was that? Why me?

24

I was still in the gallery, deep in my thoughts, when Christiansen returned alone.

'She'll be alright,' he told me. 'They're keeping her in for the rest of the night. She's lost a lot of body heat. But they say she'll be alright.'

'Thank God!'

If he saw the open cupboard door and the illuminated self-portrait, he didn't care. All his concern was for Flora.

'Why did she do it?' he said. 'She's always known she's safe here.'

'I think I'm to blame,' I said.

'Yes. I supposed so.'

He didn't ask for an explanation, but I gave it anyway. He was very tired, but at the same time not at all calm. He listened to me, frowning.

'I thought she wanted – what I wanted. Do you remember saying to me, "You must learn to make demands"?'

'Ah, yes.'

'I made demands. She became hysterical. So in the end, she told me.'

'Told you what?'

'About the rape. And the abortion. And how it's been for her since.'

'The rape. The abortion.'

He let out a long sigh.

'What a day we've had,' he said. 'My poor Flora. She succeeded in surprising me.'

'You didn't think she'd go so far?'

'No. Never. Nor am I sure that she did mean to go so far.'

'You think she didn't mean to die?'

'I think perhaps she wanted to come close to death, and to be rescued. She wanted to see the possibility of an end. Who knows what she saw? She has poor eyesight, of course.'

'Poor eyesight?'

'Didn't you know? She's extremely short-sighted. You can't have failed to notice.'

But I had. All those looks of mystery and collusion. That faraway gaze that had so fascinated me. And all the time, she was short-sighted.

'And you, amator? Do you love her still?'

'No.'

'The spell has been broken at last.'

'Yes.'

'Because now you know she can never love you?'

'Yes. I suppose so.'

'Poor Flora. It always ends this way for her. I had hoped I could make a difference. But it seems not.'

'I thought you were her lover,' I said. 'Or had been.'

He smiled. 'No. I was never her lover.'

'I understand that now. She has no lovers.'

'Not for that reason. For another reason. Why do you say she has no lovers?'

'Because of the trauma. She can't make love.'

'She can't make love?' Christiansen was clearly surprised to hear this. 'My dear young friend, she is married. Do you think Axel Jaeger would have married her if she couldn't make love?'

This had not occurred to me.

'But the rape – the abortion—'

'There was no rape. There was no abortion.'

I gaped. He shrugged wearily: his apology for all the disappointments of life.

'Flora is a liar.'

'But she hates lies!'

'Of course she hates lies. All liars hate other people's lies. Because they lie themselves, they think everyone else lies. Because their own lies are successful, they trust nothing anyone else says.'

'What do you mean? What lies?'

'Where to begin? There are so many. Did she tell you she was expelled from her school?'

'Yes.'

'Not true. Did she tell you she went out with Mick Jagger? And Lucian Freud, and David Bailey, and Terence Stamp? All lies.'

'She has a photograph of her by Bailey.'

'How do you know it's by Bailey?'

'Her cousin told me.'

'And who told him?'

'Flora.'

'All lies.'

'Did her father leave home when she was young?'

'Yes. That much is true.'

'I don't understand. Why? Why make up the story of the rape?'

'So that she would not have to make love with you.'

'But – but why? She liked me. She kissed me. I swear to you I'm not making this up. Why would I have gone on loving her if I hadn't received encouragement?'

'I believe you. For a while I had hopes that you would be the one she would trust. I think maybe she even hoped that herself. So you see, when she knew it would go with you as it has always gone before, she despaired.'

Too much past.

'Do you understand, Freddy? What is it she's so afraid of?'

'Yes, I think I understand. Like all liars, she's afraid of the truth. She believes that anyone who comes close enough to her to see the truth will abandon her. She believes she's worthless. No education, no talent, no place in the world. She believes she's nothing. But of course, she is beautiful. Men are interested in her, as you have been interested in her. They want to know her. So she invents someone for them to know, someone worthy of their interest. Then, when they come too close, she disappears.'

'Afraid of the truth.'

'So I believe.'

'No wonder you asked, Is true love possible between men and women?'

'I wanted you to convince her. Please believe me.'

'It doesn't matter now.'

Everything was slipping away from me. The night had gone on too long. But it was not quite over.

'Gandy has told me everything,' I said.

'Everything? That covers a great deal.'

'Enough, then.'

'I see.' He rose. 'Then I think I need a drink. Will you join me?'

258

So we drank brandy once more. The drink they give you when you're rescued.

'It seems you're a liar too,' I said. 'Like Flora.'

'It takes one to know one.'

'You don't sound very ashamed.'

'Ashamed? No, I don't think I feel ashamed.'

'What do you feel?'

'Proud.'

'Like Gandy. He's proud too.'

'He's a great artist. He has every right to be proud.'

'And you too. A great artist.'

I read from the letter framed on the wall.

All things happen in the same moment . . . My eternity is in his art . . . In scorn of the world.

How differently it sounded, now I knew its true authorship.

'You wrote the Left-Hand Letters too? You wrote, "Eyes dry with not seeing you"?'

'All paintings require a provenance. There had to be documents.'

'You wrote, "I leave doors ajar to feel nearer to you"? You wrote, "I am yours by the ceremony of the heart"?'

'Seventeen letters. A journal. Some scrawled messages. It takes very little to make a life.'

'You were both of them?'

'Yes.'

I was the first person he had ever told of his remarkable thirty-year-long project. He too was like an artist whose greatest work has never been seen. And I, without seeking it, had become his witness, his posterity. In a kind of controlled exultation, he detailed for me how he had woven his fictions into the known facts; and then, when those fictions had been established, how he had woven into them further fabrications. He told me how he, the forger, had also become the authenticating expert; and how careful he had been to sell his forged Marottes in limited numbers.

'In every respect we have made our invented Marotte live and work within the constraints of a real artist. He has not painted more paintings than is humanly possible; considerably fewer, in fact. His letters are the product of a continuous integrated consciousness; which is, of course, my own. His art has been taken over and developed by an artist who was drawn to his style in the first place by a genuine affinity, and who has since given his life to perfecting it.'

'You worked all this out right from the start?'

'Oh, no. Only the barest bones. But I knew from the beginning how easily people confuse feelings with art. I knew that if I were able to create a life of intense emotion, there would be many who would translate that in their own minds into significant art. So I built a simple story that fitted the known facts, but cast them in a new light. A bourgeois who longs to be an artist. A romantic meeting. The world given up for love. A few poor but passionate years. A lingering death. A suicide.

'I planted the key elements of this story in a few letters, a journal, an autobiographical fragment. Everything else has been read into it. People do it instinctively. It fits some deep need. Great art has to be the product of great love. Great love has to be won at the cost of riches, respectability, even life itself. You understand this more than most, my dear one-time amator. For here you are, at work on a book about true love.'

Transformation after all: but not as I had imagined it. I recalled the old man's dismissal of romantic biography:

260

all this gossip about love and poverty and death . . . all that matters is the work.

Against all expectation, I was smiling. Perhaps it was the brandy, or the accumulation of the emotions of the long day, but the agitation and the confusion now all dropped away from me, leaving in their place a novel sensation of warmth, and the conviction that all was well.

'You invisible man,' I said. 'The love comes from you, after all.'

He gave me the oddest look, like a child caught in a forbidden act, and at once turned away.

'The love is real, after all,' I said.

'Who's to say?'

'I say.'

I went to him and took hold of his hands and pulled at them.

'You crazy fool,' I said. 'All these years. So much love.'

He looked down at his hands, which I was pumping up and down in mine. He seemed surprised to see so much activity emanating from his own body. But I knew now that it was this he had wanted to reveal to me all along: that he too had loved, and that he could love again.

'You and Gandy,' I said. 'Two madmen forging love.'

Then I put my arms round him and hugged him. I held him close, and in a little while his arms crept round me, timid, fearful of rejection. He let his head rest on my shoulder.

'What a fool I am,' he said with a sigh.

'All fools,' I replied. 'All of us fools.'

'Ah, but you're still young.'

He opened his arms and we parted. He walked away from me and turned, as if to look out at the lake, but I knew it was so that he could not see my expression when he next spoke.

'One last confession,' he said. 'One last deception. Please regard this as nothing more than an item of information, to which you are entitled. No response is required. I hope we will continue to be friends.'

'Of course we will.'

'You see, my dear amator, something unexpected happened to me on the day that I first met you, at the Marotte Huis. I think of it as the penance imposed on me by the God who is stronger than I, for my many sins, perhaps even for my survival and my success. I fell in love.'

He shook his head and gave a sweet wry chuckle, in which were contained all the ironies of his life.

'With you, my youthful, eager, unworthy, oblivious amator. With you. And, of course, at first sight.'

25

I returned to London to find Anna was not at home in the Cross Street flat, and was not answering her phone. I called her office and was told she had taken a few days' leave. They did not know where. I had no key.

London is not a city that gives comfort to the homeless, especially in January. It was mid-afternoon. The night would be very cold. I felt confused and lonely, and wanted to be among friends. I wanted to tell somebody about all that had happened to me. I wanted to tell Anna.

I phoned Bernard. The phone rang, but no one answered. I let it ring for a long time. As it rang, and as I looked out through the scratched glass of the phone booth at the people passing in the street, I felt a longing to be at Tawhead. I wanted to be back in the woods between the two rivers. I wanted to see the mist over the valley. Devon was only a three-hour train journey away. I could be there by the evening. The gate-lodge was mine for the using, its key would be lying under the stone where I had left it. The stove would not be lit, but there were logs and kindling, and old newspapers and matches. Bernard might be away, but Dora would be there, and would let me raid the larder. And more than likely Bernard was at home, but out with his cows, beyond the summons of the phone.

I reached Paddington just as the Barnstaple train was pulling out of the station, and had to wait over an hour for the next train. As a result, it was past ten when a taxi deposited me at the gate-lodge; far too late to go knocking on the door of the main house. But the little lodge was just as I had left it, and soon enough the logs were blazing away in the stove. The bedroom was bitterly cold, so I went to bed in my clothes. As soon as I had wriggled myself into warmth, I fell sound asleep.

From long habit I woke early, and decided to make my way down the woodland path to Taw pool, as I had done each early morning when I had stayed here in the autumn. It was a chilly misty morning, but the air smelled sharp and fresh, and the rising sun, hidden from sight, was slowly melting the shadows. My low spirits of the previous day were gone. I felt that a new life was about to begin.

I reached Taw pool and came to a stop, to look and to listen. All was familiar and all was fresh-made, that dawn. I watched the water racing round the island, and thought of Flora, of that last sight of her, cocooned in a blanket, in the back of Christiansen's car. I felt no regret, no impulse to pursue.

I felt the rising sun before I saw it. Then, looking up, there it was, above the railway bridge, a brighter white on the white horizon. As I looked, a second much smaller light came rushing out of the mist: the Barnstaple train, hurrying towards Bicton. The booming rattle of the train followed, loud in the still air, startling the rooks from the elms. Then the train was gone, and the sound of the river returned.

Perhaps someone would be up and about in the big house.

I felt hungry, and in need of coffee. I turned towards the path across the sloping meadows.

And there was Anna.

I think I jumped. It was such a shock.

'Anna!'

'Bron?'

'What are you doing here?'

'What are you doing here?'

'Nothing.'

'I'm doing nothing too.'

She had made no sound approaching, so she must have been standing there, like me. Doing nothing. She had on an ancient duffel coat, with the hood up over her head.

'I thought you were in Switzerland,' she said.

'I was.'

'So what are you doing here?'

'Well, I have to be somewhere. And you weren't in your flat.'

She started to laugh.

'Oh, poor Bron. Were you locked out? I thought you had a key.'

'No. I gave it back. Remember?'

'Not really.'

'And anyway, what are you doing here?'

'Oh, I got a bit low in London. I decided I needed a break. Bernard's been so sweet.'

We walked to the big house together, over the frosty grass. We joined the woodland path and climbed the hillside and so came to the old stone wall with the two gates, and the view of the valley beyond. I held open the smaller wooden gate for her. 'My favourite view. The doors of the world.'

'Yes, I know.'

265

'What do you mean, you know?'

'I mean, it's one of my favourite views too.'

We stood and looked west over the Taw valley, while the sun crept higher into the white sky.

'You're not usually up this early,' I said.

'No. I couldn't sleep.'

'Where on earth did you get that coat?'

'I found it on a peg in the passage. I think it must have belonged to Bernard's mother.'

I kept glancing at her. She was so welcome to me, so familiar and easy to be with. Also her face looked so funny, peeping out from the hood of the duffel coat. I thought how long I had known her, over ten years now, and how pleased I was to see her again.

We walked on to the house.

'So Bernard must be home, after all,' I said.

'Yes, of course he is. I wouldn't be here on my own.'

'It's just that I called yesterday afternoon, and he didn't answer.'

'We went for a long walk yesterday afternoon. We got as far as Crown Head.'

'Long way.'

'So Bernard's not expecting you?'

'No.'

'I hope he doesn't mind.'

'Oh, he won't mind. He told me I could use the gate-lodge any time. He likes the company.'

Then, as we reached the house: 'Why should he mind?'

'I don't know. I just thought he might.'

We found Bernard in the kitchen, stirring the porridge on the Aga. As soon as he saw me I knew that Anna was right, and that he did mind. And I also knew why.

'Bron! What are you doing here?'

'Why does everyone keep asking me that?'

Bernard looked to Anna for an explanation. She gave him an apologetic shrug and said, 'I found him by the pool.'

'I've come to finish my book. Is that okay?'

'Yes, of course. Only I've not made enough porridge for three.'

'All I need is coffee.'

Bernard bustled about the kitchen seeing to Anna's breakfast, and I, with a sinking heart, understood why I was unwelcome. Anna had got a bit low in London. Bernard was being sweet.

Then I remembered something else. 'It's your birthday.'

'Whose?' said Bernard.

'Anna's. She's thirty. Today.'

Anna tried to shrug it off.

'I decided to cancel it. Due to lack of interest.'

'Your thirtieth birthday!' exclaimed Bernard. 'We must celebrate.'

'No, please, Bernard. No celebration. No flowers. You can make a donation to charity if you want.'

'What?'

'Like with funerals,' I explained.

I understood Anna so much better than Bernard did. So much better than everyone. I now knew exactly what she was doing at Tawhead. I also knew it would never work.

'You can't do this, Anna,' I said.

'I can if I want to,' she replied.

'Do what?' Bernard was baffled.

'It's not fair on others,' I said.

'Others are willing,' she said. 'And I don't see what right you have to tell me what to do.'

'No right at all,' I said.

'Stop this!' cried Bernard. 'What's going on?'

'Bron's being a dog in the manger,' said Anna. 'It's time he got out of the manger.'

'Fine,' I said.

I felt a childish desire to smack her, to make her see sense. This was getting out of hand. I poured myself a mug of coffee, and said no more.

'At least I can say happy birthday,' said Bernard.

'Alright. But no happy returns of the day.'

'You have to say happy birthday too, Bron.'

Bernard the peacemaker. But I was feeling sulky.

'Bron's feeling sorry for himself,' said Anna, acute as usual. 'Be nice, Bron, or go away.'

'If you say so.'

I took my mug of coffee down the long passage to the library. Here, away from the need to retain my dignity, and afloat on a wave of self-pity, I confronted the ridiculous truth. What had I been thinking of all these years? It was now so startlingly clear to me that I wanted to be with Anna, that it was with Anna that I was myself, that it was with Anna that I felt happy, that I had somehow assumed that Anna would always be there for me. And now, cruelly, just as I came to see this simple but immense truth, I was one day too late. Anna had come to Tawhead to let Bernard be sweet to her. They had gone on a walk yesterday that must have been at least four hours long. What had been said? Was it all already settled?

I couldn't bear to think it. Anna belonged to me. But alas, I had failed to tell this to Anna, and so had forfeited my rights. The door had closed, and I was shut out. This drove me wild. I wanted to beat on the door, and call her name.

As I stamped up and down the long library, in a mounting rage with myself and with Anna, my eyes fell on Bernard's writing desk. This had belonged to his father, and was the old kind, that comes with writing paper and envelopes laid out in a little rack. As soon as I saw this, I knew what I was going to do. I would write her a letter.

The letter was quite short. I dated it, folded it, and put it in an envelope. On the outside of the envelope I wrote: ANNA. Then I finished my coffee, and took the mug and the letter back to the kitchen. Bernard was at the sink, his back to me, washing up breakfast.

My manners had improved.

'I'm going back to work,' I said, speaking in what I meant to be a light and friendly voice. 'Maybe I'll see you both later?'

'Join us for lunch,' said Bernard, not looking round.

'Lunch it is.'

With a glance at Anna, I laid my letter on the table before her. She saw it, but made no move to pick it up.

So I left the house.

Back in the gate-lodge I sat at the table before the window, not working, not thinking, almost not living. I suspended time itself, while I waited for Anna to come.

She did not come for three hours.

Then she came.

'You bastard,' she said. 'You fucking bastard.'

Sweet joyous relief flowed through my chilled body. I hadn't even moved to feed the stove. Anything but pity. Anything but kindness.

'You're just a bloody little spoilt child, aren't you?'

'Yes, I am.'

'You don't want the toys until someone else wants them.'

'It's true. Whatever you want to say about me is true. Just don't leave me.'

'Don't leave you! Since when was I with you? You make me miserable for years and years, and then you have the fucking nerve to say, Don't leave me!'

'What did you say to Bernard?'

'That's none of your business.'

'I'm so, so sorry about Bernard. That's the worst of it. I never meant to mess him up.'

'Who says Bernard's messed up? You don't know what I'm going to do.'

'Yes, I do.'

She stood before me, trembling with anger, and she was so beautiful it bewildered me that I hadn't seen it before.

'Well, fuck you!'

With that, she fell into my arms. I held her tight, and she started to shake, and then to cry.

'It's alright now,' I said to her. 'I love you.'

'Jesus!' she exclaimed. 'What took you so fucking long?'

Anna and I have been married for twenty-four years now. We have three children. Anna's business flourishes. I make a living of sorts by writing. I am profoundly happy.

Freddy Christiansen died at the end of last year. He has been a good friend to us both. He teased me that he loved Anna far more than he ever loved me. In his will he left us his collection of Marottes. Now that he is beyond the reach of earthly laws, I feel free to reveal his secret. He deserves his curious footnote in the history of art.

Flora Freeman married again, and lives in the United States. She was unable to come to Freddy's funeral. She sent flowers. Bernard too married, over ten years ago now, and has twin boys that he spoils terribly.

Anna keeps my letter in a locked drawer of her desk. When our girls ask about our courtship, and how we came to be married, she shows them the letter.

There are three things I'm sure of. That we are right for each other. That I can make you happy. And that one day we'll be together. So please know that I'm waiting for you. When you wake one morning thinking of me, all you have to do is call me, and I'll come to you, and I'll never leave you again.

The girls think this is the most romantic letter in the world. As do I. This is, after all, a story about true love.

THE END

The artist Paul Marotte is fictional. All other historical characters referred to in the novel – the famous lovers, artists and forgers – are factual, and the statements ascribed to them are authentic.